THE RUSSIAN'S GLUTTONY

ALSO BY CAP DANIELS

The Chase Fulton Novels
Book One: *The Opening Chase*
Book Two: *The Broken Chase*
Book Three: *The Stronger Chase*
Book Four: *The Unending Chase*
Book Five: *The Distant Chase*
Book Six: *The Entangled Chase*
Book Seven: *The Devil's Chase*
Book Eight: *The Angel's Chase*
Book Nine: *The Forgotten Chase*
Book Ten: *The Emerald Chase*
Book Eleven: *The Polar Chase*
Book Twelve: *The Burning Chase*
Book Thirteen: *The Poison Chase*
Book Fourteen: *The Bitter Chase*
Book Fifteen: *The Blind Chase*
Book Sixteen: *The Smuggler's Chase* (Winter 2021)

The Avenging Angel – Seven Deadly Sins Series
Book One: *The Russian's Pride*
Book Two: *The Russian's Greed*
Book Three: *The Russian's Gluttony*
Book Four: *The Russian's Lust* (Spring 2022)

Stand-Alone Novels
We Were Brave

Novellas
I Am Gypsy
The Chase Is On

THE RUSSIAN'S GLUTTONY

AVENGING ANGEL
SEVEN DEADLY SINS SERIES
BOOK #3

CAP DANIELS

ANCHOR WATCH
PUBLISHING
** USA **

The Russian's Gluttony
Avenging Angel
Seven Deadly Sins Book #3
Cap Daniels

This is a work of fiction. Names, characters, places, historical events, and incidents are the product of the author's imagination or have been used fictitiously. Although many locations such as marinas, airports, hotels, restaurants, etc. used in this work actually exist, they are used fictitiously and may have been relocated, exaggerated, or otherwise modified by creative license for the purpose of this work. Although many characters are based on personalities, physical attributes, skills, or intellect of actual individuals, all of the characters in this work are products of the author's imagination except those used for historical significance.

Published by:

** USA **

13 Digit ISBN: 978-1-951021-28-3
Library of Congress Control Number: 2021951101

Cover Design: German Creative

Printed in the United States of America

"Gluttony and Lust are the only sins that abuse something that is essential to our survival."

—Henry Fairlie

THE RUSSIAN'S GLUTTONY

Obzhorstvo Russkikh

CAP DANIELS

1

Snova Pod Strazhey
(Back in Custody)

Vancouver, British Columbia – Autumn 2004

Anastasia "Anya" Burinkova sat on a stool with her back to the ornate bar inside the Grand Condor Inn, watching throngs of people passing the floor-to-ceiling windows only fifteen meters away. With Vancouver International Airport less than a kilometer down the road, the Grand Condor played host to wealthy jetsetters and businessmen on the go. Boasting triple-pane glass throughout and some of the finest insulation of any hotel in the world, the roaring jet engines had little hope of penetrating the fortress of the privileged. The thousand-dollar-per-night price tag, like the glass and insulation, was designed to keep out another element most luxury travelers couldn't be bothered with: the middle class.

People-watching for sport had only recently become a favorite pastime for the former Russian SVR assassin. Highly trained in the art of surveillance—as well as an impressive array of other skills—Anya saw the environment around her much differently than most anyone else. The cane hanging by its decorative handle on the back of the chair, which was occupied by a man who appeared to be well into his ninth decade on Earth, featured an unworn rubber foot that should've been unevenly stained and deteriorating, while the handle showed the wear of years in the man's grip. The smooth flesh above the old man's collar and below his hairline belied the apparent age on his lined, weathered face. He sat alone thumbing through a French newspaper, but the absence of left-to-right movement of his head told the former spy she was watching a man who was watching someone else instead of reading the lines written on the paper.

The angle at which she sat gave her the perfect vantage point from which to see through the edge of the man's rimless glasses. The out-of-focus image a magnifying lens should produce from such distance was absent, leaving the spectacles to be clear glass, or more likely, a dense polymer designed to protect his eyes rather than correct his vision.

Perhaps the foot of the cane has recently been replaced and the eyeglasses are prosthetics for vanity's sake, thought the Russian. *Perhaps the man is everything his outward appearance says he is not.*

The slightest change in the man's posture sent Anya's eyes exploding toward the opulent lounge near the entrance. A pair of Asian men in ten-thousand-dollar suits and an older man with a little too much weight around his waist strolled into the room. The Asians flanked the older man, whose features told the story of a life spent behind the Iron Curtain. His suit was well cut and tailored to fit his oblong frame, but it lacked the sophistication of the dress the Eastern businessmen sported.

Anya sent her gaze back to the man with the cane and watched him slide a napkin from the table and onto the floor by his right foot. Without scanning the room for curious eyes, he reached for the napkin and brushed his fingertips across the foot of the cane as if inspecting it for debris or obstructions.

Anya leaned forward until the balls of her feet touched the floor, giving her the ability to leave the stool and bound toward the center of the room in a fraction of a second. Whatever she was watching was about to turn into the worst day of someone's time on Earth.

The Asians and the Eastern European took seats at a table only an arm's length from the man with the cane. A cocktail waitress who looked like the seductress of every middle-aged man's fantasy glided to the table and cooed, "*Bonjour, messieurs. Que désirez-vous?*"

The table's occupants stared up at the woman with confusion masking their features, and she repeated her question in English. "Hello, gentlemen. What would you like?"

The accent of the European, coupled with his brash insistence on demonstrating his wealth and worldly experience, confirmed Anya's suspicion he had once been a member of the Communist Party of the Union of Soviet Socialist Republic, the flag under which she herself had been born and spent the first formative years of her life.

"Vodka, and only finest Russian vodka. I never drink anything less." The waitress turned to the two Asian men, but the Russian held up a hand. "Vodka for all of us!"

The two men made no effort to contradict the order, and they sat in silence.

As the boisterous Russian regaled his Eastern comrades, the man with the cane folded his paper and tucked it inside his jacket. He rose from his chair, feigning a decrepit nature, but his practiced stance and the placement of his feet directly beneath his shoulders positioned at least seventy-five percent of his weight on the balls of his feet—unlike what an octogenarian would be capable of doing. Careful to keep the foot of the cane off the floor, he lifted the ornament from the back of his chair and took two cinematic old-man steps toward the Russian. As his left foot struck the ground, he drew the cane upward, bringing its foot to bear on the Russian's back.

Anya sprang from the stool and closed the distance an instant before the foot of the cane was pressed into her former countryman's flesh. With the speed and precision of a pouncing jaguar, she struck the assailant's wrists, forcing the foot of the cane skyward and the old man stumbling forward. He regained control of the cane and thrust it toward the bulky Russian as he fell to his left, obviously determined to imbed the recessed needle into the fat of his victim's back. Anya threw a front kick, sending the cane into the air and landing harmlessly several feet away.

The would-be assassin drew his knife and sprang from the floor as if fired from a cannon, landing in a perfect fighting stance in front of Anya.

She stepped between the man and his target, shielding the Russian with her body, and whispered, "I will now kill you with your own knife."

The young man behind the makeup laughed and lunged for Anya with a straight-line attack aimed at her heart. She easily sidestepped the attack and struck the man in the side of his neck as he passed. Taking advantage of his newfound position in the room, he tossed the knife from his right hand to his left and redirected its deadly tip toward his still-seated, original Russian target. Anya sent a crushing sidekick to the man's knee before he could deliver the deadly blow, sending him, once again, back to the ground.

Patrons stood from their tables and backed away. Some ran in fear while others couldn't take their eyes from the unbelievable scene unfolding in front of them.

Anya grasped a heavily weighted tumbler full of honey-colored liquor and hurled it toward the would-be assassin's face as he scrambled backward, determined to escape her attack. The glass struck his nose and opened his flesh through the prosthetic and makeup. He pawed at his bleeding face and continued to squirm backward. Anya lifted a steak knife from a table and tested its weight in her palm. She tossed the weapon into the air and caught it by its tip. An instant later, the spinning blade left her grip and soared through the air and toward the man who no longer cared if anyone believed he was a senior citizen. With the skill of a master martial artist, he thrust his body away from the airborne blade, taking its impact on his right shoulder instead of the center of his chest. The glancing blow sent the weapon skittering harmlessly across the floor.

The Asians retreated to the relative safety of the bar, but their Soviet companion stood in awe at the battle waging just beyond his fingertips. The gleam in his eye gave him the look of a man with a million-dollar wager on the outcome of the fight, while in reality, his very life was at stake.

As the flailing assassin continued his backward crabwalk across the floor, Anya sent a thundering kick into the seat of a heavy wooden chair.

The object exploded into a dozen pieces, but the only remains of the chair she wanted lay side by side in the debris. She lifted what had been the two back legs of the chair and stepped toward the killer, who'd found his way back to his feet.

Obviously still amused by Anya's aggression, the man drew a second knife from his waist and dared her to approach. She spun the chair legs like batons and advanced on the knife-wielding man. He once again lunged for her, thrusting a killing blade before him, but Anya pivoted, clearing the centerline of the strike and sending the end of a chair leg crashing down onto the back of his hand. The sickening sound of bones collapsing beneath the blow echoed through the room, followed by his bellowing cry. As the energy of his advance carried him past Anya, she landed a second blow on the back of his neck, just below the base of his skull, and he fell limp, face-first onto the cold marble floor. She yanked a second knife from a table and leapt onto the man's back with her left knee planted in the center of his spine. The blade came to rest on the same smooth skin of his neck she'd noticed moments before the attack.

The pressure from the tip of the knife broke the flesh, but he didn't move. His shoulders never rose nor fell. He'd drawn his final breath the instant before Anya sent him into the afterlife with the broken leg of a chair.

A commanding voice filled the air of the bar. "Do not move! Vancouver Police. Raise your hands above your head, immediately!"

Anya followed the order and raised her hands, allowing the knife to remain lying on her victim's neck. A uniformed officer clasped a handcuff around her left wrist and twisted her arm to the small of her back. She allowed him to cuff her right wrist, and she stood upon the officer's urging.

The heavyset Russian stepped to the officer's side. "What are you doing? This woman saved my life. You cannot arrest her."

The officer placed a hand in the center of the man's chest and pushed him away.

The Russian swatted the offending hand. "How dare you touch me? You will release her at once. She is my personal bodyguard, and you are out of line."

"Step back, sir," the officer ordered. "This doesn't concern you."

"The hell it doesn't concern me. This man was trying to kill me with that cane." He drove a finger through the air toward where the cane had landed only seconds after the attack began.

A second officer followed the man's finger. "What cane, sir?"

The Russian scoured the area with his deeply hooded eyes. "It was there only moments ago. Someone must have . . ."

The officers flanked their cuffed prisoner and brushed past the Russian. "Step aside, sir. If this woman works for you, I recommend finding her a competent attorney."

The heavy man thrust a hip against the officer, forcing him backward a stride, and he leaned toward Anya. "Tell me your name. I must know your name."

Hiding her Russian accent as much as possible, Anya said, "First, I must know yours."

The man closed one eye as if aiming with measured precision. "My name is Zakhar Belyaev. And now yours."

I am United States Department of Justice Special Agent Ana Fulton."

2

REPATRIATSIYA
(REPATRIATION)

U.S. Department of Justice Supervisory Special Agent Ray White flashed his credentials to the desk sergeant at the Vancouver Police Department. "I'm here to see Captain Leblanc."

The young officer behind the desk looked up with relief written all over her face. "You have no idea how happy we are to see you, Special Agent White. That agent of yours has had this place turned upside down all day. Captain Leblanc is waiting for you." She motioned through a pair of double doors. "Follow that corridor to the last office on the left, and please tell me you're here to collect Special Agent Fulton, because you're either taking her back with you or you're taking me. I can't be in the same building with her for another day."

White leaned across the desk. "Do you know how to cut the heart out of a Russian mafia boss with a pair of toenail clippers?"

The sergeant recoiled. "What is that supposed to mean?"

White gave her a wink. "If you can't do that, then I'll take my agent. You couldn't possibly replace her."

A buzzer sounded, followed by the thud and click of the locking mechanism on the doors. White, followed closely by two more agents of the DOJ, pushed through the doors. Thirty-one-year-old Johnathon "Johnny Mac" McIntyre and twenty-eight-year-old Guinevere "Gwynn" Davis trailed their boss down the spotless corridor lined with photographs of men—and a few women—who must've held some importance to the country of Canada, but neither junior agent recognized any of the faces.

Johnny Mac laid a hand against the captain's door before White could pull it open. "What do you want us to do in there, boss?"

White smacked his hand from the door. "I want you to do the same thing in there I want you to do out here in the hallway—keep your mouths shut, and look menacing."

The woman sitting behind the desk in Captain Leblanc's outer office never looked up. She pointed toward a second set of double doors and pressed the remote lock.

Gwynn caught the woman's attention as they passed, and she mouthed, "Thank you."

The woman rolled her eyes and dove back into her computer keyboard.

Captain Leblanc rose from behind an elegant desk in front of a wall of glass looking out over Vancouver Harbour. He extended a hand, and White took it.

"Supervisory Special Agent Ray White."

"Nice to meet you, Agent White. I'm Captain Stephon Leblanc. I suppose you'd like to see your agent."

"I would," White said. "But first, I'd like to hear your version of what happened."

Leblanc motioned toward a collection of chairs. "You don't have to hear my version, Agent White. We've got the whole thing on digital video." The captain spun a monitor to face the three Americans and pressed a key on his keyboard.

"Property of the Grand Condor Inn" scrolled across the screen before four individual panes appeared, showing four unique views of the lounge.

The three DOJ agents studied the screen, taking in every face in the crowd, until Gwynn blurted out, "Ooh, there's Anya. I mean . . . Special Agent Fulton."

White eyed her as if to command a disobedient child to stop whatever she was doing. Gwynn stared back at the screen as the video showed Anya scanning the room like a hawk. The big man flanked by two Asians entered a frame and took their seats. The scene played out as the old man with the newspaper rose, lifted his cane, and approached his target. Gwynn gasped as her friend and mentor leapt into action. Johnny Mac's eyes widened almost as broadly as Gwynn's, but White remained stoic.

The fight played out, and the video ended with Anya being led away by a pair of uniformed officers and briefly exchanging words with the large man who'd obviously been a target of the now-dead assassin.

"Who's the man?" White asked.

Leblanc said, "His name is, or was . . ."

White interrupted. "I don't care about the dead guy. Who's the fat guy my agent saved?"

The captain cleared his throat. "His name is Zakhar Belyaev. He's a Russian businessman who apparently owns interests in more than fifty businesses around the world, including a Chinese tech company whose sole purpose seems to be the development of artificial intelligence. The two men with him are the company's chief engineer and the equivalent of a chief financial officer. Rumor has it they were negotiating a—"

White held up a hand. "Okay, that's enough. I don't need to know any more. Do you know the true identity of the assassin?"

"Not yet, but we're running his fingerprints through INTERPOL. So far, he's a ghost. We would, of course, welcome any assistance the Americans could provide."

"Copy me on the INTERPOL request." White slid a business card across the desk. "I'll personally see that his prints are run through both the FBI and Central Intelligence databases. He obviously wasn't very good at his job, so I'm betting he's a low-level nobody who wants to make a name for himself on the international scene. Do you have any pictures of his face without the disguise?"

"We do. I'll forward those, along with the INTERPOL packet."

White nodded and pulled an envelope from an interior pocket of his jacket. "Forgive me, Captain, but I'm not up to speed on legal proceedings on this side of the border. I have a formal request from the United States attorney general to repatriate my agent. Is it necessary for me to file it with your equivalent of our AG?"

Leblanc waved him off. "Agent White, even though our laws are quite different from yours, your agent isn't being charged with a crime. From all indications, she saved a man's life today, and we saved her from a swarm of media attention neither she nor your government wanted. As far as the Canadian government is concerned, your agent is free to go, but we would request that she stay in Canada no longer than absolutely necessary to board an airplane and fly anywhere south."

White tucked the empty envelope back into his pocket, thankful the ruse had at least sounded official. "I do have one more question if you wouldn't mind."

Captain Leblanc sighed. "Yes, what is it?"

"The desk sergeant—at least that's what we call them in the States— seemed anxious to get rid of Agent Fulton. Could you tell me what she did that caused so much fuss?"

Leblanc forced back the coming smile. "Apparently, Agent White, your girl back there has quite the opposition to having her fingerprints taken. She destroyed our electronic fingerprint scanner and broke two pairs of handcuffs and one officer's wrist who tried to ink her prints."

Johnny Mac gasped, and Gwynn giggled almost silently.

White shot both of them the stern parental look. "Captain Leblanc, do you make a habit of fingerprinting every foreign federal government agent who saves the life of a prominent businessman who your police force couldn't protect from a second-rate assassin?" Leblanc frowned, and White said, "Include a bill for your electronic fingerprint machine, and I'll see that you're reimbursed. Now, where's my agent?"

The captain pressed a button on his telephone, and a uniformed officer appeared in his doorway. "If you'll follow this officer, he'll take you to your agent. Oh, and one more thing, Agent White. Make it clear to your agent that her next visit to Vancouver won't be as pleasant, so she'd do well to stay south of the border."

White offered a mock salute, and the three followed the officer from Leblanc's office. He led them through a labyrinth of hallways and finally into a block of holding cells with narrow, wire-reinforced windows on heavy steel doors. The officer peered through the window of the second cell and pulled an electronic key from his belt. After a swipe of the keycard and a six-digit code, the door clicked and swung inward.

Clearly uninterested in entering the cell, the officer stepped back, allowing White and his two minions to stroll through the opening.

Anya looked up from her seat, leapt to her feet, and ran to Gwynn. "I knew you would come for me. It is so good to see you again."

White ran a hand between the two women and pried them apart. "Cut it out. This isn't some kind of girlfriend reunion. You've caused even more trouble than you usually do. Let's go."

In the van back to the airport, White hushed any attempts at conversation, but when the four were buckled aboard the U.S. government Gulfstream jet, White said, "Okay, let's hear it. What the hell was that all about?"

"Are you talking to me?" Anya said.

"No, I'm talking to the other former KGB assassin on the plane who destroyed a fingerprint machine and killed a guy in a swanky bar today."

"He was not just a guy," she said. "He was State-trained assassin, and he was not alone."

White leaned in. "What do you mean he wasn't alone?"

"It is difficult to see everything when fighting dangerous man, so I did not see person who escaped with cane, but someone did. Also, I do not know this man, Zakhar Belyaev. I have never heard of him."

"If you don't know him, what made you risk your life to save his?"

"I did not risk my life," she said. "I only stopped assassin from killing this man because it was right thing to do. Oh, and I am not former KGB assassin. KGB was dead when I completed training with SVR."

Five minutes into the flight, the pilot's voice poured from the speaker overhead. "We're now back inside American airspace. Welcome home."

Anya smiled as the pilot's words washed over her, and Gwynn seemed to notice. She gave the *former* Russian's hand a squeeze and offered a barely perceptible nod.

Unlike Gwynn's kindness, White grabbed a fistful of Anya's shirt and scowled. "Where have you been?"

3

SVIN'YA
(THE PIG)

Anya glared downward at White's fist, and he released the hold on her shirt. "Where I have been is none of your business, Agent White, but if I had not been delayed in Vancouver, I would be back in Washington D.C. by now and ready for next mission."

White growled. "You don't get to run off wherever you want whenever you want."

Anya nodded. "Yes, I do. When I am not on mission for Department of Justice and for you, I will do whatever I want. I told to Gwynn I would come back, and I would catch for you all of *Russkoye Bratstvo* you want. Holding over my head threat of prison is no longer necessary."

"It may not be necessary, but it's far more than a mere threat. It is exactly what will happen if you—"

Anya laid her hand on top of his. "Agent White, I am here to help you. I have proven I can disappear if this is what I wish to do. Obviously, this is not what I wish. I am American girl now, and I will help my country only because you ask . . . not because of threat."

White pulled his hand from beneath hers. "I can keep you in the States."

"You could *try* to do this, but you cannot. If you put for me ankle monitor, this will not keep me inside country. It will only let you know when I have left. Also, you could put me into prison like you have threatened to do, but there is no prison in all of world that can hold me. You know all of this, so your threat is empty. I am like powerful horse being ridden by little boy."

Ray White shook his head. "What?"

"Yes, I am like horse, and you are little boy. You believe I must obey when you give command, but this is not true. Truth is, I obey because I choose to do so, not because I must. Horse can throw boy onto ground and step on him but does not do this because maybe horse likes little boy."

White pinched his eyebrows together. "Am I the horse or the boy?"

Anya gave him the smile that had melted men's resolve in every corner of the globe. "I will not step on you, little boy. This I promise to you."

White unbuckled his seatbelt, moved as far away from the others as the cabin space would allow, and settled into a new seat. Sleep took him before his anger could.

Gwynn glanced between the seats to see her boss's eyes closed and his chest rising and falling in rhythmic cycles. She leaned toward Anya. "Are you going to tell me where you've been?"

"Not until we are alone," Anya whispered. "Do we have new mission?"

Gwynn nodded. "Yeah, we do. It's in New Orleans. Have you ever been?"

Anya looked toward the ceiling. "I think yes, I have been, but only once, and for only short time. It is city of uh . . . I do not know English word. In Russian is *razvrat*."

Gwynn frowned. "What does that word mean in English?"

Anya sighed. "I think this means people doing immoral things with no remorse."

"Debauchery," Gwynn said. "I think that's the word you're looking for."

"Perhaps this is word, but I do not know."

Gwynn gasped and covered her mouth. "Oh my God! I know where you've been."

Anya shot looks at White and Johnny Mac before whispering, "This is not possible."

"Oh, it's possible, all right. You've been in Russia. I can tell by your accent. You've not spoken English in three months, and it shows. Your accent is stronger, and you've abandoned English articles altogether. You've been speaking only Russian, and the only place you can do that is in Russia."

Anya said, "You are better police officer than you think."

"What were you doing over there? I thought it was too dangerous for you to go back."

"It is dangerous, but sometimes is worth danger. Perhaps, someday, I can tell you every part of me."

Gwynn grabbed Anya's arm. "Perhaps nothing! You're definitely telling me what's so important that you'd risk getting caught in Russia."

Anya glanced back at White, still sleeping away like a little boy. "Maybe, but not now."

* * *

Robert F. Kennedy Department of Justice Building at 905 Pennsylvania Avenue Northwest, Washington, D.C.

Special Agent Ray White sat upright in his plush office chair behind his power desk. Gwynn and Johnny Mac took seats beside Anya, opposite their boss.

"Don't get comfortable," White said. "You two can wait outside while Anya and I have a talk."

Without argument, both agents abandoned their seats and made their way to White's outer office.

The senior special agent pulled a bottle and two tumblers from a bottom drawer. He poured two fingers of the golden liquor into each glass and slid one across the desk.

Anya stared down at the cocktail. "No, thank you."

White huffed. "It's not vodka, for God's sake. It's good Kentucky bourbon. Drink it."

Anya lifted the glass to her nose and inhaled the oaky scent of the well-aged spirit. White raised his glass, and Anya followed suit. "To coming home."

The Russian smiled. "Yes, to coming home."

They sipped and stared for a long moment until White broke the silence. "You and I are going to cut a deal."

Anya looked over the glass at White as he leaned back in his chair. "What is deal?"

White placed his tumbler on the corner of his desk. "First, you're going to stop making me look like a jackass all over the world, and especially in front of my own subordinates."

Anya asked, "Does this mean no more horse and little boy comparison?"

"I think you know the answer to that one."

She nodded. "This cannot be all, so what is rest of deal?"

"The rest of the deal is that I'll stop hanging prison over your head. If you're serious about doing what's right, then you'll stick around. If not, I'll retire in failure."

"What does this mean, retire in failure?"

White poured another inch of bourbon into his glass. "It means my career is over when this assignment ends. I'll either retire as a disgrace to the DOJ, or I'll accomplish this mission and fade away with some dignity and one last checkmark in the win column."

Anya cocked her head. "But you are young man. I think maybe only forty-five. This is too young to no longer work."

I've been doing this job for almost twenty-seven years, Anya. Aside from college and law school, it's all I've ever done as an adult."

"You have done more than this," she said. "You have learned to cook, enjoy tea with me, and drink wonderful bourbon."

"Aside from tea with you, the other two are merely distractions from this job."

She smiled, but not the carefully crafted, learned smile. Hers was sincere and more beautiful than any she could manufacture. "So, this means you like having tea with me, yes?"

White stared deeper into his glass. "Anya, you're a thousand different people inside that flawless shell of yours, but someday I think I'd love to have tea with the real one behind all those facades."

She considered his confession and swallowed another sip of her bourbon. "The real one inside me would also enjoy this . . . someday."

Neither spoke for a long moment, each sitting in silence and pondering how life without pretenses might feel.

Supervisory Special Agent Raymond White thought of life simply as Ray, a man without a badge, a gun, or a title . . . Just a man. Anastasia Robertovna Burinkova pondered how pleasantly simple life might have been without her ability to sever life from flesh and bone, without her stolen childhood, and without her training as a master craftsman of seduction and betrayal.

White drew them both back into the reality of the moment by leaning the bottle toward Anya's nearly empty glass. She tasted the smokiness of the whiskey on her lips and slid her glass toward him. He poured until she raised a hand.

"When we started this operation, I had a list of seven nasty little Russians," he began. "They're ignoring the law and making a mockery of what's left of the goodness in this country. You've eliminated two of those men, and now you're going to help me put the remaining five in a casket or a prison cell, and you're going to do this because it's the right thing to do."

The clang of the hammer and sickle echoed in her head. "Am I to kill these men for you? If this is what you want, give to me names and photographs of five remaining men, and they will die before end of year."

He sighed and leaned back, staring at the ceiling above him. "Oh, if it were only that simple. But that's not how we do things here. We're not the Soviets. We're the good guys . . . mostly."

She savored another taste of the whiskey. "I am not good . . . mostly."

White chuckled. "Anya, compared to ninety percent of the people in this city, especially the civil servants, you're a saint. The difference between you and them is that you have a conscience. Most of them don't."

She ignored the compliment—if that's what it had been—and motioned toward the door. "We should bring back others into office so we can brief mission in New Orleans."

"How could you possibly know the mission is in New Orleans?"

She offered nothing more than a devious smile.

Ray pressed a button on his phone. "Get in here, you two."

An instant later, Gwynn and Johnny Mac were back in their seats flanking Anya, and White began the briefing. "Davis, you and Knife Blade Natasha are going to New Orleans." The two friends shared a knowing glance, and White slid a file across his desk.

Anya watched the folder come to a stop an inch from the edge of the mammoth piece of furniture. "What is his name?"

White pointed at the folder. "It's all in there."

Anya patted the file. "Yes, but inside is no feeling. Is only paper and words. Whoever is inside folder is also inside your mind. You know everything about him, and when you look into my eyes and tell to me his name, I will see and hear and feel emotion for this man inside you."

"His name is Vasily Orlov, and he's doing something we don't understand."

Anya stared into Ray's soul, then opened the file and thumbed through the pages, stopping on a photograph. She held up the picture. "This is Vasily Orlov?"

"Yes, that's him."

Anya studied the picture for a few more seconds and tossed it back into the folder. "He is fat pig. This is crime inside United States?"

"No, we're a nation of fat pigs. If that was illegal, the prisons would be overflowing."

"This is true of prisons already," Anya said.

"Yes, but they're not full because of obesity, and we're not after Orlov because of his gut. We want him because of what we believe he's bringing into the country."

4

Bol'shoy Legkiy Gorod
(Big Easy City)

Ray White flipped open the file. "This mission is a little different than anything you've done for us in the past."

Anya frowned. "I have done only two things for you in past. First one was actually done by Gwynn when she killed Leo in Miami. Second, I gave to you information on man who is stealing diamonds in New York City."

White leaned back in his chair. "That's not all you did in New York. You also fled the scene while we were raiding Viktor Volkov's warehouse and office."

She smiled. "Yes, I did this because you did not need me there, and I had things to do."

He crossed his legs. "Things to do, huh? The story I heard is that you had some important deliveries to make. Would that be an accurate statement?"

"I cannot say if statement is accurate. I did not hear anyone tell you this."

Ray shook his head. "You do that on purpose, don't you? You pretend you don't know what an English phrase means, and then you play innocent. Cut it out. You know exactly what I mean."

"I make promise to little girl, and promises like this must always be kept."

"Then stop making promises."

The Russian turned to Gwynn. "I made promise to her that I will do for you these missions without threat of prison for rest of my life. Is okay with you if I keep this promise, yes?"

White tossed a pair of antacid chews onto his tongue. "Conversations with you are like trying to pet a porcupine."

"Why would you do this?" Anya asked.

"Because it's my job," he said.

Anya narrowed her gaze. "Petting porcupine is your job?"

White huffed. "I'm going to shoot you in the face if you do that again. You're the smartest person I've ever met, so playing dumb with me is never going to work."

Anya placed her hand on her chest as if in disbelief. "Thank you. This is wonderful compliment."

He squeezed his eyelids closed as if warding off a coming migraine. "Let's focus on Vasily Orlov. We believe he's illegally importing beluga caviar into New Orleans. It's possible he's having the caviar packed beneath Chilean sea bass."

Anya screwed up her face. "Why would this be illegal?"

"It's not exactly illegal . . . yet," White said. "But it will be next year."

"We are now arresting people for things that will not be crime until future?"

White held up a palm. "No, not at all. It's ridiculously complex, but I'll try to break it down for you."

"You said I am smartest person you know, so I think I can understand."

"Yeah, anyway . . . The Chilean sea bass is one of the most highly regulated fish products shipped to the United States. Let's start with a little history lesson. Chilean sea bass doesn't originate from Chile. In fact, it's not really bass. Technically, it's two different fish—the Patagonian toothfish and the Antarctic toothfish. They're almost impossible to tell apart unless you're some kind marine biologist who specializes in Antarctic deep-water species. None of that really matters, though. What matters is that Chilean sea bass imported to the States must be caught in approved fishing grounds and managed in a sustainable manner."

"This sounds silly," Anya said. "Why does United States Department of Justice care about fish and eggs?"

White rolled his eyes. "I understand your confusion, and I feel the same, but we don't get to pick and choose which laws we enforce and which ones we ignore. There's also a lot more to the story. The U.S. attorney general believes if Orlov is skating around the rules by importing poached sea bass and possibly hiding beluga caviar in the packing ice, he's likely doing far worse things than that, and ultimately, your mission is to find out what else he's doing."

"This is joke, yes? I cannot believe this is real mission. I am highly trained *ubiytsa*, and this is mission for fishing police."

White ran his hands through his hair and sighed. "Yeah, I know you're an assassin, but you're also Russian, and that key opens doors Gwynn and Johnny Mac cannot. You can slip into Orlov's world without him suspecting you're a fed."

"Yes, of course, this is true, but I am not police officer. I am killer. Bringing into country illegal fish is not crime to be killed for, is it?"

White dug at his temples. "You're missing the point, Anya. And you *are*, technically, a police officer. You've got a badge, and a federal judge swore you in. Remember?"

"I remember this, yes, but—"

White held up a hand. "Just stop and listen. We don't want to arrest Orlov for smuggling fish or caviar into the country. We want to know what else he's doing. Think of the smuggling as a gateway crime."

"I do not know this phrase, gateway crime."

"Think of it as a relatively minor crime that leads to a much larger one . . . or several larger ones. Just like marijuana is believed by some to be a gateway drug to the far more deadly narcotics like heroin or cocaine, we believe Orlov likely started out bringing in a few cans of caviar for himself until some of his buddies wanted a case and were willing to pay for it. Orlov's ties to Russian organized crime are justification for us sticking our nose into his business and seeing what else he's hiding."

Anya nodded slowly. "And for this mission, Gwynn and I are noses of Department of Justice."

White smiled for the first time in days. "I wouldn't have put it quite that way, but now that you mention it, that's precisely what you are."

"This is boring mission. We will have another soon, yes?"

"Compared to South Beach, New York City, and where you've been for the past three months, maybe New Orleans is boring, but something tells me the two of you are going to find a way to turn it into a circus."

"You have for us apartment in New Orleans, yes?"

"Actually," White said, "how do you feel about boats?"

Anya's eyes lit up. "I love boats, and I am very good sailor. I learned this from Chase."

White drummed his fingers on the desk. "This one isn't exactly a sailboat. It's a motor yacht. The legend we've constructed for you is that you're the daughter of a Russian oligarch, and, as such, you've grown accustomed to the finer things in life. That justifies the boat, your wardrobe, and whatever you two decide Davis is going to be."

Anya gave Gwynn a wink. "I think I was wrong. This will not be boring mission, and it might take many weeks."

White drove a finger through the air. "Oh, no! That's where you're wrong. You two are not dragging your feet on this one. You'll get in, get the goods, and get out. This isn't an all-expenses-paid vacation on the taxpayers' dime."

Anya held out her hand. "Give to me file on Vasily Orlov."

White slid the packet back across the desk. "That folder doesn't leave this office. Memorize it, sing it to yourself, whatever you have to do, but it stays with me."

Anya wordlessly thumbed through the file, stopping occasionally to absorb the details. Two minutes later, she slid the file back to Ray. "I will do this for you, and I am certain my Russian oligarch *otets*—this means *father* —wishes for me to have *my* Porsche inside Big Easy city."

Ray grimaced. "Yeah, I know what *otets* means, but how many times do I have to remind you the Porsche isn't *your* car. It's the property of—"

"Yes, yes," Anya said. "It is property of United States government, but is for me to use, and I wish to now use for mission."

"That's not how this works. You don't get to decide what assets you'll have available for any given mission."

She gave him a sharp nod. "Good, then it is settled. We will have Porsche for New Orleans mission. When is starting time?"

White dove back into the antacid bottle. "Have you ever heard the phrase 'You can't always get what you want,' and doesn't *anyone* ever tell you no?"

Anya stood and stared down at him. "Yes, Chase Fulton said to me no, and from him I kept only last name on passport and driving license. From him, I could not have what I wanted, but from you, I can."

She turned for the door and took Gwynn's hand. "Come. We have shopping trip before moving onto yacht, and you are my American girl-friend. We do everything together. This is what I have decided you will be for mission. This is okay with you, yes?"

Gwynn took her hand and stood. "Oh, yeah. That's more than okay."

Before White could protest, the two women sashayed through the office door and Johnny Mac threw up his palms. "Why do you let them do that?"

White hooked Anya's tumbler with one finger and slid it toward his side of the desk. He poured half a glass and slid it to Johnny Mac. "Jealous much, Special Agent McIntyre?"

Uncertain if the drink was a test, the young agent pointed toward the glass with the question glowing in his eyes.

White waved at the drink with the back of his hand. "Oh, pick it up. We're off the clock, and you're going to need it before you hear your next assignment."

Johnny Mac eyed his boss and sipped the bourbon. "Why do I get the feeling I'm not going to like this one?"

"Because you're a good cop. And good cops have good instincts. You're going to The Big Easy with the women, and you get a clothing allowance, too. The difference is, you'll want to spend yours at the thrift store instead of Barney's. Anya and Gwynn need an invisible overwatch, and nobody is more invisible than a homeless guy in the French Quarter."

Johnny Mac emptied the tumbler and planted it back on White's desk. "You can't be serious. Those two are living on a yacht, and I'm sleeping in a cardboard box?"

"That's how the ball bounced on this one. Your day will come, but for now, the demands of the service outweigh the tenets of fairness. Remember, you begged for this job. Over two hundred agents wanted this gig in Special Projects, but you and Davis wanted it a little more than everyone else. I'll make it up to you, Johnny Mac, but you're going to have to swallow your pride on this one."

"I did want this job, and I'm thankful you chose me, but playing a homeless guy on Bourbon Street isn't exactly what I had in mind."

White poured another drink for the dejected agent. "I lived in a dumpster in New York City for four weeks in December of eighty-eight. It was the worst assignment of my career, but it got me this office and this desk. We busted Carlos Mancini, one of his lieutenants, and five wise guys because of what I heard while I was in that dumpster and the evidence I collected every time one of Mancini's thugs was too lazy to take the trash across town instead of tossing it right into my lap."

Johnny Mac swirled his drink. "Four weeks in a dumpster, huh?"

"That's right. And did I mention it was December?"

Johnny Mac sipped his cocktail. "Are you saying if I pull off this home-less-guy gig in New Orleans . . ."

White shrugged. "You never know which job is going to make your career, but I guarantee this one isn't going to hurt yours."

5
TORT PROGULKA
(CAKE WALK)

Just before ten the next morning, Ray White checked his watch for the last time before picking up his phone. "Davis, are you planning to come to work this morning?"

Gwynn stared into the phone before saying, "I've been here since seven, boss."

"You've been *where* since seven?"

"In my office."

"Find your little *matryoshka*, and get in here. We've got a mission to brief."

Gwynn followed Anya down the gray corridor and through White's office door. "I am not *matryoshka*. This is cheap Russian nesting doll. I am none of those things."

White couldn't resist. "None of what things?"

Anya frowned. "Cheap, nesting, or doll. I am not for sale, so I cannot be cheap. I have no home, so I cannot nest. And I am definitely not doll for someone to play with."

White ignored the cheap and doll denial but lingered on the nest. "What do you mean you have no home? You've got a house in Athens and an apartment you didn't think I knew about."

"Only half of this is true. I do not have house in Athens. I gave this to Irina Volkovna and daughter, Anya. And how do you know about apartment?"

White inspected his fingernails. "I'm a big-time federal agent. I know a lot of things you don't think I know."

Anya pretended to ignore his comment. "Apartment is not home. Is only temporary sleeping and eating place."

"I'm not so sure a two-bedroom, luxury apartment in downtown Nashville qualifies as just a place to sleep and eat."

"Oh, this is apartment you are talking about. Yes, of course, Nashville apartment is nice and comfortable. I thought you meant other apartments."

White raised his eyebrows. "Other apartments?"

"Yes, of course, and if you were really big-time agent like you believe, you would know of these, also."

"These? Plural?"

The Russian shrugged. "My English is not so good. Maybe I said plural when I meant only single . . . maybe."

"Your English is a lot better than you pretend. We'll get back to the apartments—plural—in a minute, but first I want you to tell me about Zakhar Belyaev."

"I told you before, I do not know this man. I only temporarily stopped assassin from killing him in Vancouver because it was convenient."

"Convenient? You killed a would-be assassin out of convenience?"

"No, not exactly, but this is not what I mean. Zakhar Belyaev will be dead soon if SVR wants to kill him. I think man I killed was not SVR. He fought more like street thug than trained officer. I think he was not Russian. Maybe Chechen . . . Yes, probably Chechen."

White cocked his head. "Why would you say that?"

Anya stared down at White, perplexed. "You know of Chechen War, yes?"

"Yes, of course. It's been going on since ninety-nine, but how could you possibly know he was Chechen?"

Anya pursed her lips. "Is just feeling I have. Maybe I am wrong, but probably not. This is not important for mission in New Orleans, yes?"

"Is that a real question?"

"No, is rhetorical question, I think. But is not important, yes?"

"Stop doing that! No, it's not important whether or not the guy you killed is Chechen. It has nothing to do with the mission."

"This is what I said. We can sit down, now, yes?"

"Yes, sit. Just stop ending sentences with yes or no. It freaks me out. Now, stop talking, and listen."

The former spy and her understudy did as they were told and nestled into their chairs.

White began. "First, don't kill anybody else. Got it?" Neither woman flinched, and White said, "Got it?"

Anya turned to Gwynn. "Is this order for you or for me?"

Gwynn whispered, "I think both of us."

"Did you kill someone I do not know about?"

Gwynn shook her head.

"It's for both of you," White said, "but mostly you, Red Sonja. You've been back in North America for an hour, and you already killed some poor guy in Canada."

"Is not some poor guy, and is much more than one hour."

White raised a hand. "Stop talking!"

"I will stop talking for now, but was not some poor guy. Was mediocre assassin."

White slammed a hand onto his desk. "You're talking, and that's the opposite of not talking. Now, listen. Do not kill anyone in New Orleans. We don't even know for sure what this guy, Vasily Orlov, is doing down there. For all we know, he could be handing out black-market caviar. If that's all he's doing, we don't care. Have you got that?"

Gwynn nodded, but Anya couldn't hold her tongue. "Yes, we do not kill Orlov unless he is doing more than smuggling caviar."

"No! We don't kill Orlov no matter what he's doing! You find out what's going on, and you make daily reports. That's it. This mission is a cakewalk."

Anya furrowed her brow and started to speak, but Gwynn put her hand on the Russian's arm. "Shh. I'll explain it later."

White said, "Orlov spends a lot of time in a restaurant called Eden's View. That's where you'll start. The chef is a guy named Christian Gerard. Here's his dossier."

Anya caught the folder before it fell from the desk, and she opened it to reveal a single sheet of paper. She scanned the document and passed it to Gwynn.

Thirty seconds later, Davis replaced the sheet into the folder and laid it back on the mahogany desk. "Do we believe the chef is part of whatever Orlov is doing down there?"

White said, "No, probably not, but he's worth taking a look into. He's a graduate of Le Cordon Bleu and the Culinary Institute of America. As you saw in the dossier, he studied under a couple of chefs nobody's ever heard of."

Anya raised a finger. "This is not true. Look again. He studied under Marcus Vikander in New York City. He is most famous chef from Norway."

"Okay, fine. He cooked with some Norwegian reindeer chef that only you've heard of. That's not the point. The point is, this guy spent a lot of time in school and working for other people, and then, all of a sudden, he opened up this joint called Eden's View, and he's instantly on the cover of every culinary magazine in the world."

Anya gazed at the horizontal line where the ceiling of White's office met the wall. "Why New Orleans?"

White lowered his gaze. "What do you mean, why New Orleans?"

"Why did Gerrard go to New Orleans to open restaurant? Where is home for him?"

White flipped open the file and ran a finger down the page. "Hmm, we don't know. But that's an interesting question. Maybe he has a weakness for Eastern European blondes who've heard of that Vikander guy."

Anya turned to Gwynn. "Or maybe he prefers beautiful American brunette girl with rich Russian girlfriend."

"Perhaps," White conceded.

The three sat in silence, pondering the possibilities until White snapped his fingers. "I almost forgot. Johnny Mac is going with you on this one, and he's not happy about it."

Gwynn leaned forward. "Not happy? He's been chomping at the bit to get into the field with us. Why isn't he happy?"

White chuckled. "He's going undercover . . . down and dirty kind of undercover. You are not to interact with him, even if you see him. Things can get, let's say, exciting on Bourbon Street for two women on their own."

Anya lowered her chin. "There is no one on Bourbon Street—or any other street—who is more dangerous than me. I think we do not need Johnny Mac to protect us."

"Don't worry. Johnny Mac isn't there to protect you. He's there to make sure *you* don't hurt anybody."

"This is good idea. Gwynn always wants to hurt other people. She is very aggressive."

Gwynn laughed. "Yeah, that's me . . . aggressive."

"Okay, that's enough fooling around," White said. "Here's what's going to happen next. We'll fly the two of you into New Orleans Lakefront Airport where you'll be met by the limo."

Anya raised a finger. "You mean, where our Porsche will be waiting, yes?"

White glared at the Russian. "Interrupt me again, and I'll send that car you love so much straight to the crusher." Anya pouted, and White continued. "The limo will pick you up, and the driver will make sure everyone notices you. He'll take you to the South Shore Harbor Marina, which is literally across the street from the airport. Your boat will be on display for you and everyone else who passes by the marina."

White paused long enough to swallow another mouthful of coffee, and Anya jumped in. "Marina beside airport will be very loud and no good place for luxury yacht."

"Don't worry. You're not staying at that marina. Once you're aboard and suitably viewed, the captain will move the yacht to the New Orleans Yacht Club, where you'll be moored in plain sight. The view won't be quite as nice as your apartment in Times Square, but you'll definitely get more attention."

"We will fly on private jet to New Orleans, yes?"

"Of course. Everything about this mission is going to be over the top. We've tried to hide you for the previous two missions, but not this time. You two will be the stars of the show in The Big Easy."

The look on Gwynn's face said she'd been taking careful notes in her head. "How quickly do you want us to hit the restaurant after we arrive?"

White rubbed his forehead. "That's the part that gives me a headache. I have no choice but to leave the operational details up to you. There are too many variables to consider in a place like New Orleans. You'll have to play it by ear, but I expect a daily report. Of course, there will be secure comms on the yacht. That'll be our primary means of communication during the mission."

Gwynn nodded. "Okay, I've got that. Now, just so I'm clear on the details, do you want us to find and befriend Orlov, or should we crawl in bed with the chef? Not literally, of course."

"I made the decision to keep you two high-profile for this one, so it's far more plausible that you'd mix and mingle with Orlov's crowd than the chef, but if those two are wrapped up as tight as I suspect, they may be practically interchangeable."

Gwynn stared at the ceiling and bit her bottom lip.

"Are you okay?" White asked.

"I'm fine. I'm just running through the logistics. This op feels a lot looser than New York and Miami."

White leaned back in his chair. "I'm glad you noticed. Here's the truth, but don't let it go to your heads. The two of you have proven to be a far better investigative tool than anyone here at Justice could've imagined. This doesn't mean you're not still on a leash. It just means the leash isn't quite as short, and the collar isn't so tight."

Gwynn and Anya shared a mischievous glance, and White punched a finger at both women. "On, no. Don't get that look. You're both doing good work, but she"—White eyed Gwynn and pointed to Anya—"she is a bad influence on you, and if you turn into her, it'll destroy your career at Justice."

Gwynn smirked. "If I turn into her, I won't need this crummy career at Justice."

6

Etogo Nikogda ne Budet (This Will Never Do)

Dawn broke over Davison Army Airfield at Fort Belvoir, Virginia, to find Special Agent Gwynn Davis and Anya Burinkova climbing the boarding stairs onto a luxurious Gulfstream business jet. The two looked as if they could've just walked off a fashion shoot in Paris.

"It's amazing what a nearly unrestricted clothing allowance can do to transform you two into"—White motioned toward the pair—"this. You both look stunning."

Anya pushed a strand of perfect blonde hair from her face. "We were stunning before you gave to us clothing allowance."

White held up his palms in surrender. "I'm not interested in ending my career with a sexual harassment complaint, but both of you certainly look the part. Do you have any questions before you soar off into the wild blue yonder?"

Gwynn asked, "Where's Johnny Mac?"

White smirked. "He's on a United flight out of Dulles."

"Oh, sorry for asking. I guess he's not happy about flying coach while we're going in style."

"Don't be sorry," White said. "He'll never know about this little ride, but what do you think? Isn't it nice?"

"It is beautiful," Anya said. "It is Air Force C-Thirty-Eight Courier, yes?"

White surveyed the cabin. "Very good. The civilian designation is a Gulfstream G-One-Hundred, but the Air Force calls them Couriers. This one doesn't have any Air Force markings. In fact, the registration number comes back to a fictional Russian company we created just for this mission."

Anya took a seat and buckled her belt. "Of course you did not forget about Porsche, yes?"

White bored holes through the Russian with his eyes. "Enjoy the flight, and call me when you make it to the yacht."

A uniformed pilot jogged up the boarding ladder and closed the door behind him before removing his cap. "Good morning, ladies. I'm Captain Stoney Burns, but as you can see, I'm a little out of uniform today. I had to trade in my Air Force flight suit for this getup. If there's anything we can do to make your flight more comfortable, just let us know."

Gwynn leaned toward Anya and whispered, "I think I'd like to have one of him to keep."

The pilot disappeared into the cockpit and closed the door.

Anya said, "He is military pilot. You would be home alone most of time. He is not proper man for you."

Gwynn leaned back and raised an eyebrow. "Do I detect a hint of jealousy?"

Anya smiled and took Gwynn's hand. "Yes, you are mine. Man—especially man like him—would only be distraction for you."

Gwynn squeezed her hand. "You're probably right, but he would be fun to play with for the weekend."

Anya shrugged. "Perhaps."

The two settled in as they climbed into the cool morning air of Northern Virginia. When they leveled off at 42,000 feet, Gwynn said, "It's time for you to tell me where you've been."

Anya stared out the window. "I made promise to you I would never lie, but I cannot always tell to you truth."

Gwynn turned in her seat. "Yes, you can."

"But you have obligation to tell to Agent White everything I say to you."

Gwynn smiled. "You heard what he said about us. We're making him look really good, so we're not on such a short leash anymore. If you ask me not to tell him something, as long as it doesn't jeopardize our operations, I can keep a secret. Besides, I already know you went to Russia, so let's hear it. Where and why?"

Anya traced the arcing line of the horizon in the distance. "This is correct. I did go to Russia, but not only Russia. I went also to see someone who is very special to me in Bern."

"Where's Bern?"

"Bern is capital of Switzerland. Everyone knows this."

"Oh. Is it a guy?"

Anya stared down at her hands. "No, this person is not guy, but this is all I can tell you for now. Please let this be only mine for now. Maybe in future I can tell you more, but it is too hard right now."

Gwynn's curiosity urged her to push Anya to come clean about who and what was so important in Switzerland, but she granted the Russian her wish and changed the subject. "Do you think you'll ever go back to Russia to live?"

"No, this I will never do. I am American now. I wish only to live inside America, or maybe on island sometimes."

Gwynn laughed. "You know, your accent has really gotten atrocious while you were gone. I think that's a good thing for this operation. It'll make our cover story easier to sell, but I'm determined to have you sounding as American as you feel."

"I am sorry. I did not realize English would suffer in few weeks."

"More like a few months. But it's okay. Like I said, we can work with it for this op, but we're going to clean it up when all of this is over."

"Yes, this we will do."

No flight attendant materialized, but a second pilot emerged from the cockpit forty-five minutes into the flight and took a seat across from the two women. "Is everything all right back here?"

"Yes, everything is perfect," Anya said, "but should you not be inside cockpit to fly airplane?"

The young Air Force officer melted in front of her. "Uh, Stoney has things under control up there. I just came back to check on you two and hit the head. I mean, use the restroom. Can I get you anything?"

Anya furrowed her brow. "From bathroom?"

The man blushed. "No, ma'am. I didn't mean I could get you something from the bathroom. I mean . . ."

Gwynn rescued the young pilot. "She's just messing with you, but we'd love a bottle of water. Just not from the bathroom."

"Yes, ma'am. Two bottles of water coming right up."

He slid open the ice drawer and pulled a pair of bottles from inside. He gave them a wipe and handed them to the two women. When Anya took hers from his hand, she let her finger trace across his knuckles slowly enough to continue the man's melting process. "*Spasibo.*"

He swallowed hard. "You're welcome, ma'am. If, uh . . . you know. If I can do . . ."

Gwynn chuckled. "Yes, we know. Thank you for the water. We're just fine for now."

Anya shot a thumb toward the rear of the plane. "Bathroom is that way, in case you have forgotten."

This time, he blushed in silence.

Gwynn gave her partner a playful slug. "You're terrible. Why do you do that?"

Anya grinned. "Because it is fun, and maybe is your turn to be jealous, no?"

Gwynn uncapped her bottle and took a drink. "You know, I really hate you sometimes."

Anya appeared shocked. "Why do you hate me?"

"Oh, relax. It's not that kind of hate. It's just that you can have any man you want anywhere on Earth. You're gorgeous—there's no denying it—but it's more than that. You have a way of disarming men that turns them into putty in your hands. How do you do it?"

"This is not true. I cannot have any man I want."

Gwynn interrupted. "Don't start again with Chase. You screwed that one up."

"Yes, this is true, but this is not subject. You asked about disarming men, yes?"

"Yeah. How do you do it?"

"Is simple. Men are creatures who respond to attention." Anya placed the tip of her finger lightly on the bridge of Gwynn's nose. "When you look to man, look only here and turn head slightly. It is sometimes good to speak softly so he will lean forward to hear. When he does this, you have him in palm of hand, and he will do anything you wish."

"Oh, come on. It can't be that simple."

The Russian leaned toward her student and whispered, "It works also on beautiful special agent like you."

Gwynn pulled herself from Anya's trance. "Don't do that. It's not fair."

Anya leaned back and put on the smile that had stolen a million hearts. "You will try this, yes?"

"Oh, you can bet your Russian tush I'm trying it. Is that how you get Agent White to do whatever you want?"

Anya's smile faded. "No, he is not little boy inside. Is not so easy with him."

"But you know you do it, right?"

Anya shrugged. "We will see if Porsche is waiting in New Orleans. If yes, it works, but if no, maybe I am losing skills."

* * *

The landing gear left the fuselage, and they touched down at New Orleans Lakefront Airport. The Air Force crew, clad in their best charter-pilot attire, taxied the luxurious jet to the ramp, and Captain Burns emerged from the cockpit to open the cabin door.

Gwynn wasted no time seductively slipping her hand into the pilot's and focusing on that spot just between his eyes. "Thank you. I'd really like for you to take me someplace again . . . maybe without so many others tagging along."

On the carpet at the foot of the stairs, Anya whispered, "I told you it works."

Gwynn gave her arm a squeeze.

If a prototypical Russian man exists, he was standing beside the open door of a black limousine. The only thing sharper than the razor-thin brim of his cap was his jawline. He continued to hold the door until Gwynn and Anya were well ensconced inside the lavish space. Although they'd spent only minutes on the ramp, the limousine alone was enough to draw the eye of a bevy of curious onlookers.

Gwynn took in the darkened limo. "I could really get used to living like this."

"Perhaps your Air Force boyfriend will have for you limousine."

Gwynn cocked her head. "Aw, isn't that cute? Jealousy, again."

The ride lasted fewer than five minutes before the driver brought the car to a stop at the South Shore Harbor Marina, where a pair of white-uniform-clad seamen stood as if ready to stop the whole world simply to please their guests.

As Anya slid from the car, she let her eyes meet the driver's. "*Spasibo, ser.*"

The driver eyed the two men waiting to receive the ladies and handed her a card. In perfect Russian, he said, "I'm Peter, and I am never more than a phone call away. It is important you read the card."

Anya gave him a barely perceptible nod and slipped the card into her clutch.

Gwynn emerged seconds later, matching Anya's elegance, if not her height. The uniformed man bearing four stripes on his epaulets bowed slightly at the waist. Good morning, ma'ams. I am Captain Charles Gordon, master of the Utrennyaya Zvezda, and this is David Young, my first officer."

Anya gave the captain her hand but looked beyond him at the magnificent yacht that lay moored alongside the seawall. "The *Morning Star* is beautiful boat, and I am pleased to meet you. This is my friend, Gwynn."

The captain kissed the back of Gwynn's presented hand, and the first officer did the same.

Captain Gordon held out his hand toward the gangway. "Paradise awaits, and your luggage is already aboard."

The former Russian assassin and the DOJ special agent let themselves be led aboard as if they were royalty. Once they were on deck, the gangway was pulled away, and the two seamen removed their hats. "Now for the real welcome, Agents Davis and Fulton. We are Captains Gordon and Young, but the formality is only for show when anyone is watching. Feel free to call us Chuck and Dave."

Gwynn took charge. "Thank you for the show, gentlemen. We're Gwynn and Anya. Obviously, she's Anya."

"Obviously," agreed Captain Gordon.

"Okay, now that introductions are done, Dave will show you your cabins and give you a tour of the vessel while I get us underway. The New Orleans Yacht Club is less than ten minutes away, so we'll be back alongside before you know it."

Dave Young led the two down a winding staircase and through a short corridor amidships. "These are your cabins, port and starboard. They are identical except for the view. While we're alongside at the yacht club, depending on the direction the captain lays us to moor, one cabin will have a city view, while the other will look out over Lake Pontchartrain."

Anya eyed the corridor and the entrances to both cabins. "Our rooms are not connected?"

Dave motioned astern. "They can be connected through a short passageway there, but we weren't briefed on the configuration you wanted."

Anya said, "Have someone open passageway. It may become necessary for us to have access without exposing ourselves into corridor."

Gwynn leaned toward Dave. "She's afraid of the dark, so sometimes I have to read her a bedtime story to help her go to sleep."

Dave surveyed the two women, clearly unsure what his newest assignment had dropped into his lap. He pulled a set of keys from his pocket. "I'll take care of that now."

They followed him into the starboard side cabin and into the rear passageway. He unlocked both doors and reclosed them. "There you go. Any time you need—or want—to cross over, just open the door. If either of you wants privacy, each door can be locked from inside its cabin."

They thanked him, and he made his way from the cabin. Before he turned down the corridor, he spun on a heel to face the women. "I still don't know for sure what's going on here. This is only my third assignment after leaving the Navy, but I've got to say, I'm not in a hurry for this one to end."

Gwynn smiled. "Neither are we, David."

The drone of the propellers came to a stop, and the yacht's motion ended with a gentle kiss of the dock. Soon, lines were made fast, and the big vessel was well on display at the New Orleans Yacht Club.

Gwynn and Anya inspected their cabins, and especially their views, before meeting back in the corridor.

"This is spectacular," Gwynn said. "What do you think?"

Anya glared at her partner. "No. This will never do. I must speak to captain, immediately."

7

PODDERZHANIYE
(MAINTENANCE)

Special Agent Gwynn Davis stared back at her partner. "What's wrong? The yacht is great. Our rooms are great. What won't do?"

"Come with me." Anya stormed up the curved stairs to the main salon, then motioned toward the wall of windows on the port side. "Tell me what you see."

Gwynn huffed. "Uh . . . windows. But I don't see how windows can be the problem."

"Windows are not problem. Problem is what is not outside windows."

Gwynn widened her eyes. "Anya, I don't know what you're talking about."

"There is no French Quarter outside windows. We are in wrong place. We cannot stay here. Chef Christian Gerard at Eden's View restaurant is inside French Quarter."

"Calm down. This is the New Orleans Yacht Club. This is where all the rich Russian girls park their yachts. We have a driver to take us to the French Quarter whenever we want to go."

Unaffected, Anya stormed from the salon, and Gwynn gave chase. "Where are you going?"

Without turning around, the Russian said, "I must find map of city with also water."

Trying to keep up, Gwynn breathed, "I'm sure they have a chart on the bridge, but—"

"Then this is where we must go to see chart."

Without knocking, Anya led Gwynn through the doorway to the navigation bridge, where they discovered a young man they hadn't met. He wore khaki pants and a blue polo with "MV Morning Star" embroidered on the left front.

The man leapt to his feet, sending the sheaf of paper he'd been holding floating to the deck. "Can I help you?"

Anya scowled. "You are not captain."

"No, ma'am. I'm the second officer, but I have the watch. Is there something I can do for you?"

"I must see map of city and water. You have this, yes?"

He moved toward an elevated table behind the helm station. "We've got a nautical chart, but that's all."

Anya leaned across the table, staring down at the chart. "Show me where we are, and tell to me your name."

The young officer pointed toward the chart. "I'm Nick Brower, and we're right here in the yacht basin."

Anya studied the chart for several minutes while Gwynn reached for Nick's hand. "I'm sorry we barged in on you like this. I'm Gwynn, and she's Anya. Even though she's a little preoccupied—she gets that way sometimes—we're both really glad to meet you."

"Okay, nice to meet you, too, but what's going on? Do I need to call the captain?"

Anya tapped her fingertip against the chart. "Make me understand map. We are inside lake?"

Nick leaned down. "Well, yes, ma'am. Technically, we're in Lake Pontchartrain, but . . ."

"This is no good. We must be in ocean and facing French Quarter."

Nick glanced at Gwynn as if begging her to rescue him, so she did. "Anya thought we were going to have a view of the French Quarter. It's kind of important."

Anya interrupted. "Is *more* than important. Show to me where is French Quarter on map."

Nick slid his finger across the chart and circled a spot near a ninety-degree bend in the river. "This is the French Quarter, but there's no ocean—just the Mississippi River."

Anya straightened and surveyed the yacht from stem to stern through the bridge windows. "This boat will fit inside Mississippi River, yes?"

"Well, yeah. They bring a cruise ship up the river. In fact, it docks right there." Nick brought his finger to rest on the cruise port.

"You will take us there now. You can drive boat, yes?"

Nick turned back to Gwynn with terror in his eyes. "Uh, is she serious?"

"I'm afraid so," Gwynn said.

"I can pilot the yacht, but not without the captain's approval. I don't have the authority to move us unless there's an emergency."

"This *is* emergency," Anya demanded. "We must be in French Quarter."

Nick's eyes remained saucers. "No, not that kind of emergency. I meant, like, if there's a fire on the dock or something like that. Something that could potentially damage the yacht. But that's not the only reason I can't move us into the river facing the French Quarter."

"What is this reason?" Anya asked.

"Because there's no place to dock over there. I mean, the only two docks are the cruise ship port and the dock for the *Belle of Orleans*."

"What is *Belle of Orleans*?"

"She's a paddlewheel steamer. You know, an old riverboat. It's not really old, though. It's just built to look old. They do dinner cruises, weddings, and stuff like that. She does a dinner cruise every night except Monday, and I think they still do sightseeing cruises up the river on weekends."

Anya stared to the south. "And we are bigger than *Belle of Orleans*?"

Nick turned his eyes toward the ceiling in thought. "I think we're more gross tonnage, but she's wider and a few feet longer than us."

"This is very good. You will move us to her dock on river, and *Belle of Orleans* will come here until we are finished in New Orleans."

Nick shook his head. "That's not really how it works. We can't just commandeer her dock and force her to go somewhere else. That's her dock, and the only times she leaves it are for cruises or when they take her to the shipyard upriver for maintenance."

Anya turned from the chart to face Nick. "When is maintenance?"

"I have no way to know, but even if the dock was empty, it's still *her* dock, and we can't just decide to use it."

"This is not true. Is time to call captain."

Unsure what to do next, but quite certain he'd identified the more rational of the two women, Nick said, "I can call the captain, but he'll tell you the same thing I told you."

Anya moved to within inches of his face. "You are certain this is what captain will tell us?"

He took a step backward. "Yes, ma'am. I'm sure."

She smiled. "You are very good second officer, Nick. I think you will be excellent captain someday. We have small boat on yacht, yes?"

"Yes, ma'am. We have a twenty-foot tender, but it's on deck. If we need it, one of the engineers can launch it for us. But why do you ask?"

"You will call for engineer and put small boat into water." She lifted the chart from the table and rolled it into a tube. "We will change clothes and you will have small boat at stern for us in ten minutes."

Nick protested, but Anya led Gwynn from the bridge with the chart rolled beneath her arm.

Descending the stairs, Gwynn said, "What are we doing?"

"We are going to change clothes. We cannot explore in small boat dressed like this."

Gwynn couldn't suppress her smile. "I've got the greatest job in the world."

Exactly ten minutes later, Anya and Gwynn arrived at the stern dressed in jeans and sweatshirts. Dave, the first officer, waited as the tender bobbed lazily against the swim platform. "I told the captain you two were going to be a lot of trouble, and it looks like I was right. Where do you want to go?"

Anya ignored him and stepped aboard the boat. She moved to the helm and familiarized herself with the controls.

Gwynn joined Anya and said, "Apparently, we're going to see the French Quarter."

Dave lowered his chin. "You want me to take you to see the French Quarter . . . in a boat?"

Anya looked up. "No, this is not what we want. We will take ourselves. We do not need you. I have chart."

Dave glanced to Gwynn, and she shrugged. "She has the chart."

He shook his head and tossed the painter line aboard the tender as it motored away.

Gwynn sidled up to Anya. "Are you sure you know what you're doing?"

"Yes, I learned from Chase. I am very good sailor."

"This isn't a sailboat."

"Yes, but I am very good engine boat driver, too."

"Engine boat. Is that what we're calling this thing?"

Anya ignored the question and pressed the throttle to its stop as they exited the yacht basin. The tender's bow rose, temporarily blinding them to the open water above, but it quickly fell as the boat rose onto plane. They accelerated as they roared along the city's waterfront.

Just before reaching the Lakefront Airport, where they'd landed less than an hour earlier, Anya spun the wheel and sent the tender gliding across the water and into the Inner Harbor Navigation Canal.

With the engine still growling, Anya kept the tender at maximum speed as the canal narrowed. Seconds later, a long, sleek patrol boat rolled behind the tender and hit their lights and siren. Neither could hear the siren, nor were they looking behind them, so they continued southbound and farther into the canal. The pilot of the patrol boat added enough power to come alongside the tender, and that caught their attention. A uniformed officer aboard the patrol boat motioned for Anya to stop, so she pulled the throttle to idle, and the hull of the tender settled into the water. The patrol boat matched their deceleration and stayed alongside.

A gold badge and black lettering reading "NOPD Marine Division" was painted on the side of the patrol boat. As the two boats came to a stop, the officer asked, "Where are you ladies going in such a hurry?"

Anya started to speak, but Gwynn laid a hand on her arm. "I've got this." She turned to the officer, pulled her credential pack from her pocket, and flashed her badge. "DOJ official business."

"Oh, really?" said the officer. "Why don't you hand me that cred-pack?"

Gwynn placed the leather wallet in his hand and stepped back as he examined the identification. "Are you armed, Special Agent Davis?"

"I am."

The officer peered across the cred-pack and toward Anya. "How about her?"

Anya said, "I have only knife. I do not need gun. I have also badge. You would like to see, no?"

The officer tossed Gwynn's pack back to her. "No, I don't need to see, but I do need for you to slow down. The canal gets crowded, and we don't want anybody getting hurt. Keep it under fifteen knots, unless you're in pursuit, in which case, you need to let us know. Got it?"

Gwynn pocketed her credentials. "We got it. Thanks."

Anya accelerated southward and planed out the tender at just under twenty knots. "This is close enough to fifteen, yes?"

Gwynn laughed. "Close enough for government work."

The canal widened as it met the Mississippi River, and the water turned from dark green to muddy brown—so brown it looked as if they could walk across the surface. Anya turned right and rounded the ninety-degree bend in the river. A tugboat pushing eight barges down the river maneuvered toward them, and she gave the load a wide berth by hugging the northern shoreline.

When the tug was well clear, Gwynn pointed ahead. "There's the *Belle of Orleans.*"

Anya slowed the tender and motored toward the paddle-wheeler.

Gwynn said, "Wow, it does look like an old Mississippi riverboat. It's gorgeous."

Anya continued surveying the ship as they drew nearer. She brought the tender alongside the riverboat and turned to Gwynn. "You can drive boat, yes?"

Gwynn pointed toward the ship. "Not that one!"

"No, not that one. This one."

"Yeah, sure, I can drive it. But why?"

The Russian stepped onto the gunwale and grabbed the railing of the first deck of the riverboat. "Come back for me right here in thirty minutes."

"What? No! What are you doing?"

If Anya heard her partner, she gave no signal. She leapt across the river-boat's railing and landed like a cat on the deck beyond.

Gwynn added just enough power to motor away from the ship as her partner disappeared inside. Accelerating away, she couldn't take her eyes off the riverboat, and minutes passed like hours. She did every maneuver she could think of to not look like she was waiting for her Russian assassin partner to emerge from the bowels of the ship.

Finally, exactly thirty minutes after she'd stepped from the tender, Anya materialized at the rail of the steamer, precisely where she'd boarded. Gwynn carried a little too much speed into the approach and sent the rail-ing of the tender crashing into the side of the ship.

A deckhand from high above yelled down. "Hey! Watch what you're doing. Get away from there."

Gwynn called up to the man. "Sorry, I wasn't paying attention, but I'm fine. Thanks for asking."

He waved her off and disappeared.

Anya jumped from the ship and landed on the foredeck of the tender in a crouch.

Gwynn demanded, "What were you doing in there?"

Any settled into her seat. "Take us back to yacht."

Gwynn spun the wheel and added power.

As they entered the canal, Gwynn turned to her partner. "Tell me what you were doing."

Anya grinned. "I was making boat ready for maintenance."

8

DEN' PEREYEZDA
(MOVING DAY)

Carefully observing the speed limit on the Inner Harbor Navigation Canal, Gwynn and Anya made their way back to the *Morning Star*, where they found Dave Young standing on the aft deck checking his watch.

Anya tossed a line to the first officer. "Hello, Dave. We are back, and we are safe, but you did not tell us about speed limit inside canal."

Dave caught the painter line and secured it to a deck cleat. "Please tell me you didn't get a ticket."

"We did not," Anya said. "But water police . . . no, this is not right. Marine police . . . yes, this is correct. Marine police made us stop and told to us speed limit."

Dave shook his head. "It's going to be this way the whole time you're here, isn't it?"

Anya cocked her head as if she didn't understand, but Gwynn jumped in. "Yes, it is. You'll get used to it soon enough."

"That's what I hear."

It was Gwynn's turn to appear confused. "Who do you hear that from?"

Before Dave could answer, Anya said, "This is not correct."

Both Gwynn and the first officer turned to Anya.

"Proper English would be, from *whom* do you hear this?"

Gwynn waggled a finger. "No, you don't get to correct my grammar, Moscow Molly."

Dave held out a hand. "Come on. There's someone waiting to see you."

Anya accepted the offered hand and stepped from the tender.

Gwynn did the same and asked, "Who's waiting to see us?"

"I don't know. Some guy who looks like a cop."

The two followed Dave through the interior of the yacht until reaching the main salon, where Agent Ray White sat with a cup of coffee in his hand. "How was your little field trip, ladies?"

Anya smiled down at him. "Is good you are here. You will make arrangements for us to move to dock of *Belle of Orleans*. We cannot stay here. No one who matters will see us unless we are at French Quarter."

White pointed toward the sofa. "Sit down, both of you. I spoke with the captain, who apparently spoke with Nick, the second officer."

Anya said, "This is good. You will make arrangements, yes?"

White took a sip. "No, that's not how this works. We can't force the riverboat to give up her dock."

"She will not need dock for many days."

White glared across his glasses. "What are you talking about?"

Anya continued smiling. "This is where we have been. We saw riverboat, and it is having problems. This means it must go to shipyard for repairs."

White redirected his glare to Gwynn. "What did you let her do?"

Gwynn snapped her head toward Anya.

"I did inspection on ship, and is definitely in need of going to shipyard."

Before White could continue his stream of questions, the captain stuck his head into the salon. "I'm sorry to interrupt, but I have some information you may want to hear." All three feds turned to face the captain. "I just heard over the radio that the *Belle of Orleans* is sinking by her stern. The Coast Guard and Corps of Engineers are responding."

White shot a glance at Anya and gave her a quick wink before turning back to the captain. "Is anybody hurt?"

"Apparently, no one was down below, so everybody got off. That dock is shallow, so she'll only sink about twenty feet. Most of the ship will still be above water."

White's throttled smile said he was finished asking questions.

The captain said, "Again, I'm sorry for interrupting, but I thought you'd want to know."

White stood. "You two wait here. I need to talk with the captain."

He followed the officer from the salon and up the stairs to the bridge. Nick was still on duty and leapt to his feet when the captain came on deck.

Chuck motioned for his third-in-command to sit. "It's okay, Nick. We'll only be here a few minutes."

Nick nodded and reclaimed his seat as Chuck and White slipped into the captain's office behind the navigation bridge.

Chuck eyed White. "Your girls sank the *Belle*, didn't they?"

White checked his fingernails. "They're not girls, Captain. They're federal agents, and federal agents don't sink civilian passenger vessels."

"That's what I thought." Chuck pulled an ancient Rolodex from his desk. After flipping through two dozen cards, he pulled one from the unit and slid it toward Ray.

White lifted the card and read its contents. Without a word, he pulled his phone from his pocket and pressed ten buttons. The phone rang twice in White's ear before a voice said, "New Orleans port captain."

White cleared his throat. "My name is Supervisory Special Agent Ray White with Justice. Are you the port captain?"

"What can I do for you, Agent? We're a little busy down here right now."

"That's the reason I'm calling. I happen to be in town and thought I'd ask if there's anything Justice can do for you."

Silence filled the line for a long moment before the port captain said, "Why do I get the feeling you're not really calling to help?"

"I have no idea why you'd have that feeling, Captain, but I'd be remiss if I didn't offer any assistance my office can provide."

"Yeah, right. You're from the government, and you're here to help. Is that it, Agent White?"

"Sure, something like that."

"How about you give me twenty-four hours to figure out what's going on down here, and then you call me back and tell me what you really want. How's that?"

"That sounds good to me. In the meantime, feel free to call me if I can help. Here's my number."

White gave him the number and hung up.

Chuck replaced the card back into the Rolodex and leaned back in his chair. "I guess that means tomorrow is moving day for us, huh?"

"I'm not a maritime guy, Chuck. How long does it take to clean up a mess like this?"

"The Corps of Engineers will already have divers in the water, and I'm sure there are already half a dozen salvage companies knocking down the door. They'll have the *Belle* back on the surface in a few hours, but it'll be tomorrow before they tow her up to the shipyard. They won't move her in the dark, and sunset is just a couple hours away."

* * *

Dawn broke over the mighty Mississippi River on the edge of the New Orleans French Quarter. Floating yellow barriers surrounded the *Belle of Orleans* and her dock, as well as most of the commercial port to contain the fuel and oil the riverboat lost during the time her engines and equipment rooms were underwater. A dozen boats with the seal of the Environmental Protection Agency patrolled the river and a bevy of EPA trucks, including a mobile command center, lined the waterfront.

Ray White's cell phone chimed as he poured his morning cup of coffee aboard *Morning Star*. He stuck it to his ear. "White."

"Agent White, this is Greg Litton, the New Orleans port captain. Did you say you were with Justice?"

White liked the way his day was beginning. "That's right, Captain Litton. I'm a supervisory special agent with Justice."

"I see. Well, you asked if there was anything you could do to help with the mess we've got down here. Is that offer still on the table?"

White took a sip of the steaming brew. "That depends on what you need, Greg."

The switch from the title of captain to only his first name wasn't lost on Greg Litton. "I'm a salty old sailor, Agent White. I don't know much about how things work in Washington, but I could sure use a little help getting these environmental guys out of my hair."

"What's happening over there, Greg?"

"The environmentalists have the whole port shut down. I've got a cruise ship full of pissed-off passengers and two freighter captains chomping at the bit to get off the dock. Do you have any pull over there at the EPA?"

White's twenty-five years playing the federal government bureaucracy game tasted even better than the coffee in his cup. "I don't know, Greg, but for you, I'll see what I can do. Those environmental guys are tough to deal with, though. I'll get back with you as soon as I have some news."

"If you can get my port open long enough to get that cruise ship and those freighters underway, I'll owe you one. A big one."

White hung up without another word and climbed the stairs to the upper deck. Overlooking the yacht club and enjoying every sip of his morning coffee, he planned his strategy for the coming day.

Footsteps on the stairs preceded the long blonde hair of White's favorite former Russian assassin with a pair of mugs in her hands.

Anya surveyed the deck and found no one except White. She placed a cup in front of him and settled into a chair across the glass-top table. "Good morning, Ray. I have for you more coffee."

He slid his empty cup away and lifted its replacement. "Are you sure you didn't slip a little cyanide in my cup?"

She eyed her mug and then exchanged it for the one she'd placed in front of White. "That was close. I almost drank wrong coffee."

White chuckled and sipped the brew. "Are you ever going to tell me what you did to the *Belle of Orleans*?"

"I believe American phrase is *plausible deniability*. Is that right?"

White raised his mug. "Here's to plausible deniability."

Anya tapped his mug with hers, and they drank in silence for several minutes, taking in the view as the city came alive to the south and the morning fog lifted from the lake.

With his second cup empty, White lifted his phone from the table and touched his finger to his lips, indicating Anya should be silent. Seconds later, an executive assistant in the Robert F. Kennedy Department of Justice Building answered the ringing phone. "Attorney General's office."

"Good morning, Megan, Ray White here. Has she made it in yet?"

"Yeah, she's here, but she's not in a good mood."

White laughed. "When was the last time the attorney general was in a good mood?"

"You've got an excellent point. Do you want me to see if she's interested in talking with her least favorite supervisory special agent?"

"No, I want you to simply put me through, and do it on the hotline if you can."

"Ray, you know I'm not supposed—"

"This one is real, Megan."

The executive assistant sighed. "Okay, but if you're lying, this is the last favor you'll ever get from me."

The line rang twice, and the attorney general of the United States picked up the phone. "AG."

"Good morning, ma'am. It's Agent White. May I have two minutes?"

"You've got ninety seconds. Go."

"I need you to order the port of New Orleans open and call off the EPA. They're overstepping their authority down here, and I . . . *we* need to get my avenging angel to work."

Silence filled the line before the AG said, "Who's the incident commander?"

"I don't know, but what we're doing is a lot more important than what they're pretending to do."

"I'll call you back in ten minutes. Answer your phone."

Before Ray could acknowledge the command, the line went dead.

Anya motioned toward the phone. "That sounded not pleasant."

"It's all a big game in D.C., and I've been playing it a long time."

Small talk followed, and the ease of conversation grew with every passing minute.

Finally, Anya said, "I do not like what you have done to me, Ray White, but I like you, this you, the one I am having coffee with."

Ray peered at the Russian across his cup. "I'm terrified of you, Anya Burinkova, but when you're not threatening to gut me like pig or destroy what's left of my career, I like you, too."

Before she could respond, the phone chirped. "White." He listened intently for half a minute. "Thank you, ma'am. You've just made one very happy port captain, and today is now moving day for our avenging angel." Silence again, and then White said, "Yes, ma'am. Of course I meant *your* avenging angel."

9

KHOROSHIYE NOVOSTI
(GOOD TIDINGS)

Ray White scrolled through his list of incoming calls and pressed send when he found the New Orleans port captain's number.

"Port captain."

"Greg, good morning. It's Supervisory Special Agent Ray White."

"Please tell me you've got some good news."

White gave Anya a wink and turned back to the phone. "Are you in your office, Greg?"

"I am."

"Can you see the EPA barricades and boats from your window?"

"Yes, I can see the whole mess. If we just had some clowns and an elephant, we'd have ourselves a fine circus. Come on, White. Cut the small talk, and get to the point before I become one of the clowns."

"Do you read the Bible, Greg?"

"What? What's that got to do with any of this?"

White chuckled. "Remember when the angel showed up and told the shepherds he was bringing good tidings of great joy?"

Litton sighed. "Please tell me you're my angel."

"Nope, not even close, but I just happen to be sitting across the table from one. Here's what I recommend. Pour yourself a nice, hot cup of coffee, and pull your chair to the window. It's time to tear down the circus tent."

A sound akin to something a death row inmate might make after hearing the news of a pardon came from Greg Litton's lips. "I have no idea what a lowly little port captain in New Orleans could ever do for you, but if you ever need anything—and I literally mean anything—on the water down here, it's just a phone call away."

"I'll keep that in mind, Greg. I'll check on things later today, and we'll see how the progress is coming along."

White thumbed the end key and slid the phone onto the table. "Well, that was fun."

Anya looked up. "You got for me dock I need?"

"Yeah, I got it, but the port captain doesn't know it yet. You can plan on watching the sunset over The Big Easy tonight from your nice, comfy spot on the Mississippi River."

Anya leapt from her seat and flung her arms around White. "I knew you could do it, but there is one more thing . . ."

He enjoyed the hug, and when it was over, he pointed toward the yacht club parking lot. Anya followed his finger until her eyes fell on her deep blue convertible Porsche 911. The next hug was punctuated with a kiss White hadn't expected, but he made no effort to shun her appreciation.

From the top step of the stairs came the sound of Special Agent Gwynn Davis clearing her throat. "Am I interrupting? I can come back later if you two need some privacy."

Anya spun on a heel and bounced across the deck to her partner. She stuck a finger through the air. "Look! Agent White brought for us our Porsche."

Gwynn glanced toward the car and back to White. "Maybe I should learn to kiss better. Nobody has ever given me a car for one of my kisses."

"I will teach you," Anya said. "Is simple. We will practice later, but there is more good news. We are moving to French Quarter today."

Everyone took seats, and White briefed the happenings of the morning. Gwynn didn't kiss him, but she shared Anya's excitement.

A man in a tall chef's hat joined the trio on the upper deck. "Good morning, everyone. Would you prefer to have breakfast up here?"

Without consulting the others, Anya said, "Yes, of course. This perfect place for breakfast. You will bring also captain when you bring breakfast, yes?"

The chef bowed and disappeared. Fifteen minutes later, two servers followed the captain onto the upper deck. Breakfast was served without the necessity of ordering.

White stood and shook the captain's hand. "Good morning, Chuck. It looks like we've turned lemons into piña coladas."

The captain took his seat. "How so?"

White reclaimed his chair. "The *Belle of Orleans* is headed up the river for major repairs after spending a few hours on the bottom. The EPA showed up and turned the site into a three-ring cluster. Fortunately, our boss, the AG, was able to call them off and reopen the port. That leaves the *Belle*'s dock empty, the port open for business, and the port captain in my debt."

The captain took a bite of his omelette. "I guess that means we'll be tossing off the lines and moving south."

"There are still a few details to work out, but I recommend planning for an early afternoon departure."

Breakfast continued until plates were empty, stomachs were full, and Ray White's cell phone came to life. "White."

"Agent White, it's Greg. I don't know what kind of strings you had to pull or favors you had to call in to make this happen, but the cruise ship is gone, the freighters are right behind her, and a pair of tugs just showed up to tow the *Belle* to the shipyard. All of that is great, but the best part is there's not an EPA vehicle in sight."

"I'm glad to hear it, Greg. I'm glad I could help. See? Not all of us government types are hard to work with."

Greg said, "Thank you again, and don't forget, if there's ever anything I can do . . ."

White put on his victory smile. "Now that you mention it, there is one little thing maybe you could help me with."

"Name it, my friend. If I can't do it, I'll find somebody who can."

"Well, the truth is, it's a bit of a hush-hush kind of thing. Can you be discreet?"

"After what you did for me, you can cut out my tongue if you want."

White laughed. "I don't think we'll have to go that far, but if it comes to that, I know just the person."

Greg let out a hesitant chuckle. "Okay, I guess you would have people like that, huh?"

"Don't worry about that. What I need is the name and number of the person who manages the dock the *Belle of Orleans* uses."

"The *Belle* belongs to the city, and her dock is owned by the port, so I manage her dock, as well as the rest of the commercial port, but why do you need to know any of that?"

"As I said, it's hush-hush, but I've got a little operation underway in your city, and I need a place to park a big yacht for a couple of weeks. I've got some VIPs who demand a view of the French Quarter from the yacht. What would it take for me to get use of the *Belle*'s dock for, ah, maybe three weeks or so?"

"A big yacht, you say? Bigger than the *Belle*?"

"No, she's a few feet shorter than the *Belle* and considerably smaller in the hips."

"I've got to be honest with you, Agent White. I've never had a request like that before, but there's no way the mayor will bite off on a private yacht at the city dock. The liability is just too much. Imagine what your VIPs would do if their yacht suffered the same fate as the *Belle*. The city doesn't have insurance to cover anything like that."

White scratched his chin. "What if we waived liability? After all, I've got the attorney general on speed dial. It's not like we'd have any trouble whipping up a waiver."

The port captain hesitated. "I suppose it's time for a confession. I was married to the mayor's sister for almost eighteen years. Now that she and I are no longer basking in wedded bliss, so to speak, I'm not on particularly good terms with the sitting mayor. So, now you know all the moving parts. As far as I'm concerned, the *Belle*'s dock is yours until she comes back from the shipyard, but I'm afraid I'm in no position to negotiate on your behalf with the mayor."

"I understand, and it's not a problem. The mayor knows we're here and has a rough idea what we're doing. When the U.S. attorney general calls, mayors tend to answer the phone. You can expect a beautiful yacht full of beautiful people on the *Belle*'s dock just after lunch. Oh, and Greg? We'll call it even."

Captain Chuck rapped on the tabletop. "It looks like I'd better make ready to get underway."

"That's right, Captain. Put her on the *Belle of Orleans* dock when you're ready to go."

Without another word, the captain disappeared, leaving only the feds occupying the breakfast table. A waiter cleared the plates and glasses and offered more drinks that were promptly declined.

When they were alone, Anya took Gwynn's hand and gave White a nod. "We are good team."

White rolled his eyes. "Just don't sink anymore ships, okay?"

"This is not what I do. I cannot sink ship. Only water inside can sink ship. It looked like very old ship, and old ships have sometimes water coming inside."

White held up a palm. "Just stop talking, and go get dressed like a spoiled Russian rich girl." Anya stood, and Gwynn eyed White. He waved toward the stairs. "You, too. Go play dress-up with your friend, and don't start thinking you can get away with the crap she pulls. Got it?"

Gwynn stood and offered a sharp salute.

An hour later, the engines came to life aboard *Morning Star*, and Captain Chuck stood behind Nick, his third-in-command, as the junior officer piloted the yacht away from the dock. Nick's skill at the controls of the ship grew every time he handled her, and the captain had come to trust the young man, even in the tight confines of the yacht club and the canal.

When Gwynn and Anya emerged from their cabins, they played the part of trust-fund babies to the letter. They ignored the longshoremen mooring the yacht to the *Belle*'s former dock as if they were nothing more than hired help. The champagne in their flutes, however, was only a prop to support the ruse.

Anya tried a sip and recoiled. "What is this?"

"It's sparkling white grape juice. We're on the job. We can't be drinking at eleven o'clock in the morning."

Anya set the flute on the table. "Tell me when it is time we can have real champagne. I do not like fake."

Gwynn pretended to enjoy her glass, "Oh, you're right. That *is* bad. I think I'll also wait until it's five o'clock somewhere."

The massive yacht immediately drew the attention of dozens of tourists and locals alike as the captain shut down the engines. Passersby waved at the two beautiful women aboard, but Gwynn and Anya ignored them.

Gwynn shot her chin toward the crowd. "It looks like it's working."

"Of course it is working. We are beautiful girls on beautiful yacht inside a city that is not so beautiful."

Gwynn frowned. "Oh, I disagree. You'll see. New Orleans is gorgeous. You just have to see it from the inside. Trust me, you'll love it when we go out tonight."

Anya shrugged. "I always love when we go out to paint new city red. This is saying that also works for New Orleans, and not only for New York, yes?"

Gwynn grinned. "Oh, yeah. We can paint any city we want—probably even Moscow."

"You would maybe love Moscow for short time. Perhaps I will take you there when we are no longer doing this thing we are doing."

Gwynn stared up at the Russian. "I like that."

Anya wrinkled her forehead. "You like what?"

"I like that you think we'll still hang out when this assignment is over."

Anya shrugged. "I am not certain we will both survive this assignment, but if we do, I would like this to be friendship and not only working partners."

"Yeah, that's exactly what I meant," Gwynn said. "By the way, where's Agent White?"

"I do not know. He sent me away from table to get dressed, and now he is not here. Perhaps he is bringing our car from yacht club to here."

Gwynn giggled. "You've reduced that poor man to a valet. I want you to know that no one else in the world could do that to him. He's got a soft spot for you, and I suspect it has something to do with you looking like"— Gwynn waved her open hand down Anya's body—"that."

"I do not think this is true. I think he is not used to people challenging him, and it is game for me to do so."

"He'd kill you if he heard you say that."

"He will not kill me. You and I are his swan song. He needs us so he can retire and live in house on bank of river and catch trout."

"How do you know things like that about him? I've worked for him for three years, and I don't know stuff like that."

Anya held up both palms. "I cannot help it. Sometimes, men tell to me things even when I do not ask. I only listen and remember."

10

Prosto Idi s Etim
(Just Go With It)

Anya pulled the chauffeur's card from her clutch and read the face.

Peter Evans, U.S. Department of State.

"Our driver is not only driver but also diplomat."

Gwynn stuck her head out from the bathroom. "What makes you say that?"

"His card says he is spy."

Gwynn stepped into the hallway. "A spy?"

Anya handed her the card, and she examined it carefully. "This says State Department. Not *everyone* at State is a spy."

"Yes, everyone in State Department is spy. You would know this if you were also spy."

"How would you know? You're not a spy."

Anya planted both hands on her hips and eyed her partner.

"Okay, so maybe you're right. I'll be ready in ten minutes."

Anya chuckled. "This means thirty minutes. We are sometimes like married couple. I am ready fast, and you are ready slow."

* * *

The two found Peter waiting beside the open rear door of the limousine as they strode across the gangway from the yacht.

Anya gave the driver a wink and whispered, "You must be terrible spy to now be driver for us."

He leaned close. "I'm the worst spy, but I am an excellent killer. No one will harm you tonight."

She ran a hand across his bicep. "Look at my hand, Peter."

The driver followed her toned arm past the elbow and wrist to find the blade of the assassin's favorite fighting knife protruding from her palm. "You are maybe second-best killer inside car tonight. You will not intervene unless I am losing, yes?"

He shook his head. "I guess they were right about you."

"Yes, *they*—whoever they are—were quite right, but please watch for my friend. She is still learning to defend herself. Always help her first. I can take care of myself."

He carefully slid a finger between her blade and his arm. "I can see that. I promise not to get involved unless you're dead—or about to be dead—and Gwynn is in danger."

The two women slid into the back of the impossible-to-ignore car, and Peter took his place behind the wheel. Anya leaned forward and tapped on the glass separating the privileged from the indentured. "You did not ask where we want to go."

Peter met her gaze in the mirror. "It's New Orleans, and you two are supposed to be noticed. There's only one place for getting noticed in The Big Easy."

Anya turned to her partner. "I like Peter. We will keep him, yes?"

Gwynn raised her eyebrows. "Oh, yeah. We're definitely keeping him."

They stopped just before the intersection with one of the most famous streets in the world, and Peter stepped from the car and held open the door. Gwynn stepped to the curb first, followed closely by a pair of legs every supermodel on Earth would kill to have. The Russian keeper of the legs stood to her full height and straightened the skirt designed to turn every head on Bourbon Street.

Gwynn checked her reflection in the glass of the limo and recoiled. A filthy man dressed in even filthier clothes stood from his perch—an overturned bucket against a brick wall—and stepped toward her. Before she could react further, Anya stepped between the bum and her partner. Moving too fast for the human eye to see, she drew the same knife she'd shown Peter and placed it not-so-gently beneath the bum's right eye. "We have nothing for you. Sit down, or I will sit you down in pool of your own blood."

Special Agent Johnathon McIntyre threw both hands into the air and stepped back until he collided with the wall behind him. "Relax, Anya. It's me."

Gwynn giggled. "Johnny Mac, what are you doing here? And why are you dressed like a homeless guy?"

Anya returned the knife to wherever it had been hidden, and Johnny Mac stepped back toward the pair.

He held up one finger. "First, no more pulling knives on me. Got it?"

"I did not pull knives on you. It was only one knife."

"And second," he said, "I'm here to watch your back."

Anya frowned. "But this is why Peter is here, and we do not need either of you."

Johnny Mac held up a finger again. "First—"

Anya stopped him. "You cannot have another first. You already had first, and it was do not pull out your knives again. You can now have third, but not again first."

His finger turned to a fist. "Shut up and listen to me. That guy"—he motioned toward Peter—"he doesn't even work for us. He's on loan from somebody."

"Yes, he is spy from Department of State, and he is very strong."

Johnny Mac growled. "Fine, whatever. He's the driver. I'm on the street. We're making sure no one gets too close to you."

Anya turned to Gwynn. "This makes no sense. We are here for exactly purpose of getting close to Vasily Orlov. Peter and Johnny Mac should not prevent this."

Gwynn checked for nearby ears. "Don't worry. This is protocol. They won't intervene when it comes to Orlov, but strange, unexpected things happen in the French Quarter. There's nothing wrong with a couple of very capable guys watching our back."

Anya turned back to Johnny. "But why are you dressed like this?"

"It's called undercover. It's the easiest way to blend in. Nobody pays any attention to homeless people on the street."

Anya smiled. "I paid attention with my knife."

"Yeah, of course *you* did, but normal people don't pay attention."

Anya chuckled again and surveyed the four of them. "We are American spy who is now driver, Russian assassin who is now federal officer, special agent dressed like bum, and beautiful Gwynn who is also special agent but looks like secret Victoria model. Is this what is normal?"

"It's Victoria's Secret, and thank you for the compliment," Gwynn said, "but trust me, it's all good. Just go with it."

Anya gave the driver and the homeless guy one more glance before taking Gwynn's arm and setting off into the raucous throngs on Bourbon Street.

Their desire to be noticed quickly morphed into the two of them growing more fascinated with the absurdity of the street. A performer swallowing flaming swords while riding a unicycle stopped Anya in her tracks.

She studied the spectacle. "I do not believe this is real. It is only trick, yes?"

Gwynn watched in equal fascination. "I don't know. Go ask him if you can examine one of his swords. Maybe he'll let you."

The Russian crossed the street and approached the performer. He was focused on his flaming sword and didn't see her coming. As he tilted back his head and poised the blade above his tongue, Anya gave the single tire of his perch an abrupt tap with her heel. The performer recovered before falling from his unicycle, but the flaming sword fell to the sidewalk.

As Anya knelt to lift the sword, the performer's spotter stepped from the shadows and grabbed her arm. "Hey, lady! What are you doing? This is a dangerous act. You can't be doing that. Now, step back!"

Anya glanced down at the man's grip on her forearm. "Take your hand from my arm now, or I will take it from yours."

"Are you crazy, lady? Get out of here!"

With the speed of a puma, she reached across the aggressor's grip, took his hand in hers, and stood while rotating the man's arm through an arc above her head. Her victim bent at the waist and bellowed in pain.

Seeing the commotion, the performer leapt from his unicycle, landing on the sidewalk with athletic poise, and lifted the unicycle like a giant hammer. Anya saw the coming assault and tightened her grip on the spotter's wrist. Still moving like a jungle cat, she slid her foot beneath the flaming sword and flipped it into the air. With one precise motion, she swung the sword through the night air, sending the flaming blade into the rubber of the approaching tire. The blow stopped the stunned performer in his tracks, and the spotter tugged against her grip. She swept his feet, sending him face-first onto the sidewalk.

The performer dropped the now flat-tired unicycle and threw both hands into the air as he faced the beautiful woman wielding his still-flaming sword. Seeing the man's surrender, she released the spotter's wrist and lifted a plastic cup from a stunned bystander. She poured the contents of the cup down the length of the sword, extinguishing the flames. Anya examined the weapon and even fenced with an invisible opponent for three strokes before handing the sword back to the performer, who tentatively took it from her hand.

"Is real sword," she said, "but not very good one."

Anya rejoined her partner just as a filthy homeless man stepped between astounded onlookers.

Gwynn ignored Johnny Mac and leaned toward Anya. "That's not ex-actly what I meant when I said ask him to let you inspect his sword."

"Yes, I know this, but my way is more fun and also gets for us more at-tention."

"I've got an idea," Gwynn said. "Let's just assume we're getting plenty of attention without starting any more sword fights on the sidewalk. Are you good with that?"

"But I did not start . . ."

"You're missing the point," Gwynn said. "Just do that second thing you're best at."

"What is second thing I am best at doing?"

Gwynn made a show of ogling her partner. "Looking hot."

One block and a thousand catcalls down Bourbon Street, Gwynn nudged Anya down a side street.

The Russian asked, "Where are we going?"

"You'll see." Gwynn pointed to a well-lit sign hanging above a pair of French doors.

Anya smiled. "Eden's View. This is restaurant with chef who is friend of Vasily Orlov."

"You *do* pay attention. I like that."

They two stepped through the double doors to find an impeccably well-groomed young man in slacks and a crisp white shirt and tie with a black vest buttoned from top to bottom.

"Good evening, ladies. Do you have a reservation?"

Gwynn leaned toward him and took his hand. Just as Anya had taught, she let her eyes explore his face before settling on a spot just between his eyebrows. "We're just here for dessert," she whispered. "Surely, we don't need a reservation for something sweet, do we?"

The man cleared his throat and adjusted his vest. "Uh, let me see what I can do. We're pretty full tonight, but . . ."

Gwynn moved in closer and centered his tie. "You obviously have the power to make things happen. We saw that as soon as we came through the door."

He bit his bottom lip as a bead of sweat rolled from his sideburn. "Yeah, well, maybe I can get you a table in the bar. It'll be near the kitchen. I'm sorry, but that's the best I can do."

Gwynn planted a delicate kiss on his cheek. "That would be perfect. Thank you."

He cleared his throat again and stumbled as he turned away. "Okay, just follow me."

Anya leaned into her partner. "I told you it works every time."

Gwynn sighed. "I've still got so much left to learn, but I want to be just like you when I grow up."

The maître d' pulled out first one chair, then the other as Gwynn and Anya took their seats.

Gwynn covered the man's hand with hers. "Thank you for making room for us. Perhaps later, you and I could . . ." A jacketed waiter stepped to the table before she could finish, and Gwynn offered the maître d' a wink and mouthed, "We'll chat later."

"Ladies, good evening. I'm Landon. What is your pleasure this evening?"

Anya curled a finger, and the waiter leaned toward her. She took his arm and motioned across the room. "This man—the big man—what is his favorite dessert? He looks like a man who loves dessert."

The waiter straightened. "Oh, you mean Mr. Orlov. Well, he, uh . . . he doesn't really order from the menu. He and the chef are very close friends. He eats from a personal menu and only what the chef makes. No one else is permitted to cook for him when he is here."

"He is here every night, yes?" Anya asked.

"No, not every night, but several nights every week."

Anya cast an eye toward the kitchen. "How can I become close friend with chef and eat only from private menu?"

The waiter spoke as if recruiting a co-conspirator. "You could start by lending him a million dollars like Mr. Orlov did. At least that's what I heard."

Anya sat erect. "In this case, we will order from dessert menu and continue to not be close friend with chef."

The waiter rattled off the dessert list, and they chose something chocolate that sounded decadent and irresistible. When it arrived, they devoured the confectionary slice of Heaven with sighs of delight following every bite.

When the waiter returned, he trailed one step behind a tall, lean man in a tall white hat. The pair approached the table, and the man removed his hat and bowed slightly. "It would appear that you enjoyed your dessert."

Gwynn sighed as if she'd never been more satisfied. "It was delightful. Thank you so much."

"You are quite welcome," he said. "I am Chef Christian Gerard. It's delightful to have the two of you inside Eden's View. I do hope you enjoyed your dessert enough to come back for a full meal next time."

In an intentionally strong accent, Anya said, "This we will do, but perhaps you can make for us special dinner that is not on menu."

The chef instinctually turned toward Vasily Orlov and back to Anya. "It would be my pleasure, Miss . . ."

"I am Ana, and this is my friend, Guinevere."

He kissed each of their offered hands. "I'm charmed, and I look forward to seeing both of you again soon. Next time you come, though, let the maître d' know you're my guests, and I'll see that you have a much better table."

11

Utracheno pri Perevode
(Lost in Translation)

The following morning, Anya pulled Peter's card from her nightstand and dialed the number. "Good morning, Peter. Is Anya."

The State Department driver chuckled. "Yes, I can hear this, plus I saved your number, and I have caller ID."

"You have not so visible car?"

"Is that a question?" he asked.

"Yes, is question. We need car that is inconspicuous. You have one like this?"

"I can get one," he said, "but it'll take an hour or so."

"Good. You will pick us up at southeast corner of Jackson Square in one hour." She ended the call before he could protest or confirm, and she slinked through the passage to Gwynn's cabin. "Good morning."

Gwynn jumped. "You've got to stop doing that! You scared me out of my wits."

"If you are going to be good federal police agent, you have to have much better awareness of what is happening around you. We will work on this."

"Sure, we'll add that to the list of the forty-seven other things I'm terrible at."

Anya frowned. "You are not terrible at forty-seven things . . . only four."

Gwynn felt a pang of truth in Anya's backhanded compliment. "Thanks, I guess. Only four, huh? So, other than environmental awareness, what are the other three?"

"If you do not know, then there are five things. Is okay, though. We will fix all of these. Is only matter of time."

"Only a matter of time, huh? I guess it's really a matter of time and staying alive."

"Yes, this is correct, but I will not let you die. But even if I could not keep you alive, we have strong Peter and Johnny Mac dressed like bum."

Gwynn let the picture soften the mood, and she even chuckled. "He does make a pretty good bum, doesn't he?"

"Speaking of bum, dress in yoga pants, sweatshirt, and running shoes today. You will also need jacket. It is raining."

Gwynn pulled the curtains aside and watched the drops of water draw long vertical tracks down the window. "Ooh, you're right. It's nasty out there this morning. What's the plan?"

"Plan is to meet Peter at Jackson Square in fifty minutes. We are going to do something you are probably very good at."

Gwynn raised an eyebrow. "Oh, what's that?"

"*Nablyudeniye.*"

Gwynn smiled. "Surveillance. Yeah, I'm really good at that. Who, and/or what, are we surveilling?"

Anya took a glance through the window. "First, we will watch morning delivery at restaurant, and then maybe Vasily Orlov."

Gwynn rubbed her palms together. "Now, that sounds like fun."

The two pulled on light rain jackets over their sweatshirts and set out on foot toward one of the world's most famous parks. When they arrived, Anya led the way to the center of the square, where a statue of Andrew Jackson mounted on horseback rose above the grounds.

Gwynn stared up at the figure. "I guess I should be ashamed, but I never knew Jackson Square was named after Andrew Jackson."

"How could you not know this? You were born inside America, and you went to American school, yes?"

"Yes, but that doesn't mean I know everything about every park in the country."

"But Jackson was seventh president of United States and also victorious general at Battle of New Orleans in eighteen-fifteen. This is important history for America."

"You're right, of course, but I bet you can't find more than two people in the whole park who know what year the Battle of New Orleans was fought. And I'll double that bet to say you can't find a single person who knows which number president Jackson was."

"This cannot be true," Anya said. "Surely these people who come to see statue know these things."

Gwynn shrugged. "I think I'm right on this one."

The drizzle stopped, and several vendors and artists began setting up their workspaces and stands. Anya approached a man of perhaps fifty with a long gray ponytail protruding from beneath a beret. "Good morning. I am from other country. Can you tell me of this person Andrew Jackson?"

The man placed a metal can of paintbrushes on a cloth-covered table. "You know, with that accent, you don't have to tell people you're from another country. That's pretty obvious. But yeah, about Jackson . . . He was like the fifth or sixth president, maybe."

Anya sighed and looked at her partner.

Gwynn mouthed, "I told you."

She turned back to the painter. "Was President Jackson in battles, maybe?"

The man cocked his head and eyed the gray cloud cover. "You know, now that you mention it, I think he was. If I remember correctly, they called him Old Hickory, but history isn't really my thing."

Anya said, "Yes, this is also obvious. How about swallowing sword? Do you know how this is done?"

The painter took a step back. "What's wrong with you, lady?"

"I told you. I am from other country, and I am curious about American things."

The man turned away and mumbled, "Whatever."

Anya checked her watch and took Gwynn's arm. "We are to meet Peter in two minutes."

They walked through the throngs of artists, most of whom knew little more than the ponytailed painter about American history.

When they arrived at the corner of Saint Peter and Decatur Street, their own Saint Peter was waiting beside a nondescript blue sedan with Louisiana plates.

Anya slid onto the back seat. "You will ride in front with Peter. You are better than me for surveillance."

The compliment brought a broad smile to Gwynn's face, but uncertainty soon followed, and she turned to the Russian. "Are you just saying that to make me feel better about the four things I'm terrible at?"

"I do not say things I do not mean. You are well trained as surveillance officer. This not what I do. I am person of action, not person of watching."

"Okay, fine, but at least tell me what we're looking for."

Anya laid her hand on Peter's shoulder. "Please take us to back of Eden's View restaurant. We wish to watch morning deliveries."

Without a word, Peter pulled into the light traffic and soon had the sedan tucked behind a stack of wooden pallets across the street from the restaurant's service entrance.

"I do not know exactly what we are looking for," Anya said, "but it would be nice place to start if we know what happens inside restaurant when customers are not there, yes?"

Gwynn nodded. "You're right, but so far, it just looks like normal restaurant stuff. The liquor guy came and went. There's a meat truck coming up the road now. Let's see if he backs in."

Just as she'd expected, the truck bearing the logo of Silver's Meat and Poultry backed to within a few feet of the restaurant's back door.

Gwynn leaned toward the driver. "I can't see. I don't have the angle. Can either of you see what they're unloading?"

Anya opened the door and slipped from the car. With her rain jacket and hood still in place, she strolled across the street and stood against the corner of the building. Five minutes later, the truck pulled away, and Anya returned to the car. "It looked only like meat, but it was heavy. Delivery man was very strong, but he sometimes struggled, and tires on cart were pressed out of shape."

Gwynn said, "I thought you said you weren't very good at surveillance. You picked up on things most people would've missed."

Anya pulled off her hood. "I did not say I was not good at surveillance. I only said you are better."

They sat for thirty minutes as people came and went through the service entrance.

Gwynn yawned. "All of this looks pretty normal for a restaurant, don't you think?"

"Yes. Perhaps we have seen everything for this morning. I think we should—"

Peter held up a hand. "Wait. There is another truck coming down the alley."

"What kind of truck?" Anya asked.

Peter kept his eyes focused out the window. "I don't know yet, but it'll be here in thirty seconds."

An all-black refrigerated truck with no lettering or logos backed to within a foot of the door. The driver tapped the horn three short blasts, and Chef Christian Gerard stepped from the restaurant wearing a black baseball cap and full-length apron. He scanned the area and froze when he eyed the stack of wooden pallets partially hiding the blue sedan.

"What's he doing?" Gwynn asked.

"I do not know, but he moves like man who is nervous. I think maybe he saw our car."

Suddenly, the chef spun and moved back through the door. A few seconds later, a trio of workers pushed three tall racks on wheels from the kitchen onto the back parking lot. They lined the carts beside the truck, completely hiding the activity at the rear of the truck from the sedan.

"That's not good," Peter whispered. "They're definitely hiding something."

Anya opened her door again, but Gwynn said, "No! Stay in the car. They're obviously nervous enough already. We don't want to spook them."

Anya closed the door, obeying Gwynn's command. "You are correct, but we must know what is inside truck."

Gwynn said, "Whatever it is will be inside that kitchen soon, and the cool thing about restaurant kitchens is that you can't drive away with them. We've just got to find a way into the kitchen after the truck leaves."

Peter said, "I'm not trying to work my way into your investigation, but maybe following the truck to see where it goes would give us—I mean— would give *you* some answers."

"I think this is very good idea. What do you think, Gwynn?"

She continued peering through the windshield, willing her eyes to pierce the barricade of carts. "Yeah, that's a good idea, but I've got an even better one. Peter, you follow the truck and call us when you find out where he goes. Anya, you come with me. We're going to put your feminine charms, and your acting skills, to the test."

Gwynn exited the car and pulled open the back door as she passed. "Come on. Let's go."

Anya slid from the car and looked up to see her partner sprinting down the alley. She gave chase and quickly caught her. "What are you doing?"

"What's it look like? We're running. Now, try to keep up."

Gwynn quickened the pace, and Anya easily kept in stride. They continued north for two blocks and then turned east. By the time they'd circled back to the restaurant, both the black truck and Peter were gone.

"What is plan?" Anya said.

"Don't worry. Just trust me, and keep running."

They rounded the corner to the front of Eden's View. Four strides from the front door, Gwynn gave Anya's trailing foot a sharp kick, sending the Russian crashing to the sidewalk. Gwynn patted to a stop and knelt beside her partner.

Anya growled, "Why did you do that?"

"It's all part of the plan. Just trust me, and go with it. Now, stay down."

Gwynn stepped across her partner and pounded her fist against the glass of the restaurant's double doors.

Seconds later, one of the doors opened a few inches, and Christian Gerard's voice came through the opening. "We're not open until four."

Gwynn stuck a foot into the opening and gave the door a yank. The chef followed the door as it flew open.

Gwynn gasped. "Oh, my gosh. You're that chef from last night. How lucky are we? Ana and I were running, and she fell right here in front of your restaurant. I think she may have sprained her ankle. We need some ice."

Gerard gazed back inside the restaurant. In a moment of uncertainty, he stammered, "Uh, just wait here, and I'll have someone bring you some ice. Do you want me to call for an ambulance?"

Gwynn looked up into the chef's blue eyes and suddenly remembered where her focus should be. She took a step toward him. "I'm afraid it's going to start raining again. Can we please come in and sit down while you get the ice?"

Gerard hesitated, and Anya joined the cast of actors by forcing a pained sigh.

Gerard's resolve melted, and he took a knee beside Anya. "Here, put your arm around my neck. I'll get you inside."

Anya laced her arm around his neck and let him lift her from the sidewalk. She shot a wink toward her partner as the chef carried her through the door and placed her on an upholstered chair.

Gerard knelt in front of Anya and reached for her foot. "Let me take a look."

Gwynn nudged him aside. "No! You go get the ice. I'll get her shoe off."

Gerard wiped his hands on his apron and turned for the kitchen as Gwynn remained at Anya's feet. She pulled off her shoe and ground her knuckles into the ankle bone.

Anya yanked her foot away. "What are you doing? That hurts!"

"It's supposed to hurt. Now, shut up and give me your foot. We have to make it look like you sprained your ankle."

Hesitantly, Anya surrendered her bare foot back to her partner, who made short work of making it look badly swollen and red. When Gerard returned with a bag of ice and a towel, Gwynn stepped away, revealing the ankle and her handiwork.

Gerard gasped. "Ouch. That definitely looks sprained, but it might be worse than that. Here, let me get you a stool."

He pulled a small stepstool from beneath the maître d's stand and slid it into place. He gently placed Anya's foot on the step and draped the towel across her ankle. When he laid the bag of ice on top of the towel, Anya gasped in mock pain. He carefully held her foot in place and situated the ice directly over the most seriously reddened area just above the ankle. "I don't know. It looks pretty bad. Maybe you should let me call an ambulance just to make sure it isn't broken."

"This is not necessary. I will be fine."

The chef started to look over his shoulder to protest to Gwynn, but Anya rolled her foot sharply to the left, sending the ice bag crashing to the floor. Before Gerard could turn to notice Gwynn's absence, he reached for the ice and carefully repositioned it back on the ankle.

Anya whimpered. "You will please hold ice in place, yes?"

Gerard's eyes widened in realization. "You're the two from dessert last night. I didn't recognize you in your running clothes."

He turned again to include Gwynn, but Anya jerked and gasped. "Please just hold in place. I'm sure my friend is calling for our driver."

"You have a driver?"

Anya nodded. "Yes, my father is wealthy man back in Russia. He makes certain I have everything I want, and also he is generous for people who care for me like you are doing now. My father would be pleased."

"Wait a minute. Are you the ones on that yacht out there where the *Belle* used to dock?"

Anya nodded. "Yes, this is my boat. It is *Utrennyaya Zvezda*. This means—."

He interrupted. "*Morning Star*. Yes, I know."

Anya smiled. "*A ty govorish' po russki?*"

He blushed. "I only speak a little. I have some friends—well, just one friend . . . I mean, he's more of a business associate, you might say, but he's Russian. I've picked up a few words and phrases from him over the years."

Anya tilted her head and found that perfect spot just between his eyes. "What is your friend's name?"

"Vasily."

Anya kept her gaze focused on her victim. "Vasily is only one name. Do you know what this name means?"

"No, I don't. What does it mean?"

"It is difficult to translate perfectly, but in English, Vasily would be 'king' or maybe 'royalty.'"

Gerard let out a huff. "Yeah, that sounds about right. Vasily is definitely up on a throne of his own making."

"What is surname of Vasily? If he is your friend—or maybe business partner—surely, you know his name."

"I didn't say he was my partner—just an associate. I'm not in business with him. He spends a lot of time in my restaurant, and sometimes we invest in some things together. It's like that."

Anya smiled. "So, he is man who wants to be important, but he needs money from you for investments, yes?"

"No, it's not like that. I mean . . . oh, never mind. It doesn't matter. The truth is, I only know about ten Russian words, and most of those aren't appropriate for polite company, especially company like the two of you." Gerard looked up to see Gwynn standing over his shoulder.

"How's the patient?"

He lifted the ice and pulled the towel away. "It looks like the swelling has stopped, but it's still pretty red."

Gwynn said, "Thank you for the ice and for letting us come inside. I'm sure you must be busy getting ready for another day as the city's top chef."

He situated the towel and ice back in place. "I'm far from the city's top chef, but I appreciate the confidence." He stood and shot a look toward the kitchen. "I'm sorry, but I really need to get back to work. I've got a lot going on back there, and . . ."

Gwynn traced her hand down the outside of his arm. "It's okay, really. I called for our car, and you've been more than kind. We'll get out of your hair and out of your restaurant. But before we go, is that offer for a better table still available? After Ana's ankle heals, of course."

"I'll save the best table in the house, just for you."

"I think this is not true," Anya said. "I think best table is for always your friend Vasily."

He held up both hands. "Okay, you caught me. I'll save the second-best table just for you. Tonight?"

Gwynn looked to Anya, who said, "Yes, tonight. I will have probably cast on broken foot, but you will make me forget pain of leg with best food in all of city, yes?"

"I'll do my best."

Their limo pulled up in front of the restaurant, and instead of Peter stepping from the front seat of the long black car, Dave Young, the first officer, stepped from behind the wheel. He opened the rear door and strode for the double doors of the restaurant.

Gerard helped Anya to her feet, and she rewarded him with a suggestive kiss to his cheek. "*Spasibo, povar i vrach.*"

"You're welcome, daughter of rich, generous Russian father. But please tell me *povar i vrach* means something good."

She smiled as she hopped toward the limo. "Ask your friend . . . or business partner. He will tell you what this means."

12

Fol na Vecherinke
(Party Foul)

The limo ride back to the *Morning Star* was brief but full of questions. Their first-officer-turned-driver eyed them in the mirror. "What was that all about, and do I need to take you to the ER?"

Gwynn met his gaze. "That was about getting inside the restaurant when no customers were there to screw up our surveillance, and no, we don't need an emergency room. We could use a really good first-aid kit, though."

Dave Young shook his head. "You two certainly live an interesting life. Oh, and we can do a little better than just a first-aid kit back on the boat. We've got a full medical suite and a nurse practitioner on board."

Anya said, "This is not our life. This is our work. Our life is what we choose when we are not working. This is not same for you?"

Dave considered her explanation. "I guess you're right, but my work seems to consume my life most of the time."

"This is also true for us."

Dave watched Anya step from the limo and up the gangway with no sign of injury. He turned to Gwynn and pointed toward the Russian. "So, that was all an act?"

"Something like that," Gwynn said. "She used to be an actress back in New York."

"On Broadway?"

Gwynn smiled. "No. She did most of her performances in the Diamond District."

Dave held the questions that were obviously straining behind his eyes. "The medical bay is on deck one forward in the forecastle."

Gwynn scowled. "I've never liked that word."

"What word?"

"Forecastle. It looks like it should be pronounced *for castle*. How did it ever come to be pronounced *fokesal*?"

Dave watched Anya as she disappeared inside the yacht. "How did a Russian foreign intelligence officer ever come to be working with the FBI to spy on restaurateurs in New Orleans?"

Gwynn planted her hands on her hips. "First, I'm not FBI. I'm DOJ. And second, how did you know she was . . . you know."

Dave stuck out his hand. "It's nice to meet you, DOJ. I'm Lieutenant Commander Dave Young, U.S. Navy intelligence, retired."

Gwynn playfully shook his hand. "Nice to meet you, too, but if you were a lieutenant commander, why aren't you captain of the *Morning Star* instead of the first officer?"

Dave tapped his chest. "Intel officer . . . not boatswain."

"For the record, *boatswain* is a stupid word, too."

Dave's infatuated smile was suddenly impossible to ignore, and Gwynn was horrified by how she must look after her morning run. She took a step back and pinned her arms to her sides.

"What's wrong?"

She blushed. "I'm a hot mess. We've been . . ."

Dave gave her a wink. "That's my favorite kind of mess."

Gwynn glanced up the gangway. "Yeah, well, I should probably . . ."

Dave nodded. "Yeah, you probably should."

Gwynn stepped into Anya's cabin to find her partner wearing only a University of Georgia T-shirt and her hair wrapped in a towel. "Oh, hey. I didn't mean to barge in on you."

"Is okay. I needed shower while you were flirting with second captain."

Gwynn blushed. "I wasn't flirting. Well, maybe I was flirting a little. He's really nice. And he's the first officer, not the second captain."

Anya pulled the towel from her head, allowing her hair to fall across her shoulder. "What is difference between first officer and second captain?"

Gwynn pondered the question. "Never mind. Do you want to know what I saw in the kitchen while Mr. Mc-Hottie-Chef was playing with your foot?"

"I am listening."

"I didn't see much, but what I did see raised a lot of questions. White was right about the caviar. I caught a glimpse of at least four cases of beluga."

Anya perked up. "This is good."

Gwynn continued. "Yes, it's good in that we're at least on the right track for some violation of import laws, but that's not the interesting part. There were several bundles of something bound in brown burlap and tied with twine."

"What was inside bundles?"

"I don't know, but we're going to find out. Whatever it was, they were handling it with extreme care. But that's not all. The people who were moving the bundles weren't the regular kitchen staff."

"How do you know?"

"Because they were dressed in jeans, sneakers, and sweatshirts. The kitchen staff were all wearing aprons and hats."

"How many of these people were inside kitchen?"

Gwynn closed an eye in thought. "There were seven or eight kitchen staff, not counting the chef, and I think five people in jeans. The kitchen staff were obviously avoiding the guys carrying the bundles."

"Where did they put wrapped-up things?"

"They put them in a second freezer or cooler. I couldn't get close enough to tell, but they definitely *weren't* putting them into the regular freezer."

"How do you know this?"

Gwynn huffed. "Because I watched them put fish into the first freezer."

Anya pulled on her jeans and sat on the edge of her bed. "What kind of fish?"

"How should I know? I don't know anything about fish. They were big, ugly fish with huge eyes and a lot of fins on top."

Anya frowned. "A lot of fins?"

"Yeah, you know how a normal fish has one big fin on top? It wasn't like that. There were like three or four fins down the spine. I don't know. It just looked weird."

Anya took Gwynn's hand. "I have idea. Come with me."

She led her partner through the interior of the yacht until they came to the galley, where a woman stood kneading dough on a stainless-steel table.

The woman looked up and dusted her hands on her apron. "Well, hello. You must be Gwynn and Anya."

Gwynn nodded. "That's us. Are you the chef?"

Before the woman could answer, Anya belted out, "Do you know about fish?"

The woman shook her head in surprise. "Yes to both questions. Do you have an allergy to fish? If so, no one told me about it, but I can add it to your preference sheet."

"No, we are not allergic, but we need to know about fish." Anya turned to Gwynn. "Tell to her description of fish."

Gwynn obeyed and described what she'd seen in the kitchen at Eden's View.

The chef said, "That sounds like a Chilean sea bass. How big were they?"

Gwynn held her hands outstretched. "Some of them were four feet long or more."

The chef nodded. "Yep, that's probably Chilean sea bass. It's actually called a toothfish, but somebody came up with a more appetizing name, and you'll never see a picture of a whole fish on a menu. Like you said, it's ugly."

Gwynn turned to Anya and held up two fingers.

Anya gave a nod. "Yes, this is two things on list, but what about bundles?"

The chef cocked her head. "Bundles?"

Gwynn said, "At the same time I saw the sea bass, I also saw some people carrying bundles of something heavy wrapped in burlap and tied with twine."

The chef recoiled. "Where did you see that?"

"Uh . . . in a commercial kitchen."

The chef shook her head. "Like in a restaurant? *That* kind of commercial kitchen or a processing plant?"

Gwynn turned to Anya, and the Russian said, "You can tell her."

"It was a restaurant kitchen."

The chef laid a towel across the dough she'd been working. "Are you sure it was burlap?"

Gwynn replayed the scene in her mind. "I'm pretty sure. At least that's what it looked like. I was about fifteen feet away, so I got a pretty good look."

"There's no acceptable reason why there would ever be anything in a restaurant kitchen wrapped in burlap except coffee beans and maybe a cured ham."

Gwynn shook her head. "It definitely wasn't coffee beans. They would have conformed to the shoulders of the guys carrying them, and the pig would've been ten thousand pounds if they were hams."

The chef raised her shoulders. "I got nothing."

Anya took control. "Thank you. This is exactly information we needed."

As they left the galley, Gwynn motioned toward Anya's foot. "We've got to get you to sick bay."

"This is silly. There is nothing wrong with foot."

"You and I know that, but Chef Gerard thinks you're a hobbler now, and we can't disappoint him."

Twenty minutes later, Anya left the medical bay with a pneumatic walking cast in her arms.

"I thought that was supposed to go on your foot," Gwynn prodded.

"It will go on foot only when absolutely necessary for playing game at restaurant. It is ridiculous."

Gwynn laughed. "Yeah, but I bet you look so cute with it on."

"If you continue this, you will learn how this thing tastes."

Suddenly, Gwynn's verbal abuse halted.

Lunch was served aboard *Morning Star*, and the captain and first officer joined the feast. It was traditional English fish and chips, but the chef's touch turned the common meal into a dining experience instead of simple pub food.

Captain Chuck wiped his chin. "I heard a rumor the two of you have reservations at Eden's View this evening."

"Yes," Anya said before placing another piece of the flakey, white fish between her lips.

"I've heard great things about that place. You'll have to tell us all about it tomorrow morning."

Anya swallowed the fish and eyed the captain. "I am not sure if this is possible or permissible. This is classified operation."

"Eating dinner is classified?" The captain stared back and forth between his guests.

"It is tonight," Gwynn said, "but I think we can get away with telling you about the meal without going to prison for divulging State secrets."

The captain slapped Dave, the first officer, on the back. "Okay, then. We look forward to hearing all about it, but for now, we've got work to do."

Gwynn watched Dave walk away, and Anya gave her arm a playful slug. "You are staring . . . again."

"Stop it! I was not! Well, maybe a little. He's got a cute butt. I'm allowed to stare. By the way, did you know he's a retired naval intelligence officer?"

Anya tossed a fry at her smitten partner. "No, I did not know this, but you are correct. His butt is very cute. There is no time for this thinking inside your head right now. We have mission. You can play with his butt when mission is finished."

Gwynn picked up the thrown fry and bit it in half. "You're right. I just want to make sure you know I'm calling dibs. You can't have him."

Anya laughed. "This is crazy thought. I could not take man from you. You are younger, prettier, and smarter than me."

Gwynn rolled her eyes. "Come on, Anya. We both know only one of those things is true, but seriously, I'm calling dibs."

"I promise I will not flirt with Second Captain Dave."

"He's the first officer! How many times do I have to tell you that?"

"Does he have captain's license?"

"Okay, I give up. I'm not playing semantics with someone who refuses to use English articles."

Anya put on a mischievous grin. "I will ask again question. Does he have *a* captain's license? If yes, he is also captain and will be first captain if first captain falls into water."

Gwynn pushed her plate to the center of the table. "You know what? You're right. Dave is now Second Captain Dave."

"I knew you would see it my way. What time are we going to dinner?"

Gwynn checked her watch. "It's just after one now, and we need to check in with Agent White and bring him up to speed. I'm thinking eight o'clock."

"Eight o'clock is good time. I wish now to have beignets and tea from Café Du Monde."

"Absolutely not! Tea with beignets is a party foul, and I won't stand for it. We can have beignets, but only with coffee."

13

KRICHASHCHIYE DUSHI (THE SCREAMING SOULS)

The confectionary clouds of bliss arrived dusted with powdered sugar and piled on a white ceramic plate that had likely seen the passing of two centuries. The petite mugs containing the café au lait appeared only a few decades younger than the plate.

The bewilderment on Anya's face left Gwynn barely able to contain her amusement. "What's the matter? Haven't you ever seen a plate of beignets before?"

Anya continued staring at the delights just waiting to be devoured. "No, this is first time. I feel like a little girl again. I am excited, but I do not know what to do next."

Gwynn giggled. "Here. I'll show you."

She lifted a beignet, tapped it on the side of the plate to remove a little excess powdered sugar, and cautiously bit off a third of the pastry. With eyes closed, she let out a sound of primordial pleasure and licked her lips, determined to savor every bit of the sweet drops of Heaven.

Anya watched in curious delight. "I think even Second Captain Dave cannot make you have that reaction. Maybe now I am afraid to try beignet."

Gwynn wordlessly sipped her steaming coffee and leaned back in her chair. "I think I'd enjoy being Second Captain Dave's little beignet."

Anya playfully slapped her partner's wrist. "You are terrible, but I am sure he would love this."

She lifted her first beignet to her lips and followed Gwynn's lead. As the sweet sugar and piping hot pastry melted onto her tongue, she instantly realized Gwynn hadn't overplayed her reaction. After a long moment of allowing the dessert to take her five thousand miles away to a sidewalk café on the Champs-Élysées, Anya sighed and lifted her coffee cup. "I think I will never eat anything else. This is perfect food."

Gwynn touched the rim of her coffee mug to Anya's. "I love your idea, but we'd weigh three hundred pounds in a month."

"I do not understand why I have lived so long and never tried beignets."

"You never forget your first. Now, eat up before they get cold."

They devoured the plate of pastries and two more cups of chicory coffee. With at least half of the powdered sugar now sprinkled across their shirts, they made their way back to the *Morning Star* and the main salon, where they collapsed and dialed Agent Ray White's office number.

"White."

"It's Agent Davis. We have a report."

White loosened his tie. "Well, if it isn't my two Southern belles. I hear you're lightly dusted with powdered sugar and hyped up on café au lait."

"How could you know that?" Gwynn questioned.

"I've got eyes and ears everywhere. Never forget that. So, let's hear this report of yours."

Gwynn briefed for ten minutes, covering their surveillance, the mysterious black truck, the broken-ankle gambit, and finally, the burlap bundles.

The sound of White scribbling furiously punctuated the briefing. He asked, "What about Peter?"

Anya palmed her forehead. "I cannot believe we have not heard from him yet. We should call him now."

She pressed send and listened for the ringing tone, but she got a recorded message instead. "We're sorry. The cellular customer you are calling is either unavailable or is outside the coverage area. Please try your call again later."

Anya mumbled, "This is not good sign. His phone will not ring."

White said, "That's not a big deal down there. Cell service is sketchy south of the city, so if he's moving toward the Gulf, he won't have any coverage."

"I do not think you understand why is not good sign. Is Peter armed?"

White said, "I don't know. Why?"

"These people he is following may be dangerous if my—I think word is —*hunch* is good. Is this right?"

Gwynn asked, "You mean, like a gut feeling?"

"Yes, this is what I mean. I have gut feeling burlap wrappings are something illegal inside wrapping for coffee beans."

"Ouch," White hissed. "If it's a drug-smuggling operation, we never saw that one coming, but if you're correct, Peter is chasing a bunch of cocaine cowboys, and we have no way to know where he is."

Anya closed her eyes in thought. "Peter is spy. He will be ready for fight, but someone at State Department will be able to find him with use of satellite and cellular towers, even if only one or maybe two towers."

White said, "He's not a spy, but you may be onto something. I'll get State on the line and see what they can do. In the meantime, what about Skipper?"

Elizabeth "Skipper" Woodley, a dedicated intelligence analyst for a team of covert operatives led by Chase Fulton—the man Anya had originally been dispatched to find, interrogate, and flip—had helped Anya on her previous mission in New York City when all other avenues failed.

"I can make call to her, but surely State Department has analysts who can do simple job of finding their own spy."

"He's not a spy," White demanded. "But you may be right. We might have the resources to locate him. I'll get back with you as soon as I hear back from State. Is there anything else?"

"No, Agent White," Gwynn said. "That's all for now."

The line went dead, and the two women were left staring at each other in the silence of the luxury yacht.

Gwynn looked up. "Why didn't you tell me about your hunch about what's inside the burlap bags? We're partners. We're not supposed to keep things like that from each other."

Anya frowned. "I did not do this on purpose. I only thought of hunch while on phone with Ray. Sometimes, smugglers will use smell of coffee to make dogs confused. This might be what they are doing, but I do not think Ray is correct. If inside burlap is cocaine, corners would be square. You said shapes were not regular, yes?"

Gwynn nodded. "That's right, and they weren't really bags. They were more like long sheets of burlap wrapped around whatever was inside. It definitely wasn't bricks of cocaine. Whatever it was, every bundle looked different."

"I do not know what could be inside bundles, but probably not drugs."

Gwynn sighed. "That's good for Peter."

"This might be true, but because we do not know what is being smuggled, it could be even worse for Peter. How long will it take for State Department to find him?"

Gwynn shrugged. "I don't know. That's way outside my box."

Anya checked her watch. "It is has been now eight minutes. This is too long. I will call Skipper."

Instinctually, Gwynn checked her phone, and as she palmed it, it vibrated. "Wait!" she said. "This is Agent White."

Gwynn hit the speaker button. "Davis."

Without preamble, White said, "He's on his way south toward Grand Isle."

Anya asked, "What is Grand Isle?"

White softened his typical tone. "It's the end of the world, though that's not the bad news. We don't have any satellites in position for a live feed, but there's a cell tower just north of a town called Golden Meadow on Bayou Lafourche. They got a solid hit on his cell there about twenty-five minutes ago."

Anya said, "This does not sound like bad news."

"Let me finish. There's a cellular relay tower in a tiny community of Leeville, ten miles south of Golden Meadow. We've not gotten a ping from that tower, and Peter should've been there no more than fifteen minutes after leaving Golden Meadow."

Gwynn jumped in. "They could've made a stop for some reason. It doesn't necessarily mean something's gone wrong."

"I like the optimism, Davis, but there's nowhere to stop on that stretch of road. Literally, there's *nothing* there. It's a swamp full of snakes and gators."

Anya stood. "We must have helicopter!"

"Calm down," White said. "I'm already on it. The Coast Guard is en route in one of their MH-Sixty-Five Dolphins."

"No!" Anya demanded. "We must have helicopter."

White exhaled a long breath. "I was afraid you were going to say that. There's an old Air Force Huey at NAS New Orleans, and they're expecting you."

Anya smiled. "We are becoming excellent team. You now anticipate and give to us what we need."

* * *

Well armed and anxious, Gwynn and Anya slid into the Porsche and made what should've been a forty-minute drive to the naval air station in just over twenty. The UH-1 Huey was perched on the ramp in front of base operations with the rotor spinning and a pair of helmeted pilots in front. Gwynn ran to the open cabin door and leapt inside, but her partner didn't follow. Instead, she twisted the handle on the left side front door and yanked it open.

The shocked copilot looked down at the Russian with her blonde hair flying in every direction, and he threw a thumb into the air. "Get in the back!"

Ignoring his command, Anya reached inside, disconnected the man's harness, and pulled him from the seat. He landed off balance on the concrete beside her, but she steadied him and held out a hand. "Give to me helmet!"

The confused copilot stared back into the cockpit at the higher-ranking pilot in the right seat. The senior pilot nodded, and Anya climbed into the copilot's seat with his helmet now controlling her unruly hair.

She plugged the helmet into the communications panel. "Golden Meadow!"

Before she'd finished the command, the pilot pulled the skids from the ground and pointed the nose of the aged chopper to the southwest. The bayou flew beneath the Huey at two miles per minute, and soon, Golden Meadow came into view.

Anya flipped the switch, opening comms with Gwynn and the former pilot in the back. "There is town of Golden Meadow. Look for blue car." She turned to the pilot. "I have controls."

He glared back over the rim of his glasses. "Are you sure?"

Without another word, she slid her feet onto the pedals and grabbed the cyclic and collective.

The pilot shrugged. "Okay, you have the controls."

She lowered the nose, sending the chopper diving toward the bayou and banking to the south.

The seasoned pilot in the right seat folded his arms and grinned. "So, a blue car, right?"

Anya kept her eyes pinned to the road leading south out of town. "Yes. Blue, four-door car, maybe ten years old. One person inside."

Everyone aboard the chopper gazed toward the two-lane road cutting through the mud and muck of Bayou Lafourche. The ten miles between

Golden Meadow and Leeville passed beneath the skids in less than five minutes with no sign of the sedan.

Anya banked hard left and brought the Huey around to the north. "We will make one more pass. Look also for small black refrigerated truck."

Everyone acknowledged the new instructions, and Anya pulled the collective to gain enough altitude to expand the search. Five minutes passed without a sighting, so Anya said, "We will search for two minutes north of town."

No one answered, but every eye aboard scanned the wetlands below. No sign of either vehicle materialized north of Golden Meadow.

Anya asked, "Does anyone have ideas?"

The pilot in the right seat said, "I'm not sure how I got involved in whatever this is, but I might be able to help if you can answer a couple of questions for me."

Anya turned south, taking them well west of the town and over vast emptiness, where only the fiercest of creatures survive. "What is question?"

"I have more than one, but let's start with, who are you?"

"I am Anya, and in back is Gwynn with your other pilot. I do not know his name."

He shook his head. "No, that's not what I meant. But I have a feeling you're not going to tell me much more than that, are you?"

"Your gut feeling is correct. What is next question?"

He motioned out the windshield. "My most pressing question at the moment is, are you planning to hit that Coast Guard chopper up there?"

Anya glanced up to see the bright orange helicopter less than a mile away. She pulled the chopper to the southeast to miss the Dolphin. "Thank you for seeing him."

The pilot laughed. "No, thank you for missing him. Can you lay out the situation for me? Who's in the blue car, and what does the black truck have to do with any of this?"

"I can tell you only this. Blue car is good guy, and black truck is maybe not good guys."

"That gives us a place to start. I'm Tiptoe, by the way. It's nice to meet you, Anya."

She turned in disbelief. "Your name is Tiptoe? This is terrible name."

"It's actually my call sign. When I was a young Air Force lieutenant in flight school, I was hesitant to step on the pedals, so the instructors started calling me Tiptoe, and it stuck. I see that you don't have any problem at all stepping on the pedals. You fly this thing like you stole it."

Anya gave him one of her patented smiles. "I think maybe I did steal it."

"Maybe you did. So, back to the manhunt . . . Can we shoot the guys in the truck?"

Gwynn's voice suddenly filled their headsets. "No! In fact, we don't want them to know we're here."

"Let me get this straight. You're chasing bad guys with the loudest helicopter you could find, and you don't want them to know you're chasing them?"

"Yes, this is correct," Anya said.

Tiptoe threw up his hands. "Well, I figured it out. This is some craziness only the federal government would pull, so you guys have to be feds."

Anya's smile returned, but no one spoke a word.

Tiptoe situated himself in his seat. "In that case, I have the controls."

Anya surrendered the chopper back to its rightful driver, and he made a poorly coordinated turn to the south.

Anya gave the left pedal a little extra love to bring the tail around where it should be. "Now I understand reason for name Tiptoe."

He ignored the jab and pointed ahead. "See that terrible-looking road running to the southwest?"

Anya followed his finger. "Yes, I see it."

"If I was going to lure someone away from my real destination and put a bullet in his head, that's where I'd go."

"Then take us there," Anya ordered.

"I just have one more question, then I'll stop asking. If we catch these guys in the act of shooting your boy in the blue car, are we going to intervene?"

Anya opened her mouth to answer, but Gwynn's voice came first. "No!"

Tiptoe flipped the switch to isolate the internal communication to just the cockpit. "What was *your* answer going to be?"

Anya bowed her head. "I do not know, but is difficult to let innocent person die when I can save them."

"That's what I thought," he said. "Maybe just our presence will be a deterrent, even if we don't directly intervene."

"Maybe this is true," Anya whispered.

With the comms switched back in the full cabin configuration, Tiptoe said, "I'll take us down the north side of the road so you young folks can use those eagle eyes of yours." He pushed the nose over and accelerated in the dive. When he leveled the chopper, the rotor wash left a wake in the black water below. Ninety seconds and three miles later, he said, "Hey, comrade, is that your car?"

Anya, once again, followed his finger to the blue sedan with the front half disappearing into the bayou. As they drew nearer, Anya focused intently on the car and ordered, "Climb and make perimeter turn!"

The nose came up as the airspeed bled off, and Tiptoe banked left in a climbing three-hundred-sixty-degree turn.

Anya said, "Everyone search for black truck." The turn continued until they made a complete circuit around the wrecked car. "Did anyone see the truck?"

"Negative," came three replies.

She turned back to the pilot. "Get us onto ground beside car."

Without hesitation, he dove for the deck and stuck the skids to the ground twenty feet away from the car. Gwynn and Anya hit the ground with their pistols drawn and approached the car with fear for what they expected to find. Seven bullet holes laced their way diagonally up the driver's door, and shards of glass hung where the window used to be. Dark-red-blood spatter patterned the interior of the passenger side.

Reaching the car, Anya yanked open the driver's door to reveal Peter's body lying across the front seat. She shoved her pistol back into its holster and reached across his body in a desperate hope to find even the faintest of a pulse. Gwynn turned, just as she'd been taught, with her back to the scene, providing as much security as possible.

To her amazement, Gwynn heard Anya's voice over the still-spinning rotor blades.

"Get for me medical bag!"

The copilot who'd ridden in the back with Gwynn leapt from the chopper with the bag thrown across his left shoulder and his Glock held firmly in his right hand. He threw the bag at Anya's feet and skirted around the car to cover the scene from the west while Gwynn stood security to the east.

Without the necessity of being instructed to do so, Tiptoe spooled the engines back to full power and pulled the Huey off the ground. He flew a continually expanding orbit around the site until his copilot waved for him to return. As soon as the skids hit the muddy ground, Anya and the copilot laid Peter on the floor of the cabin. Gwynn, followed by the copilot, mounted the chopper, but Anya grabbed the pilot's leg and motioned toward the cockpit. In wordless acknowledgment of her direction, he climbed into the cockpit with Tiptoe, and seconds later, the old workhorse was airborne with her original crew at the controls.

Peter lay on his back with three entry wounds and two horrific exit wounds. He'd lost more blood than most people can survive, but miraculously, his heart pounded on, and his one remaining lung pumped every twenty seconds. What life remained inside the man was fighting desperately to escape his battered shell.

Anya hung a bag of fluid from the med bag and skillfully inserted an IV needle into the only vein she could find. She checked and tightened the pressure bandages she'd applied while Peter was still inside the car. His bleeding had slowed, but only because the quantity of blood left inside his body had reached dire limits.

Starting at his head, she worked meticulously to his feet, examining every inch for wounds she'd missed in the initial assessment. When she finished, she gave the IV bag a squeeze and pulled the one remaining bag of fluid from the medi kit. As she worked to replace the soon-to-be empty bag, Anya caught Gwynn staring wide-eyed at her. "What is wrong?"

Gwynn shook off the bewildered look. "Nothing. It's just that I've seen you take more lives than anyone I know, but this is the first time I've ever seen you try to save one."

Without a reaction to Gwynn's observation, Anya returned to her patient, and moments later, the skids of the Huey touched the helipad on top of University Medical Center, where a gurney and four medics waited.

As the engines and rotor spun down, the medical team rolled the gurney beside the chopper, and a woman leaned in. "What have you got?"

Anya spoke over the waning mechanical sounds of the chopper. "Thirty-year-old male Caucasian, multiple GSW, at least three with two exits. No breath sounds on left, two bags of fluid in ten minutes, pulse ten, respirations three to four."

The woman in scrubs nodded. "Okay, we've got him. Hand down the IV bag."

Anya pulled the bag from its hook and handed it from the chopper as three men pulled Peter onto the gurney. In seconds, they were gone, and the Huey sat silently on the pad with Anya and Gwynn sitting in the doorway with their legs dangling toward the skids.

Anya held up her blood-covered hands and breathed in a long breath. "He will die, and is my fault."

Gwynn gasped. "Don't say that! You were amazing. If he lives, it'll be because of what you did. He's strong and—"

Anya laid a bloody hand on Gwynn's thigh. "No. He will die, and this will be one more soul I hear inside darkness."

Gwynn cocked her head. "What?"

"Their souls . . . They call to me in darkness, and I cannot stop them. This punishment for me maybe from your God. This is reason you can never be like me. I do not wish for you to lie in darkness and hear their screams. Is maddening."

Gwynn laced an arm around her partner and friend. "I don't know what to say, but I'm sorry."

"Do not be sorry. Is not your fault. Others are to blame, and also me."

Silence prevailed until Tiptoe leaned against the side of the Huey. "I'm sorry about your friend."

Anya held up a hand to block the afternoon sun. "I think he tried to leave message for us, but I do not understand."

Gwynn said, "What? What kind of message? How?"

"Inside car," Anya whispered. "In blood on dash of car, he wrote ONA with finger. Does this mean something in English?"

Both Gwynn and Tiptoe mouthed, "Ona." Tiptoe shook his head, and Gwynn said, "I don't know. It doesn't make any sense."

"I am trying list of English words beginning with these letters, but nothing is coming to me."

Tiptoe asked, "Do you want to go back to the scene and have another look?"

Anya shook her head. "No, this will not help. Please take us home."

14

Luchshaya Tablitsa
(A Better Table)

On the drive back to the yacht from the naval air station, Anya put the convertible top down and let the cool autumn wind blow through their hair. "Fresh air is good, yes? Smell of death is no good."

Gwynn tried to smile. "Yeah, the fresh air is nice. It's not your fault, you know."

"I should have gone with Peter to follow black truck."

Gwynn argued. "If you—or we—had gone with him, we wouldn't have gotten inside the restaurant, and maybe all three of us would've wound up full of bullet holes. You've got to stop second-guessing yourself."

When they arrived back at the yacht, Anya poured herself into the shower and stood under the cascading water with steam enveloping her body and mind.

With the yacht's supply of hot water depleted, she stepped from the shower and pulled on the University of Georgia baseball T-shirt she'd worn earlier and let the soft cloth brush against her skin.

She found Gwynn and Captain Chuck in the main salon, each with a glass of wine.

Gwynn motioned toward the bar. "I poured a glass for you."

Anya lifted the stemmed glass from the elegant bar and joined her partner on the sofa. "Is there any news from hospital?"

"Not yet," Gwynn said. "But I talked with Agent White. He's obviously not happy, but he's mostly concerned that whoever was in the black refrigerated truck now knows someone's watching them. They're going to be more cautious and might even stop whatever they're doing for a while."

Anya sipped her wine. "Yes, this is likely, but we already saw delivery. We now need to know what is inside burlap packages. We have to get inside restaurant when no one is there."

"That shouldn't be too hard," Gwynn said. "It's not like it'll be the first time we've gotten a warrant to search a business."

Anya inspected her nails and watched imaginary blood drip from her fingertips. "This is now investigation of murderers and also restaurant. We will get inside without warrant."

Before she could protest, Gwynn's phone chirped.

"Davis."

"Davis, it's White. I've got some good news, or at least better news than we were expecting."

"Hang on a second, Agent White. Let me put you on speaker. It's just Captain Chuck, Anya, and me." She pressed the button and laid the phone on the table. "Okay, go ahead."

"I just spoke with the hospital, and Peter's out of surgery. He's still in critical condition, but it looks like he's going to live. He's in a medically in-duced coma due to the severity of his injuries, but you two saved his life."

Anya sighed and leaned back against the plush cushions of the sofa. "This is good news, but we must talk to him. He will be outside of coma today, yes?"

"Not hardly. It'll be at least several days. He'll need additional surgery, but they have him stabilized."

"This is not good enough," Anya demanded. "Did Gwynn tell you of message Peter tried to leave?"

"Yes, she did, and I've got a team on it now. They'll figure it out. In the meantime, you two have to get back inside that restaurant and make con-tact with Orlov. Don't worry about Peter."

"We will do this tonight," Anya said.

"Okay, that's all I've got for now. No matter how late it is when you get back to the boat tonight, I expect a full briefing."

Gwynn said, "Yes, sir. You'll have it. But before you go, do you think we can get a warrant to search the kitchen?"

"Warrant? No, Davis. You and the Baltic Wonder Woman there aren't getting a warrant, but I suspect you can get it with that magic lasso of hers. Now, get to work."

The line went dead, and Anya smiled. "I told you there would be no warrant, but I do not have magic lasso."

* * *

Gwynn led the way down the gangway in a gown that would turn heads on any red carpet anywhere in the world. Anya, on the other hand, hobbled down the ramp with one foot encapsulated in the pneumatic cast. Aside from the monstrosity, she wore an equally stunning dress, cut just low enough to garner exactly the attention she desired.

Dave Young, their first officer turned temporary chauffeur, stood by the open door of the limousine as the ladies slid inside. In five minutes, Dave brought the conspicuous car to a stop at the steps of Eden's View and climbed from behind the wheel. The street lighting cast a yellow haze on the two most beautiful federal agents who'd ever graced the streets of The Big Easy.

As Anya passed Dave, he leaned toward her. "I'll be just around the corner, and the HRT is staged less than a minute away."

She gave him a nod and accepted the arm of a gentleman climbing the stone stairs to the restaurant's double French doors. Inside, Gwynn spoke softly to the maître d. "I believe Chef Christian has a private table for the two of us."

The tuxedoed host let his eyes wander momentarily before bowing slightly. "Yes, ma'am. Of course. Please follow me."

They allowed themselves to be led to a dimly lit table only a few feet from where Vasily Orlov had been sitting the night before. The maître d said, "Thomas will be your private waiter this evening. He will ensure you have everything you desire."

A thin-bearded sommelier approached with a wine list and took their drink order.

The instant he vanished, Chef Christian Gerard materialized beside their table. He removed his hat and bowed. "Good evening, ladies. I'm so glad you could come, despite your injury, Ms. Ana."

"Is fine. Thank you. It doesn't even hurt. I will probably run again to-morrow."

He laid a hand on the edge of the table. "I'm not sure I'd recommend that, but tonight, I promise you a meal you'll never forget."

Before he'd finished his speech, a commotion sounded near the front of the restaurant. Gerard turned to see Vasily Orlov wading through the tables and chairs with his four-hundred-pound girth carving a swath across the elegant dining room.

Gerard spoke barely above a whisper. "Please forgive me, but I must go. Your first course will be out soon."

Gwynn said, "But we've not ordered . . ."

He gave her a wink. "I've ordered for you. Enjoy." He turned on a heel and held an oversized chair for Orlov, who plopped into the seat as if he'd crossed a desert to be there. The chef shook Orlov's hand, and the Russian looked around him and toward the kitchen. "You have for me the wine, yes?"

"Of course, my friend, but you don't want it now, do you?"

Orlov scowled. "Only a taste for now." He snapped his fingers as if encouraging a child to hurry up, and Gerard vanished into the kitchen.

Four other men and two much younger women arrived and joined Orlov simultaneously with the delivery of his cordial of wine. Ignoring his guests, he snatched the small glass from the waiter's hand and examined it from every angle.

Gwynn leaned close to Anya. "What's he doing?"

"I do not know. Is strange."

The glass looked like a child's miniature toy in the hand of the enormous Russian. He pressed the glass beneath his nose and inhaled as if receiving the breath of life. With his eyes closed, he touched the rim to his lip and felt the viscous flow. As the wine coated his tongue and filled his mouth with its essence, Orlov rolled his head skyward before bowing as if in fervent prayer, and allowed the wine to fall into his throat. The others at his table sat in reverent admiration of their host as he continued the ritual.

The sacrament continued in prolonged displays until the glass sat empty on the edge of the table, its former contents now warming to the temperature of the big man who'd savored its every intricate detail. When he opened his eyes, his guests sat as if terrified to speak until Orlov raised a hand and bellowed, "Why do my guests have no wine?"

As if summoned from the air itself, a pair of waiters appeared pouring bulbous glasses of wine, but not the same as Orlov had just enjoyed. Glasses were raised, and cheers resounded from the round table.

Anya and Gwynn sat in silence, completely mesmerized by the scene, as a waiter placed hors d'oeuvre boards resembling small charcuteries with glasses of an elegant, light white wine.

They ate slowly, savoring every bite, but never ignoring Orlov's table. If they weren't watching every move, they were listening and memorizing every word. Orlov and his guests spoke English most of the time, but occasionally, one of them would drift off into Ukrainian-laced Russian. Gwynn couldn't decipher it all, but Anya never missed a syllable.

Soup came next. It was a light fish broth that paired perfectly with the wine from the first course. Unlike the precision of service at their table, Orlov's dinner was served family style with large bowls and platters with three full charcuterie boards and half a dozen bottles of wine. Although occurring only feet apart, the experiences of the two tables couldn't be more opposed.

When the soup was cleared, an appetizer of pickled shrimp made its way to the table. Gwynn bit into the crustacean and couldn't believe the array of flavors. "This is amazing. I've never had pickled shrimp, but I think I have a new favorite."

Anya said, "I do not care for it. You may have mine."

Before Gwynn could claim the shrimp, a waiter stepped beside Anya. "I'm so sorry you didn't enjoy the shrimp. I will order another appetizer for you in a moment. Would you care for bread to clean the palate?"

She waved a hand and exaggerated her accent in a voice a few decibels louder than necessary. "No, thank you. Is fine. I will not have appetizer."

It worked. Orlov paused, turning an ear slightly toward Anya.

Gwynn whispered, "You're so good at this."

Anya only smiled.

Nearly an hour into the finest meal either woman had experienced, the salad course arrived on small plates elegantly arranged with greens, candied nuts, shaved carrots, curls of perfectly ripened tomatoes, and drizzled with truffle oil.

"This is magnificent salad. Only in Moscow could I find better," Anya said just loud enough for Orlov to hear.

And he heard. His finger went into the air, and a tuxedoed waiter stepped to his arm. "Yes, sir. What may I get for you?" The massive Russian curled a finger, and the waiter leaned in. "Who is the blonde woman at the table behind me?"

With a noble attempt at discretion, the waiter glanced at Anya, and she gave him the smile and a tiny nod. The waiter swallowed hard and whispered, "I'm sorry, sir. I don't know her name, but someone in the kitchen said she is staying aboard the yacht docked where the *Belle* usually sits."

Orlov's hand went into his jacket and returned with several folded bills. He tucked the cash into the waiter's vest. "Next time you come to my table, you will bring me her name."

The waiter nodded. "Yes, sir. Right away."

"It is time to have some fun," Anya whispered.

A look of panic overtook Gwynn's face. "What are you going to do?"

"Relax. I am only going to give him my name. This is all."

"Anya, don't screw this up. We're just supposed to watch, listen, and find a way into the kitchen."

"Do not worry. I will be good . . . mostly."

The conversation halted when Orlov's waiter knelt beside Anya. "Please pardon the intrusion, ma'am. I know this is extremely unorthodox, but Mr. Orlov would like to have an introduction if you wouldn't mind."

Anya eyed Orlov and then the waiter. "How much?"

The waiter frowned. "How much what, ma'am?"

"How much money did he give you for this?"

The waiter stammered. "Uh, I'm sorry . . . what?"

She held out her palm. "Give to me money he gave you."

Terrified, the waiter withdrew three one-hundred-dollar bills from his vest and laid them in Anya's hand. She thumbed through the money and pulled her clutch from beside her hip. She pulled five crisp bills from inside, folded them in half, and slipped them into the waiter's hand. "My name is Go Away . . . but not back to his table."

The waiter wore Gwynn's same panicked expression, and he froze in place.

Anya placed her lips beside his ear. "Just go to kitchen for three minutes, and then do as you wish." She pressed a delicate kiss just below his earlobe.

The waiter gasped, and still uncertain what was happening, he stood, nodded sharply, and paced to the kitchen.

Anya rose from her seat and dragged her cast foot toward Vasily Orlov's table, stopping just beside his chair.

The Russian glutton raised his chin and slowly surveyed Anya's body. When he reached her feet, the sight of the cast left him curious.

Anya lightly touched a finger just below Orlov's chin and raised his eyes to hers. She studied his expression and finally laid her hand in his. "I am Ana, and it is great pleasure to meet you, Vasily."

He recoiled. "How could you know my name?"

"Who else could you be? I do not come to city without knowing who owns it."

He couldn't look away, and in his native Russian, he said, "You have me at a decided disadvantage at the moment. You seem to know everything about me, and I know only your name . . . or the name you told me is yours."

"Perhaps in time—if I am inside city long enough—you will know more, but for now, my name is enough."

He motioned toward her cast. "You did this here in New Orleans?"

"Yes, I was running—for pleasure and exercise, not in fear—and I fell on the sidewalk just outside this spectacular restaurant."

Vasily pulled a cell phone from his pocket and scrolled through a list of names. "I will send my private physician to you first thing tomorrow morning. You are aboard the *Morning Star*, yes?"

She laid a pair of fingers against his phone and pushed it away. "I have my own physician, thank you."

He let the phone fall to his lap. "In that case, I will buy your dinner, and of course your friend's as well."

Switching to English, Anya laughed. "I think you do not know who my father is, Vasily. Your money is nothing but doormat for my father. Instead, I will pay for you and your guests."

While Orlov sat in stunned disbelief, Anya slid the three bills he'd given the waiter beneath the edge of his plate. "You did not have to pay for an introduction, Vasily. You only had to ask. Please, enjoy your dinner."

She hobbled back to her table to find Gwynn covering her mouth to hide her laughter. "That was fantastic. I can't believe you did that."

"I told you, was time for fun. It was fun for me. And you?"

"Oh, yeah. I loved every minute of it."

Their dinner continued for three more courses and ended with the most delectable chocolate cake either had ever had.

Chef Christian Gerard returned to the table. "I trust you enjoyed your evening with us."

Anya said, "It may be the finest meal we've ever experienced."

"I'm so glad you came. Please consider the table your private seating anytime you'd like."

After sliding back inside the limo, Anya pulled a small cordial glass from her clutch and presented it to her partner. "Perhaps your laboratory can have some fun of their own with this."

15

Vnutrenneye Chuvstvo
(Gut Feeling)

Gwynn sat with her legs curled beneath her on the sofa in the main salon of *Morning Star* with her oversized Columbia Law sweatshirt pulled across her knees. "Why on Earth would you steal a tiny wineglass?"

Anya sat across from her partner with a mug of steaming tea in her hands, but instead of an alma mater sweatshirt of her own, she wore the same University of Georgia baseball T-shirt she seemed to consider a security blanket. "I do not know why I seized glass. This is better word, *seized*, instead of *stole*. Something about how Orlov kept wine all for himself and did not offer to friends, and how he made ceremony of drinking it. I want to know what it is. Your lab can do this, yes?"

Gwynn's smile broadened. "I don't know what the Russian word is for *gut instinct*, but you've got it in spades. Yeah, the lab can figure out what was in the glass, but what if it's just really expensive wine?"

Anya sipped her tea. "Then I want to have a glass. Don't you?"

"I guess so, but you think it's something more than just wine, don't you?"

"It might be nothing special, but like you said, gut instinct says it is more."

Gwynn lifted her mug from the side table and blew across the steaming surface. "What kind of tea is this?"

"Is lemongrass and orange, I think."

"If it tastes as good as it smells, I can't wait."

After a tentative sip, Gwynn wrapped her hands around the mug. "Excellent choice."

Anya checked the clock hanging above Gwynn's head. "Is almost midnight, and Ray said for us to call with report, no matter how late."

Gwynn cocked her head. "Ray? So, now it's a first-name-basis thing, huh?"

"This is his name, yes?"

"Maybe for you it is, but for me, it's Agent White. He's our boss, remember?"

Anya shook her head. "He is not boss for me. For me, he is captor."

Gwynn sighed. "Do you really believe that?"

"I do. It is true. He captured me and is holding me to do his will. This is meaning of word *captor*, no?"

Gwynn frowned. "That's not exactly what's going on, but we'll talk about it after we make our report."

She lifted her phone from the table, pressed Agent Ray White's speed-dial number, and put the phone on speaker.

It rang four times, and the voice of disturbed sleep boomed through the speaker. "What!"

"Agent White, it's Davis and Anya. You told us to—"

"Yeah, yeah. I know. Give me a minute."

Shuffling sounds echoed through the phone until White said, "Okay, let's hear it."

Gwynn began. "We made contact with Orlov, and Anya left quite a lasting impression."

White grumbled. "That sounds like the makings of an international incident."

"No, it was good. Believe it or not, she was well behaved. She hasn't even killed anyone yet."

"That's progress, I guess. Go on."

Gwynn briefed every detail of the evening and finished with, "And Anya lifted the wineglass. I have it sealed in an airtight plastic bag for the lab."

White said, "Okay, I've got it, but just hang on to the wineglass. Put it in the refrigerator or something. Lab time is hard enough to get without flooding them with tasks like 'name that vintage.' If it becomes important before this thing is over, we'll have it analyzed. Is there anything else?"

Gwynn looked up at Anya, who shook her head. "That's all for tonight."

"All right. Do you have a plan for the next contact?"

"After Anya's performance tonight, I'm confident the next contact will be initiated by Vasily Orlov. You know how it is when she gets under a man's skin . . . He'll do almost anything to see her again."

He huffed. "Somehow, I don't think Vasily Orlov is her type."

Anya spoke for the first time. "This is true. I prefer man who is lawyer with badge and gun."

"Cut it out. I'm going back to bed."

The line went dead, and Gwynn looked up. "You're not really hitting on our boss, are you? It's just a game, right?"

Anya smiled. "I told you, he is not boss of me."

"Okay, whatever, but I have to know the story on that T-shirt. Spill it."

Anya tugged at the soft cotton shirt. "This one, I did steal. It was inside boat, and it was Chase's shirt. He liked for me to wear it. He never said this with his words, but only with his look."

"Well, in his defense, every man on Earth would give you that look if you were wearing their shirt. You're not exactly an ugly duckling."

Anya scowled. "Ugly duckling? What does this mean?"

"You know what it means, but I'm not letting you change the subject. Chase was the one, wasn't he?"

Anya stared into her mug. "There was time I thought he was my person. For him, I turned away from my country and my home, but this doesn't matter now. Is water under bridge, as you say."

"Does he know?" Gwynn whispered.

"I do not think so. He is happy with wife and job and friends. He does not think of me anymore."

Gwynn tried to smile. "We've got a name for that in English. It's called *the one that got away*."

"Maybe this is true. I do not know. But I have things he should know."

"What kinds of things? Do you mean like intel? State secrets? Things like that?"

Anya stood and placed her empty mug on the service tray. "Good night, Gwynnechka. I will see you in morning."

Gwynn beamed. "That's the first time you've ever called me that."

"Perhaps is first time out loud, but this is how I think of you inside my mind. Is name meaning *special friendship*."

Gwynn stood. "Yeah, I know what it means, Anyechka."

Halfway down the stairs to their cabins, Gwynn's phone chirped, and she glanced at the screen. "It's Agent White."

"Answer, or he will be angry with you."

Gwynn stuck the phone to her ear. "Davis."

"Put the Russian on the phone."

She held out the phone. "He wants to talk to you."

Anya lifted the phone from Gwynn's hand. "Hello."

"What do you think is in that wineglass?"

"I do not know, but I have gut feeling it is something important."

"Okay, I'll have an agent come to the boat tomorrow morning and pick it up. There's an FBI lab in New Orleans. I'll get it on their schedule, but if it turns out to be nothing, you and your gut feelings are reimbursing the lab for the expense. Got it?"

She ignored the question and handed the phone back to Gwynn. "Tell to him my gut has large pocketbook."

Gwynn spoke into the phone. "She said she understands."

* * *

Gwynn stopped and spun on the step beneath Anya. "Tell me what was in that glass. We're partners, Anya. We don't keep things from each other."

Anya froze. "Yes, we do. There are many things about me you do not know, and you have some things you believe I do not know about you."

"Wait a minute. What do you mean by that?"

"Is simple. I know many things you have not told me about you, and this is fair because you read file and background about me many weeks before Ray, *your* boss, caught me."

Gwynn swallowed hard. "Let's take this conversation somewhere other than the stairs."

"Is very late, and we need to sleep."

"Yeah, right, like I'm going to sleep after what you just said. Follow me."

She led the Russian into her cabin and planted herself on the edge of her bed. "Okay, so let's hear some of these things you know about me that I've never told you, *and* I want to know how you found them."

Anya perched on a small dressing chair beside the vanity. "I think you have wrong thought about these things. None of them change how I am your friend."

"Friends don't really check up on each other's background, now do they?"

"You did this to me, though."

Gwynn squeezed her eyes closed. "Because it was my job."

"It is also my job to know you. We are partners. You said this just now on stairs."

"You're missing the point, but go ahead. Let's hear what you think you know about me."

Anya set her eyes on the floor.

"Come on. Don't get shy now. Let's have it."

Anya took a long breath. "For example, I know about right after you graduated from law school."

Gwynn held up a hand. "Oh, just wait a minute. I was studying eighteen hours a day and sleeping two hours. Besides, everybody was doing it. I was just the lucky one who got caught, and that's why my father took the blame. He said they were his drugs because they were in his car. I was driving it because, well, I guess you already know I fell asleep at the wheel and ran into a city bus. What do you expect? There was so much pressure to pass the bar the first time, and if I'd gotten busted for the uppers, I wouldn't have been admitted to the bar, even if I passed. Oh, and my shot at working for the Justice Department would've flown right out the window. How! How could you possibly know about any of that?"

Anya stood, crossed the room, and sat next to her partner. "Gwynn, I'm sorry we did this. No, not we . . . me. I am sorry I did this to you. It was supposed to be lesson from my training."

"What are you talking about?"

"I do not know anything of your past. I only know what you have told me. I have no way to investigate anything about you before we met. This was only exercise in making subject believe I knew, to get you to tell me what you *thought* I already knew. I know I said this wrong, but I think you understand, no?"

Gwynn shoved Anya away. "Damn you. I can't believe you'd do that to me."

Anya held a pillow between them. "This is classic interrogation technique. I cannot believe you did not learn this in Academy."

"What's with the pillow?"

"I don't want you to shove me again. This is all."

Gwynn yanked the makeshift shield away from the Russian and leaned toward her.

Anya sat motionless, unsure of what was coming next. To her relief, Gwynn extended her arms and pulled her in for a long, silent hug. As she released Anya and leaned back, Gwynn stopped inches from her partner's face and whispered, "You know, if Second Captain Hottie Pants weren't around, I just might be tempted to . . ."

Anya sat without breathing as Gwynn's breath brushed across her skin.

She traced her hand up Anya's spine and across the scar from the bullet wound until her fingertips came to rest against the smooth flesh of her neck. She cupped her hand just beneath Anya's ear and hissed, "I hope you feel that."

Uncertain how far her partner was going to take the moment's intimacy, Anya tried to relax until Gwynn whispered, "I hope you feel it. It should be quite familiar to you. It's your knife, and if you ever do anything like that to me again, I will gut *you* like pig."

Anya looked away from Gwynn's passionate gaze to see the tip of her favorite fighting knife barely touching the thin cloth of her T-shirt just above her belly button.

A soft smile of pride for her student came, and she said, "Second Captain Hottie Pants does not know what he is missing."

16

Ne Dumay
(Don't Think)

As promised, a young FBI agent who looked like someone central casting had sent over to play a fed showed up on the gangway just after eight a.m.

Nick Brower, third-in-command aboard *Morning Star*, met the agent with, "Good morning. I'm going to need some ID before I can let you aboard."

Anya and Gwynn watched the exchange from high above on the yacht's sundeck as the fed produced his credentials. As Nick stepped aside to allow the agent access to the gangway, the obvious rookie agent appeared to take exception to being questioned. Although neither woman could clearly hear the confrontation, the agent's body language made it clear he was above being detained. His right index finger came to rest only inches from Nick's nose, and his back stiffened. As his volume rose, Nick stood in a relaxed posture, carefully watching the area for interested onlookers.

From above, the scene looked like a low-budget acting lesson of how to play the role of a jackass. Nick took a short step sideways to clear the agent's finger from his face, but the fed stepped even closer.

Finally, his volume reached the point at which it could no longer be ignored. Gwynn set her juice glass on a table and turned for the stairs.

Anya took her arm. "Wait. Watch Nick's feet."

Gwynn leaned back toward the rail and focused on the man's stance. As the agent continued to yell, Nick slowly slid his right foot backward a few inches and focused his attention fully on the furious agent.

Anya said, "FBI officer has made terrible mistake. He is clearly right-handed and is giving his strong hand to Nick."

"What do you mean he's giving his strong hand?"

Anya pointed toward the agent. "Look at bulge under left arm. This is his pistol in shoulder holster. If Nick controls his right hand, the agent cannot draw his weapon, and he has lost."

Gwynn gasped. "You don't think Nick is going to attack him, do you?"

Anya shook her head. "No, Nick is being attacked, but he will soon stop this. Watch for next his shoulders to rise."

Gwynn watched, and right on cue, Nick lowered his chin and raised his shoulders to protect his head. Reading his lips, Gwynn thought Nick said, "Calm down and stop making a scene."

The command served only to energize the young agent, whose face grew redder with every breath. In one swift and decisive motion, Nick raised to the balls of his feet, grabbed the FBI agent's right hand, and gave it an inward twist. It took less than a second for Nick to have the agent immobilized and facedown on the sidewalk.

Anya chuckled. "Perhaps now you should go."

Gwynn bounded down the stairway four steps at a time until she reached the gangway. Ten more strides put her practically on top of the scene. She took a knee beside the supine agent and whispered, "I'm going to have Nick let you up, and when that happens, you're going to straighten your jacket, apologize for causing a scene, and walk aboard the yacht. If you do anything other than those three things, you'll be lucky to find a job as a mall cop in Nebraska. Got it?"

The grounded agent roared. "I'm going to bury this bastard."

Gwynn pressed a knee into the side of his face. "What you're going to bury is your career if you don't shut up and get aboard now."

She looked up at Nick and gave him a wink. "Let him up. I have him."

"Are you sure?" Nick asked.

"Oh, yeah, I'm really sure."

The man who would be in command of the yacht should Captain Chuck and Second Captain Hottie Pants fall overboard, tentatively stood and released the pressure from the FBI agent's wrist. Like a man just released from the stockade, the agent leapt to his feet, spun to face Nick, and shot his pain-filled right hand inside his jacket for his pistol. When he felt the empty shoulder holster, he twisted his upper body to see Gwynn with his Glock dangling from her fingertips.

"Looking for this?"

He lunged for the weapon, but Gwynn's agility and speed made the side-step a simple maneuver. Using the momentum the agent had built during the lunge, she gave him a little shove toward the gangway. He staggered up the ramp without looking back.

Once inside the yacht, Gwynn stuck the butt of the pistol firmly into the center of the agent's chest, shoving him backward against the wall. "I don't know who or what you think you are, but you've stuck your nose into something that's none of your business. And that's not all. Your little show out there came dangerously close to exposing a multi-million-dollar, undercover DOJ operation. You're extremely lucky Nick was there to greet you. If you'd pulled that crap with anyone else on this boat, you would've been in the river. Now, put this pistol away and stand right here. Don't move. Don't breathe. Don't think. Just stand."

He took the Glock from her hand and seated it back into his holster without a word.

She stepped away and returned less than a minute later with a plastic bag in her hand. "Take this directly to the lab. Do not pass go, do not collect two hundred dollars."

He took the bag containing the wine glass and gave it the once-over. "There's no evidence tag or case number. How's the lab supposed to know who—"

"Remember that part about 'don't think'? Yeah, do that. If anyone at the lab needs a case number, you can tell them the attorney general ordered the analysis."

Anger wrestled with submission behind the agent's eyes, but he made the only good decision of the morning when he turned without a word and disappeared down the gangway.

Back on the sundeck, Gwynn grinned when she found Anya laughing hysterically by the rail. "That was fun."

Anya regained her composure. "That was fun to watch. I am proud of you for lifting his gun so easily. I like seeing you do things I taught you."

"Me? What about Nick? He deserves some of the credit."

Anya smiled. "Yes, he was also very good. We must know his story soon. Maybe you can get your lover boy to tell you about him."

"Second Captain Hottie Pants isn't my lover boy, yet, but I'm sure I can get him to talk."

Anya said, "You can get him to do many more things than only talking. I am sure of this. I can teach you some more tricks if you would like."

"Thanks, but I think I have plenty of tricks on my own for this one."

Breakfast arrived, and although it wasn't as elegant as Eden's View's fare, it more than justified the daily exercise routine that had become part of life for Gwynn and Anya.

In the gym beneath the navigation bridge, between circuit reps, Dave Young stepped through the door, and Gwynn caught his reflection in the mirrored wall. She stepped from her machine and brushed her hair out of her face. "Oh, hey, Dave. What's up?"

Despite his desire to avoid staring, he couldn't look away from the most beautiful example of a federal agent he'd ever seen. "I'm sorry to interrupt, but there's something you two should probably see."

Anya pulled out her earbuds and stepped from the treadmill. "What is happening?"

Dave turned for the door. "Come with me, but stay away from the windows."

Gwynn tossed her towel into the bin and stepped in front of Anya as they headed through the door, then positioned herself directly behind the first officer.

He led them up the stairs toward the bridge and held up a hand when they reached the top. "Wait here while I pull the shades."

They stood still while Dave continued onto the bridge and pulled down the shades, limiting visibility from the outside. With the shades in place, he motioned for them to continue.

Anya and Gwynn stepped onto the bridge and followed Dave's outstretched finger toward the French Quarter. They scanned the streets and rooftops, but neither noticed anything out of place.

"What is it?" Gwynn asked.

Dave said, "Step a little to the left, and look at the black Lincoln on the corner."

Both Anya and Gwynn found the car he described and watched it for several seconds.

Anya wiped a drop of sweat from her face. "How long has it been there?"

Dave nodded. "That's the right question. I noticed it at nine thirty-eight and added it to the ship's log."

Gwynn checked her watch. "That's been almost fifteen minutes. Nice catch, Dave."

"It's what I do. Remember, I'm an old intel officer. It's in my blood."

Anya studied the car and then turned to the first officer. "We can get aboard small boat from port side, yes?"

Dave touched his index finger to the tip of his nose. "It looks like it's in your blood, too. The tender is already in the water and situated amidships on the port side. There's a pilot hatch four feet above the waterline."

"You will take us there, yes?"

"I thought you'd never ask," Dave said. "Follow me . . . again."

Just as before, Gwynn stepped between him and Anya. She whispered, "Hands off. He's mine."

Anya looked around her and shrugged. "Maybe."

A step through an inconspicuous hatch placed the three of them on a steel grate with a steep ladder descending from the right. Dave slid down the ladder in an impressive exhibit of seamanship. Anya and Gwynn made the descent a bit less gracefully but arrived at the bottom unscathed. Dave spun the wheel on a hatch and swung the hinged door inward. The rush of cool morning air was a welcome break from the heat of the mechanical areas of the yacht.

Tied alongside was the same tender they'd used to reach the paddle-wheeler a few days before. Gwynn stepped through the hatch and landed silently on the deck of the boat. Anya followed and stumbled when she landed aboard the tender. Catching herself, she stepped from the foredeck to the helm, where a man in khaki coveralls waited by the wheel.

The man gave a quick nod and motioned toward a tarp near the stern. "I'm Gavin. Get under there. That'll provide enough concealment to get us away from the yacht without you two being seen."

They knelt and covered themselves with the tarp, carefully tucking the edges so it wouldn't blow away when Gavin motored away from the yacht, but it didn't pick up enough speed to disturb the hiding duo.

Gwyn said, "We're flanking him, right?"

"Yes, he is clearly watching yacht and probably not looking behind, so we will have perfect opportunity to surprise him."

"I like it, but what's the plan after we surprise him . . . or them?"

"That is fun part. We will play by ear, but we will not hurt him . . . or them."

Gavin stuck a toe beneath the tarp. "Okay, we're out of sight."

They crawled out, folded the tarp, and scanned their position.

Gwynn leaned near Gavin so he could hear her over the roar of the engine.

"Where are you going to put us ashore?" she asked.

"I'll drop you at the Canal Street Ferry Terminal, unless there's another spot you'd prefer."

"No, the Ferry Terminal should be great. Are we on our own when we hit the street?"

"I don't know. I'm just the engineer. But I'll call the yacht when we slow down at the terminal."

Just as promised, when Gavin pulled the power back to idle into the terminal, he cocked his head toward the microphone clipped to his epaulet. "Morning Star, Launch One."

"Go ahead, Launch One," came Dave's confident voice over the radio.

"Our guests want to know if they should expect any other good guys onshore."

"Affirmative. Tell them to expect their favorite homeless guy near the objective."

"Roger." Gavin turned away from the mic and relayed the message, which got a chuckle out of Gwynn.

He brought the boat to rest as gently as a kiss against the ferry dock. "Okay, here we are. Do either of you have a radio or cell phone?"

Gwynn said, "No, we were working out when Dave came to get us. We don't have anything."

Gavin pulled the radio from his belt and unwound the cord leading to the mic. Once he had the kit bundled in his hands, he held it out toward Anya.

She took it from him and clipped it to her waistband, then removed the mic and tossed it back to Gavin. "This will only be in my way. It will work without mic, yes?"

"Yeah, just talk into it like a handheld. I can wait here for you if you'd like."

Anya pointed toward the radio built into the helm station. "That radio is on same frequency as this one?"

Gavin nodded. "No, but it can be. I'll make the switch." He spun a dial and looked up. "Now it is. I'll be right here unless you radio and tell me to be someplace else. Do me a favor, though. If you head back to the yacht, at least let me know so I don't sit here all day waiting for you."

Anya gave him a nod and stepped from the tender and onto the dock. They jogged up Canal and made a right onto Chartres. A quarter-mile jog put them on Toulouse Street with the black Lincoln still parked less than four hundred feet away. In less than two minutes, the question of who was watching them would be answered, but too many questions would remain to declare the operation a success.

From their new vantage point at the corner of Chartres and Toulouse, the massive yacht dominated the landscape. Anya looked away from the target vehicle parked only a few hundred feet away. "Is beautiful boat. We should keep it when all of this is finished."

Gwynn laughed. "Yeah, wouldn't that be nice? I don't think we get that option, but I do wonder how the federal government came to own it."

"Is most likely seizure from drug arrest."

"I don't know," Gwynn said. "I think I would've heard of a drug bust that produced such booty. We'll ask Agent White when we talk to him next."

Anya motioned toward the parked car. "Look. Brake lights are on."

"Is he leaving?"

"Let's get to car before he gets away."

They ran down Toulouse as if they were out for a morning jog. Halfway to their target, Anya said, "You go to right side and take front seat, and I will go left and give him big surprise."

They split based on her plan and closed the distance to the car in thirty seconds. Moving to stay out of the mirrors as much as possible, they arrived at the car simultaneously and yanked open the doors. Gwynn landed on the front seat beside the driver, sending a stack of strip club fliers sailing in every direction at the same instant Anya laced her arm around the driver's neck from behind with just enough pressure to convince him she could take his life with one final squeeze.

Reacting initially, he clawed at her arm with his meaty paws until he accepted the fact that he wasn't going to force his way out of the viselike hold. Ignoring Gwynn, he leaned as far as Anya would allow and thumbed open the glove compartment. Inside were a stack of fast-food napkins, a pair of handcuffs, and a Thirty-Eight Special. The snub-nosed revolver was his only possibility of freedom, so he wrapped his sausage-like fingers around the wood grip half a second before Gwynn kneed the glove compartment closed on his wrist, leaving him stuck between a trapped right hand and a Russian choke hold.

Unwilling and unable to take the struggle any further, the man relaxed. "Who are you, and what do you want?"

Anya hissed, "These are questions for *you* to answer. Why have you been sitting here for half hour?"

His thick Russian accent said he was fresh off the boat and already in over his head. "I was only resting because I am tired."

Anya tightened her grip as Gwynn pressed her knee into the glove compartment door a little harder.

The man winced. "Okay, I am Vladimir, and I am watching boat."

Gwynn pressed her thumb against the car's cigarette lighter, pressing it past the click and holding it in place. "Why are you watching our boat?"

"This is what boss told me to do."

Gwynn gave Anya a glance and leaned toward the driver. "We're going to play a little game now, Vladimir. I'm going to ask you some questions, and you're going to answer them. The fun part is that I already know all the answers. So, if you get any of them wrong, my friend behind you is going to shorten your time on the planet. Blink if you understand."

He sat motionless as his face changed colors.

Gwynn gave his cheek a little slap. "It's okay, Vlad. You don't have to blink, but if you don't understand what I'm saying, then you're no use to us, and I'll have to tell my friend to kill you now."

He strained to speak. "Okay, I understand. What is question?"

"Questions . . . plural. That means more than one. Got it?"

He nodded with the limited range of movement Anya's choke hold allowed.

She began. "You look uncomfortable, Vlad. Your face is turning blue, and your wrist is starting to bleed. Would you like for me to release your hand from the glove compartment?"

"Is this first question?" he asked. "If so, you already know answer."

"Ah, we've got ourselves a wise guy. This is going to be more fun than I thought." She withdrew her knee, freeing the man's hand, and he took full advantage of what he thought was a mistake on Gwynn's part. Although his grip on the revolver had softened during his confinement, he hadn't let go completely. Gwynn watched the butt of the revolver clear the lip of the hinged door, and she sent a crushing hammer fist to the back of the man's hand, breaking several small bones and causing him to release the weapon. Before he could withdraw the battered appendage, she scooped up the handcuffs and laced one around his bulky wrist.

Anya watched with delight and set her knees against the back of the seat, giving herself the leverage she needed to pin the driver to his headrest. The motion sent his left hand rising from his lap, and Gwynn threaded the cuffs through the steering wheel, then cuffed the man's left hand before he could lash out again.

She pulled the cigarette lighter from its hole and turned to Anya. "You can relax now. I think we've got his attention."

Gwynn laid the edge of the lighter just beneath Vladimir's eye. "So, let's start our little game. Remember, I already know the answers, and my friend behind you hasn't killed anyone yet today, so she's a little anxious. Are you ready?"

He turned his head, stretching and flexing his neck. "You are making terrible mistake."

Gwynn turned to Anya. "I guess I'll have to take that answer as being nonresponsive. Show him what he's won, Vanna."

Anya ripped the headrest from the back of the seat and drove a fist into the back of Vladimir's neck, where his spine entered his skull. The momentary shock of the strike left his vision blurry and pain radiating down his back. Smoke rose from the burn beneath his eye as he cried out in pain.

"Let's try this again. I think we can all assume you're ready now. So, tell us, Vlad. Who's your boss?"

The look on the big Russian's round face said he was trying to decide whether to spill his guts or swallow the cyanide capsule he wished he had. Both actions would likely end in the same result. Surprising everyone in the car, perhaps even himself, the man yanked the car into drive and crushed the accelerator. His wrists cuffed through the steering wheel made steering a challenge, but from the looks of things, he wasn't concerned about the well-being of the car.

As they accelerated forward, the front bumper collided with three steel bollards protruding from the asphalt and then kept moving forward. Steam exploded from beneath the hood, and Gwynn braced herself with both feet digging into the floorboard and each hand gripping whatever she could find. The car continued south, picking up speed as it went, until it collided with several tables and chairs outside a gumbo restaurant, sending late-morning diners scattering in all directions.

The driver yanked and twisted with every ounce of strength he could muster to either break the steering wheel or separate the chain holding the handcuffs together. The harder he pulled, the more erratic their course became. They bounced across a curb and collided with several more bollards designed to keep cars in their lane, but the pipes were failing miserably.

The man's continued battle with the steering wheel and cuffs became more violent and desperate as the steaming, crippled car careened toward the *Morning Star*. With the Mississippi River looming ever closer by the second, Gwynn lunged for the shifter in a daring attempt to stop—or at least slow—their forward motion. Her effort was rewarded when they left the ground momentarily and bucked across a much higher curb. Although she couldn't get the car in neutral or park, she yanked the shifter downward, forcing the transmission into low. Their momentum slowed, but the river and the starboard side of the *Morning Star* were still coming quickly, and the driver was oblivious to everything beyond the steering wheel that had become his life-or-death hitching post.

The lower gear slowed the car, but Vladimir kept the pedal pinned to the floor. Gwynn fell away, landing on the floorboard with her head dangerously close to the man's right foot. As hard as she struggled and squirmed, trying to climb back onto the seat was little more than wasted effort. Vladimir saw his opportunity and raised his right leg around the wheel, then sent it crashing back to the floor, missing Gwynn's head but connecting with her collarbone and shoulder.

She felt as though she'd been hit by a train, but she remained conscious.

Vladimir moved his left foot onto the accelerator and continued the punishing kicks with his right. Anya thrust herself forward and over the front seat as the massive white hull of the *Morning Star* filled the windshield. Hitting the yacht would be certain death for everyone in the car, so she grabbed the steering wheel with both hands and yanked it downward with all of her weight and momentum. As the engine roared, Vladimir bellowed in agony as his cuffed hands were wrenched through the full turn of the wheel.

Anya felt the wheel crumble in her hands an instant before they launched from the brick-paved street, over the seawall, and into the filthy river water. The car hit the river, nose-first, and the cold water poured in through the driver's open door. The collision had driven Anya's head into the dash and her body on top of her partner on the floorboard.

The cold, dark water made it impossible for either to know where they were or even which direction was up. The car filled in only seconds and plummeted through the darkened abyss toward the muddy bottom of the river, where the *Belle of Orleans* had rested only days before. The breath Anya had taken when she leapt over the seat had been solidly knocked from her lungs the instant the car hit the water, leaving only seconds for her to find the surface, but finding Gwynn and dragging her from the car-turned-sinking-coffin was her new primary mission.

Exploring the interior of the car with her hands, feet, and elbow, Anya formed a rudimentary mental picture of her situation. Gwynn's leg felt like a limp rag in her hands, but even if she'd drawn her last breath, Anya had no other option than to get her friend and partner back into the sunlight.

The car nestled softly into the muck of the bottom of the river the whole world had dubbed the "Big Muddy," sending silt and filth into the car and serving only to decrease the near-zero visibility they were already ex-periencing. With the mental roadmap of escape glaring in her mind, Anya slid an arm beneath Gwynn's body and kicked for the open driver's door. Vladimir's body wasn't there to block the way, which was a stroke of spec-tacular luck, but it likely also meant he'd escaped on or near the surface. Through the unobstructed space, Anya kicked for purchase against the now slick, slimy interior until the solid metal of the door landed beneath her foot. Hoping they'd landed at least somewhat upright, she pushed away from the car and toward what she prayed was the surface.

The Russian's lungs burned with the fires of desperation as she as-cended, but with no light penetrating the grimy water, nothing but hope guided her toward the surface. She was certain she had no more than ten seconds before her lungs would demand air and find, instead, only the darkness of death in the torturous water.

Finally, as desperation turned to near panic, Anya kicked and pawed at the water, expending the final ounce of will and strength she possessed. Ac-cepting her fate, she buried both hands beneath Gwynn's arms and shoved her body in the direction she hoped would lead to the surface, where some tiny glimmer of waning hope waited.

With the burden of Gwynn's weight no longer holding her down, Anya felt herself being buoyed upward as if by an unseen hand. Her chest ached as if it were imploding beneath a crushing force, but the torture of her body clawing for precious air softened as the darkened world into which she'd been plunged began to brighten. She didn't know if it was a cruel illusion or the blessing of the sun high in the November sky, but the hope it delivered replaced the terror she felt with euphoria. Involuntarily, she allowed her hand to rise above her head as her body succumbed to the watery grave, but before the water could fill her lungs, a hand found her and dragged her through liquid space and endless time.

When the light finally penetrated Anya's veil behind which she'd fallen, blurred figures loomed over her like ghostly apparitions hovering in the mist. The figures began to shake and tremble like flames atop candles until her vision cleared and her mind regained its ability to decipher the environment around her. The figures weren't vibrating. It was her own body shivering involuntarily beneath the solar blanket she wore like a cocoon, and the figures were those of her rescuers, First Officer David Young and the engineer who'd driven the boat—but his name wouldn't come. Instead, the one-word question that consumed her newfound consciousness poured from her trembling lips. "Gwynn?"

18

NE MOY RUKOVODITEL'
(NOT THE BOSS OF ME)

A woman with short, dark hair and soft features came into focus. The face was familiar, somehow, but no name formed in the Russian's mental Rolodex. The absence of a name wasn't startling, but the woman's face was situated near the top of Anya's mental friend-or-foe catalog. She fell solidly into the friend category, so Anya relaxed.

The woman leaned down and shined a penlight into each of her eyes. Her breath smelled of coffee and peppermint, and the recognition bell rang in Anya's mind. "You are nurse on yacht, yes?"

She laid a hand on Anya's shoulder. "Yes, I'm Cynthia, the yacht's medical officer. Do you know your name?"

Anya scowled. "Which one?"

"Yours."

Anya squinted in a wasted effort to focus. "Gwynn?"

Cynthia frowned. "You think your name is Gwynn?"

Anya shook her head slowly. "No, I have two names. First is Anastasia Burinkova, and better name is Ana Fulton. Where is my friend, Gwynn?"

The nurse practitioner held up a hand and spread her fingers. "How many fingers do you see, Ms. Fulton?"

"Four."

Out came the penlight again, and Cynthia examined each of Anya's eyes more closely than before. "And you're sure you saw only four fingers?"

"Yes, only four fingers and one thumb. Where is Gwynn?"

The tone of the question made it clear Anya was finished answering questions until she learned her friend and partner's condition, so Cynthia stepped aside and motioned across the medical suite. "Gwynn is going to be fine, thanks to you."

Anya lifted her head and pushed herself to a sitting position with her head throbbing in time with every beat of her heart. Special Agent Guinevere Davis lay on her side, covered with a white blanket with *Morning Star* printed across its surface.

"Friend Gwynn, you are okay, yes?"

Gwynn showed no reaction to Anya's voice.

Anya slid off her bed and took a step toward her partner, but Cynthia took her arm. "You need to—"

Anya brushed her hand away. "No, you need to step out of way. I am going to my friend."

Instead of protesting, Cynthia spun and crossed the room in locked step with Anya, constantly ready to arrest a fall should her bullheaded patient stumble.

Having crossed the room without incident, Anya eased herself onto the edge of Gwynn's bed and took her hand. Looking up at Cynthia, she said, "She is hurt badly, yes?"

"Yes. It's likely she has a concussion. We don't have an MRI on board, so I'm sending her to the medical center for some imaging and observation."

"She will be okay, yes? And you are certain of this."

Cynthia pulled up a high stool and took a seat. "It's likely she'll be fine, but we won't know the extent of the injuries until we see the imaging."

"She is inside coma?"

"Yes, she's in a coma, but that's actually a good thing. Based on the initial hematomas and swelling, it's likely she'd be in enormous pain if she were awake. She must've taken quite a beating when you hit the water."

Anya squeezed her partner's hand. "No, this is not correct. She was kicked in head several times by man who is now very lucky if he is dead at bottom of river. If he is not dead, I will find him and make him beg for coming of death."

Cynthia held up both hands. "That's outside of my realm. What you guys do out there is pretty much the opposite of what I do in here." She leaned toward Gwynn and gently pulled open each eyelid. "But if you need any help making whoever did this to her pay for his sins, I have a bagful of handy little medical implements I'd love to put to use."

Anya smiled. "I will not need help. I am very good at what I do. But maybe you can perform autopsy if there's enough left of him when I finish."

Cynthia straightened her scrubs and chewed on the corner of her lip.

Anya noticed. "You have something to say, yes?"

"No, not really. It's none of my business. I just had an idea."

Anya's interest was piqued. "What is idea?"

"I don't know. I'm not an operative. I'm a medical officer. But I read a lot of Cap Daniels books, and I was just thinking if we sent a pair of body bags away in the back of an ambulance, that just might convince whoever's watching you that both of you died in the car crash. I know it sounds far-fetched, but it's the kind of thing they'd do in the books. Having your enemy believe you're dead could come in handy."

Anya eyed the ceiling for a moment. "Is ambulance coming now?"

Cynthia checked her watch. "Yes, I called them just a few minutes ago. They should be here any minute."

"They will be coming with lights and sirens, no?"

"Probably not. It's important that we get a look inside your partner's skull, but she's stable, and her vitals are strong. They'll likely come without running their siren."

"You can call hospital and say to them, 'Do not do siren,' yes?"

"Yeah, I guess so, but . . ."

"Make call, now!"

Cynthia dialed and gave the instructions. "Okay, they won't run code."

"This means no siren?"

Cynthia grinned. "Yes, this means no siren, but I can't believe you're going to do this."

"It is a good idea. I wish I had thought of it. I now must decide if I am going to hospital with Gwynn."

"Like I said, I'm just a medical officer, not a tactician, but I know what they'd do in the books."

Anya glanced between Gwynn and the nurse. "I think I do not care what would be done in make-believe books. I am going with my friend, and yacht must leave."

"Do you really have the authority to make a decision that big?"

Ignoring the question, Anya said, "How did we get out of water?"

Cynthia motioned toward the corridor. "Ask that guy."

Dave Young stepped through the hatch wearing a pair of khaki shorts and a *Morning Star* T-shirt. "It's good to see you up and moving under your own power."

Anya gave him a smile. "You pulled us from water?"

Dave pointed toward Gwynn. "No, I only pulled her from the water. She didn't put up a fight. You, on the other hand, were a bit of a challenge."

"What does this mean, bit of a challenge?"

"Nick and Gavin wrestled you out of the drink, and you tried to drown both of them. I've never seen anybody fight that hard on dry land, let alone in the Mississippi River. What were you thinking?"

Anya frowned. "I do not have memory of this. I thought I was dying, so I shoved Gwynn toward top of river, and then I saw light. This is all I remember. I do not think I was fighting."

Dave held up a finger. "Hang on just a second." He pulled his radio from his hip pocket and held it to his lips. "Nick, David . . . over."

"Go ahead, David," came a crackling voice through the radio.

Dave keyed the mic. "Go find Gavin, and meet me in the medical bay."

"Roger."

Two minutes later, Gavin, the engineer, stepped into the bay carrying his left arm in a sling and bearing scratches on both sides of his face as if he'd been wrestling a cougar. When Nick walked in, both of his arms were still functional, but he wore a patch over his left eye, and the early stages of a nasty shiner shone beneath the bandage.

Dave motioned toward the pair. "Still think you didn't put up a fight?"

Anya gasped. "If I did this to you, I am so sorry. I did not do this on purpose. I didn't know I was doing it. I believed I was dying."

In a groggy, almost pitiful tone, Gwynn groaned, "Hey, you used a contraction."

Cynthia stepped beside the bed and shouldered Anya out of her way. Leaning down to peer into Gwynn's eyes, she said, "Welcome back. We missed you. How do you feel?"

Gwynn's eyes surveyed the room. "I feel confused."

"That's to be expected, but how do you feel physically?"

"Nasty headache. Could you turn off the lights?"

"Sure we can," Cynthia said. "Do you know where you are?"

Gwynn continued the pained, puzzled look. "No, not really. I remember being in the floorboard of a car with a crazy Russian kicking me in the head, but that's it."

Gavin glared at Anya. "Were you the crazy Russian kicking her in the head?"

"No, I was not! His name is Vladimir, and I think he is dead."

Dave spoke up. "I'm sorry to disappoint you, but we think he got out of the car the second before it left the dock. The ship's security cameras caught him diving from the car with his hands cuffed together and then disappearing in the Quarter."

Anya's broad smile returned, and Dave took a step back. "What's that look all about?"

Anya said, "I am happy to hear he is alive. This means I can now kill him slowly with Dr. Cynthia's tools. I will make sure he will wish he had died inside car."

"That's not really how these things work," Dave said. "Special Agent White is going to call off the operation. Too much has gone wrong. He'll make the call to pull everybody out and take another look in a year or so."

Anya shrugged. "This does not change what I will do to Vladimir. Just look what he did to my friend. I do not care what Agent White does. He is not boss for me."

Dave closed one eye and considered what she'd said. "I don't think that's how White sees things."

"I will talk with him now," Anya said. "Does he know what happened to us?"

"Yes, the captain briefed him as soon as we got the two of you out of the river. He knows you're alive, but that's about it. I'm sure he's writing an exfiltration plan as we speak."

She held out a hand. "Give to me phone. I must call him now."

Dave produced a cell phone, stepped around the Russian, and stood by Gwynn's bed. The concern and pain on his face was not the expression he would've worn for just any passenger on his yacht; his was one of a man who feared losing someone important to him, and that look set Anya's resolve even deeper in stone.

Seconds later, Ray answered his phone. "White."

"Agent White, is Anya. We are alive, but Gwynn is badly hurt. Medical officer and I have plan. Ambulance is coming to get Gwynn to have tests at hospital. I will go with her, but we will both go in body bags so people who are watching will believe we are dead. When we leave, yacht must also leave. They would not stay if we were really dead, so we have to give this impression. You understand, yes?"

White said, "Slow down, and put the doctor on the phone."

She handed the cell to Cynthia, who listened carefully for several seconds. "Ms. Burinkova is going to be fine. She's ambulatory with only minor injuries, but I'm afraid Special Agent Davis is another story. She has moderate to severe head trauma, apparently caused by the shoe of some Russian named Vladimir, who by all indications escaped before the car hit the water."

"What a minute. What?"

"It's a long story and far too early to make a prognosis, but early indications are good. She came to for a few seconds and spoke to Ms. Burinkova, but she quickly fell unconscious again. Her pupils were reactive to light, but she wasn't awake long enough for me to know much more than that."

"Okay, put Anya back on the phone."

"Yes?"

"Listen to me, Anya, and don't argue. This is how it's going to be."

Anya braced herself for the coming order to stand down, but to her surprise, White said, "When you find that SOB, make sure he feels every second of the pain you're going to inflict on him. And may the devil receive what's left of his soul when you're finished with him."

She squeezed the phone. "I think maybe this time you *are* boss for me, and I will do exactly as you say."

19

Krov' Tigra
(Tiger Blood)

A pair of ambulances pulled to the base of the gangway, and two teams of medics rolled gurneys up the ramp and aboard the *Morning Star*. When they rolled the gurneys back down the gangway, they each contained a black body bag. With the doors closed and the lights off, the ambulances pulled away without ceremony. Minutes later, the motor yacht, *Morning Star,* cast off all lines and motored south toward the Gulf of Mexico with two empty cabins.

Inside the hospital, an image technician unzipped the first body bag, revealing Special Agent Gwynn Davis with an oxygen cannula laced beneath her nose. Two orderlies carefully lifted her from the black plastic bag and placed her on the patient table of the MRI machine under the watchful eye of Dr. Patricia Sharp, the neurologist assigned to her case.

Across the room, the second body bag appeared to unzip itself, when in fact Anya had laced a finger into the track and peeled away the zipper. In any other environment, the sight would've been horrifying, but not in the clinical environment of the U.S. Naval Hospital at Naval Air Station New Orleans.

Anya sat up, pulled the oxygen mask from her face, and crawled from the gurney. "She is okay, yes?"

Dr. Sharp said, "Your partner's condition hasn't changed since you left the yacht. We'll know more as soon as we see the imaging, but you can't stay in the room."

"She is my partner and my friend. I will stay with her until she is—"

"You don't understand. It's not safe for you to remain in the room while we're doing the MRI. You'll have to either stand behind the shield with the tech and me or wait outside."

Anya said, "I am sorry. I did not understand. I will stay with you, and you will tell to me everything you see."

The doctor shrugged. "Suits me. Let's go."

Behind a lead-lined barrier, the technician launched the computer program, and the MRI machine came to life. The electronic motorized bed moved, carrying Gwynn into the body of the device. A few seconds later, images appeared on a display, and Dr. Sharp pulled her glasses from her pocket and leaned toward the monitor.

She made a few comments, apparently to no one, before giving instructions to the tech that involved a configuration change in the computer. The tech followed the instructions, and another set of images appeared on the screen that looked nothing like the brain Anya imagined.

"This is good or not so good pictures?"

Dr. Sharp held up a finger and leaned in closer to the screen. "It appears to be very good news. We'll have the radiologist take a look, but I don't see anything that gives me reason for concern. It looks like your friend is going to have a nasty headache for a few days, but other than that, everything looks relatively normal."

"We can now wake her up, yes?"

Dr. Sharp chuckled. "You could try, but I ordered a nice little cocktail for her from the NP on your ship, so she'll likely need a few hours to sleep it off. I'll do a full exam when she rejoins us and probably keep her overnight for concussion observation. I do have a couple more questions, though."

"Yes, what are questions?"

"Why is her hair wet? Did someone bathe her after the head trauma?"

Anya chose the best lie she could create. "It was boat accident."

"Oh, that makes sense, but why the body bags?"

Relieved that she could tell the truth, Anya said, "Is classified."

The same pair of orderlies who'd placed Gwynn on the table of the MRI machine so gently returned and eased her onto a hospital bed. "Follow us, ma'am. We'll take you to her room."

Anya trailed behind the orderlies as they rolled the bed down a long corridor and onto an elevator. Once inside a private room, the orderlies locked the wheels of the bed and turned for the door. "A nurse will be in shortly to check on her. You're welcome to stay in here with her as long as you'd like. There's coffee and tea just down the hall, and the call button is on the remote by the bed. Do you have any questions?"

Anya perched on the edge of the mattress. "No, thank you. I will be right here with her."

As promised, the nurse arrived, repositioned the bed, and started an IV.

Anya asked, "What is this medicine?"

"Oh, it's not medicine. It's just a slow drip of fluids to keep her hydrated. Can I get anything for you?"

"No, but thank you for caring for my friend."

The nurse smiled. "That's our job, ma'am. But it's nice of you to say that."

Someone from outside rapped sharply on the door. Immediately following the knock, a uniformed Marine wearing a pistol belt stepped into the room. "Hello, ma'am. I'm Corporal Adams, and I'll be on your door." He held up a folded sheet of paper. "No one gets in except the people on this approved list."

"Thank you, sir. It is kind of you to offer to protect us, but we will be okay. Could I see that list, though?"

The Marine stood wide-eyed. "You don't have to call me sir, ma'am. It's Corporal Adams. And I'm not *offering* to protect you, ma'am. I was *ordered* to protect you by my platoon leader. I don't have a choice, ma'am."

Anya gave him a smile. "It is still very nice of you. What is first name?"

"Mine, ma'am?"

"Yes, yours."

"Uh, it's Blake, but you can call me Tiger. Everybody does."

"Tiger? How does someone get nickname of Tiger?"

Corporal Adams checked across each shoulder and closed the door behind him. To her amazement, the young Marine unclipped his pistol belt, laid it on the floor beside his feet, then began unbuttoning his shirt.

Anya slid a hand beneath her shirt and gripped her knife. "What are you doing, Corporal?"

He pulled off his camouflage shirt and pulled up his green T-shirt, exposing dozens of scars like tiger stripes encompassing his torso.

Anya released her knife. "What happened to you?"

"I was captured in Afghanistan, ma'am. I didn't know anything classified, but my captors didn't believe me. They kept whipping me every three or four hours to get me to tell them things I didn't know. All I could do was take the beatings until I was rescued. I tried to escape a bunch of times, but that just earned me more stripes, ma'am."

"I am sorry this happened to you, but thank you for making such sacrifices for our country."

Corporal Adams redonned his uniform and gun belt and furrowed his brow. "Our country, ma'am? Forgive me, but you don't sound like you're American."

She pulled from her pocket the tiny plastic American flag that she carried everywhere. "I was born in Russia, but I am American because I chose to become so."

The Marine gave her a sharp nod. "Good choice, ma'am. Anyway, I'll be on your door for the next twelve hours, then somebody'll come relieve me. If you need anything, you let me know, Miss American By Choice."

He closed the door and left Anya alone with Gwynn in the hospital room. Anya watched her friend and partner sleeping like a baby and took a seat on the edge of her bed. Even though Gwynn would never hear her, she spoke softly as if to no one. "Is nice room. Room in military hospital in Russia is not so nice. I have been to rooms in places like that. Never is there only one person inside room. Is always many people in room in Russia. You are very lucky to be born here inside America."

Gwynn continued breathing deeply in perfect, silent sleep as Anya continued. "Did you see Marine? His name is Corporal Adams. He is good soldier, I think. He took off shirt and showed to me his scars from torture. He did not do this to be arrogant, I do not think. I think he has scars to remind him of duty. Many people will not do this. Many people will do everything to be unhurt, but Corporal Adams is Marine and strong."

Gwynn's breathing changed, and she rolled onto her side.

Anya watched as she nestled back into the pillow, then she whispered, "Are you okay?"

Gwynn nodded but didn't open her eyes. "Who are you talking to?"

"No one," Anya said. "I am sorry. I will be quiet."

Gwynn slid her hand into the Russian's. "No, I like it. You're not bothering me. I like knowing you're here. Am I going to die?"

Anya squeezed her hand. "Yes, someday you will die, but not soon, and not from this injury. You have only concussion and bruises, but they are bad. You need only rest and time."

"That's good," Gwynn mumbled through her narcotic haze.

Anya leaned close. "I will make him pay for this."

Gwynn tried to smile. "I know you will, but don't screw up the mission for revenge."

"You are always police officer, even when inside hospital with concussion."

"What were you saying about the Marine and scars? What Marine?"

"There is Marine named Corporal Adams standing outside door and making certain you are safe. He has scars like stripes of tiger from torture in Afghanistan."

"A tiger?"

Anya leapt to her feet. "Yes, just like tiger. This is what Peter was writing inside blood in car!"

Gwynn forced open her eyes. "What are you talking about?"

Anya yanked open the drawer of the bedside table and pulled out a pen and paper. She wrote feverishly and held up the pad."

Gwynn struggled to focus on the letters. "I don't know what that says."

"Of course you don't," Anya said. "Is written in Cyrillic and not in English. Remember inside car, Peter wrote ONA in blood with finger. You remember this, yes?"

Gwynn blinked rapidly. "Yeah, I think so, but what does that have to do with anything?"

"Peter is like me. He is Russian when born, but now American. Sometimes when I am hurt or afraid, I think only in Russian and not English. I think brain does this naturally."

"What are you talking about? None of this makes sense, Anya."

"It *does* make sense. Is not English. Is Russian. We thought he wrote ONA, but inside his mind, he was trying to warn us of danger."

"Don't you think finding him shot and left for dead did a pretty good job of warning us of danger?"

"Yes, of course, but this is not enough. Danger is specific kind. I think he was trying to write *опасный противник.*"

"I still don't get it."

Anya continued. "This means extremely dangerous enemy like wild tiger. This is very specific in Russian, and if this what he was trying to write, I know what laboratory will find inside wine glass and also what is inside burlap wrappings at restaurant."

20

SAPOGI NA ZEMLE
(BOOTS ON THE GROUND)

Gwynn blinked the sleep from her eyes and reached for the bed controller. Squinting to focus on the controls, she raised the head of her bed and smacked her lips. "I could really use some water."

Anya poured a Styrofoam cup of water from the bedside pitcher and handed it to her partner.

She took the cup and slowly sipped through the straw. Her thirst quenched, Gwynn cleared her throat. "I'm not sure I'm following, but it's rare to see you this excited about anything."

Anya gathered her composure and returned to her previous spot on the edge of Gwynn's bed. "Do you know of tiger bone wine?"

Gwynn made a face. "No, and it sounds nasty."

"Is ancient Chinese medicine and very rare. If they are making this wine at restaurant, this means body of tiger is what we saw at Eden's View. This is illegal, yes?"

Gwynn scoffed. "Yeah, you could say that. It's definitely illegal to import poached tiger carcasses into the States, but there are about a thousand other federal laws that cover the production of alcohol, even if it doesn't have dead tigers in it."

"Good. This will make Agent White happy if it is true. You will tell him of this, yes?"

"Yeah, I can brief him, but he's going to have a lot of questions I can't answer. I think you should be here when I call him."

"This will not be necessary."

"I think it *will* be necessary. Besides, where do you need to go right now that's more important than calling Agent White?"

"Calling him is what is unnecessary. He will be here soon."

"What do you mean? Why would he come here?"

Anya sighed. "His favorite special agent is in hospital with concussion, and his name is on access list Corporal Adams has."

"That's what I need," Gwynn said, "Agent White yelling at me while I have the worst headache of my life."

"He will not yell. He will be happy we have made break in case. He will be only worried for you."

Gwynn rolled her eyes. "He's not really the worrying kind when it comes to somebody being hurt. He worries that criminals might get away, but he doesn't worry about stuff like this."

Anya laid a hand on Gwynn's leg. "Do not worry. You will be fine. Ray will not yell at you. And I will now go and make *sapogi na zemle*."

Gwynn closed her eyes and let the Russian phrase run through her head. "Does that mean something about shoes and dirt?"

"Very good. You would say 'boots on ground' in English. I will come back when I am finished in a few hours. You have young, handsome Marine just outside door. You will be fine."

"No, wait! I don't want you to go without me."

Anya pulled away. "This is silly. You cannot go with me. You must rest."

"That's not what I mean," Gwynn said. "I meant that I want you to wait until I *can* go with you."

"This is not possible. I must go now before Vasily Orlov knows what is happening. For now, he believes we are dead, and this is good."

Gwynn sighed in resolution. "Okay, just don't get hurt. There's enough of that going around."

Anya pushed through the door, and Corporal Adams leapt to his feet. "Is everything all right, ma'am?"

"Yes, is fine, but I will be gone for some hours. You will protect Gwynn, yes?"

"Of course I will. That's my job. But I don't think your name is on my access roster." He pulled the paper from his pocket. "There aren't any names that sound like they could be you."

Anya ran a finger down the page and stopped on a name near the bottom. "This is me. I am Special Agent Ana Fulton."

The Marine eyed her. "Your name is Ana Fulton?"

"Yes."

Without another word, she made her way from the hospital and into the backseat of a taxi headed for the French Quarter. When she stepped from the cab, the world around her felt somehow clearer, as if she'd stepped into a scene where everything she knew fit perfectly in place.

The two previous missions she'd completed for the Justice Department had been cut from the same cloth. She and Gwynn found their way inside the organizations they'd been tasked with investigating and built a case against both Russian mafia bosses, resulting in the termination of each enterprise. The Miami investigation wilted to the ground in a bloody heap aboard *Leo*, the Lion's yacht. The diamond manufacturing scheme in New York City had ended in textbook fashion with the arrest of the key players. In both cases, Anya found herself well outside her comfort zone, pretending to fit into a level of society she could never make her home. With Vladimir's decision to turn a simple episode of questioning into a violent and potentially deadly encounter, all the rules by which Anya had been forced to play sank with the car that nearly became a tomb for her and Gwynn. Everything had changed, and the gloves were off. Supervisory Special Agent Ray White's avenging angel had been unleashed on a city where lesser angels feared to tread.

Vladimir, the man who nearly killed both Anya and Gwynn, would be easy to find. His boss, Vasily Orlov, would be even easier. And the chef, Christian Gerard, remained a wild card. Was he innocently caught up in a game of corruption he could never win, or was he a key player in the game?

In an alley off Bourbon Street, Anya spotted an ally and placed a boot between his filthy canvas shoes. "You are terrible actor, Special Agent McIntyre."

Johnny Mac looked up through tortured eyes. "I thought you might show up. Is Gwynn okay?"

Anya checked the alley for prying ears and eyes. "She is hurt, but yes, she will be okay soon."

"That's what I figured. I like what you did with the body bags. Nice misdirection."

"Thank you, but was not my idea."

He gave a half smile. "That Gwynn is a pretty smart cookie."

"Yes, she is, and you are brave cookie to live on street like this. Most police officers would not do what you are doing."

He laughed. "Yeah, well, I'm not most police officers. I'm on my way up, and assignments like this one are the key."

"We are now same," Anya said.

"What does that mean?"

"I am now dead woman who can only come out in darkness after today. I must move unseen, but I do not have disguise like you."

"I don't think we'll ever be the same. You're a Russian defector who doesn't have to play by the rules, and I'm an American who has no other choice."

"There is always choice," she said. "Now is very good example of this."

"What are you talking about?"

"I am going to have conversation with Vladimir . . . No, this is not true. I am going to *talk* to Vladimir. He will not talk back, so this is not conversation. To do this, I want your help."

"My help? What do you want me to do? I'm just supposed to watch your back and keep you alive down here in this mudhole. I'm not operational until you're in trouble."

"This is what I mean when I say now is time for choice. Mission is to discover what Vasily Orlov is doing and stop him. First part is done. I know what he is doing, but there are many other things that must be done before we can stop him. First among these things is, I must make Vladimir pay for hurting Gwynn."

Johnny Mac raised a hand. "Hey, wait a minute. That's not the business we're in. We're not the executioner. We build cases and make arrests. The judiciary hands out the punishment."

"This is not how it will work this time. You can choose to help me, or I can avenge Gwynn without you. It would be better with your help, but I understand if you are person who only does what he is told. These people are necessary also in government, but nowhere else."

Johnny Mac chewed on the flesh of his jaw and tried to ignore the stench of his clothes. Finally, he scampered to his feet. "What do you want me to do?"

The smile that said her ploy had worked came to her face. "You learned inside Academy to put someone onto ground and hold him there, yes?"

"Yeah, sure, I did. We all learned how to do that."

"This is what I want for you to do. I will have Vladimir brought from inside club and into alley, where you will put him on ground with face on street. You can do this, yes?"

"I can do it, but what am I supposed to do then?"

"Nothing. I will do everything else. For you is only to make him stay on ground while I talk to him."

He checked the area. "Does Agent White know about this?"

Anya leaned close. "He is one who ordered this."

The lie was little more than a delicate rewording of White's instructions to make Vladimir pay for hurting Gwynn.

Johnny Mac nodded. "Okay, then. When?"

Anya motioned toward the river. "There is gentlemen's club three blocks down on other side of Bourbon Street. You know this place?"

"I know the place."

"Vladimir will be inside. I will have him brought into alley at nine o'clock. You have watch?"

"No, I don't have a watch. I'm supposed to be a bum, and bums don't generally wear a timepiece."

"Is okay. There is clock on street. It is high on pole, and you can see it from inside alley. Use clock, and be ready at nine, okay?"

"You got it. Nine o'clock. I'll be there."

Anya said, "Please be careful. Vladimir is very strong, and I do not want him to hurt you also."

"Don't worry, Red Sonja. I can handle him any day of the week and twice on Sunday."

"What does this mean, twice on Sunday?"

"Never mind. Just have the guy in the alley at nine. I'll take care of the rest."

* * *

An hour after sunset, Anya watched as the young women who danced at Vladimir's favorite club walked into the back entrance with their bags of stage clothes and makeup slung over their shoulders. At least half of the women bore the striking features of the women of Vladimir's home in Eastern Europe. Straggling behind the rest of the women was a stunning brunette who looked far too young to be inside a club, either on the stage or at the bar. She wore a white sweatshirt with the Polish flag emblazoned across the back.

Anya stepped from her perch and between the Polish dancer and the rest of her coworkers. In flawless Polish, Anya said, "Hello. I am Anastasia, and it is nice to meet you."

The dark-haired beauty looked up. "We haven't met, and I'm late for work, so excuse me."

She tried to push by, but Anya placed a stack of folded one-hundred-dollar bills into her palm. Continuing in Polish, she said, "There is a man named Vladimir. He will be inside the club. I need to talk to him. If you will bring him into this alley at exactly nine o'clock, I will double the money you are holding."

"There's a lot of guys named Vladimir around here. How will I know which one you want?"

Anya squeezed the dancer's wrists. "He will have bruises here from handcuffs."

The woman looked down and spread the money in her palm until she counted ten bills. "There's a thousand dollars here."

"That is correct," Anya said. "And there will be a thousand more when you bring Vladimir through that door at exactly nine o'clock."

She tucked the money into the pocket of her jeans. "You're not going to kill him, are you?"

"Not tonight," Anya said.

"Okay, I'll do it, but if the cops come sneaking around, I'm not going to lie about it. I may be a stripper, but I'm not willing to lie for you, whoever you are."

Switching to English, Anya asked, "Can you keep secret?"

Hesitance shone on the dancer's face. "This depends on secret."

Anya pulled her credentials pack from her pocket and flashed her Department of Justice badge. "The police will not ask questions."

Again, the dancer thumbed through the bills in her palm. "And you will give to me another thousand if I bring Vladimir to you?"

Anya nodded. "I will."

"Let me see the money."

Anya produced another folded stack of bills, and the dancer couldn't look away. "Okay, I will do this for you, but you must promise to stop Vladimir from killing me . . . or worse."

Anya knew all too well the bevy of tortures that qualified as worse than death.

* * *

Waiting for nine o'clock to roll around, Anya bought a black sweatshirt and a pair of gloves from a Bourbon Street shop. The sweatshirt warmed the chill in the air, and the gloves would serve to protect her hands from what was to come.

A few minutes before nine, she watched Johnny Mac stagger into the alley behind the strip club. He sat beside the hinge side of the door so he would be momentarily hidden from view when Vladimir stepped out. After situating himself, he scanned the area, apparently searching for Anya, but he found only darkness. A quick check of the clock on Bourbon Street told him showtime had arrived.

As if on cue, the back door of the club swung open and struck Johnny Mac's raised foot. Vladimir stepped through the door and onto the filthy bricks of the alley. Johnny Mac leapt from his crouch and delivered a crushing sidekick to the man's knee, sending him to the ground. Johnny's next move put him behind the kneeling Russian, and a powerful thrust forced him facedown onto the grime and filth.

Vladimir lashed out, slinging his arms in every direction until Johnny Mac closed a handcuff on his left wrist. The Russian swore and struggled even harder than before, but he was no match for Johnny Mac's speed and strength. Soon the growling Russian bear found himself pinned down with his hands tightly cuffed in the small of his back. Resistance, he determined, would only result in further confinement, so he lay still, awaiting the coming fate.

Anya stepped from the shadows as if stepping between dimensions of time. She knelt beside the prone Russian and whispered into his ear. "Are you afraid of angels, Vladimir?"

"What?" he growled with his face still pressed to the bricks.

"Angels," Anya repeated. "Are you afraid of us?"

Abandoning his previous submission, Vladimir dug a toe into a crevice and thrust in a wasted attempt to face his attacker. Anya drew her knife and pressed the point into the back of the man's neck. "You will lie still, or you will die. This is power I have over you."

"Who are you?"

"I am Avenging Angel, and you are man who will soon pay price for sins."

He bucked again, and Anya sank her blade into his flesh. "It is not yet time for you to die, but blood from your neck will remind you I am always watching."

"You have no idea who you're playing with. You will be dead before the sun comes up!"

Anya laughed at the empty threat. "You have made terrible decision. Do you read Bible?"

"What are you talking about, you crazy—"

Anya laced her gloved hands around his face, pressing her right index finger against his eye. "I am talking about an eye for an eye, Vladimir."

The popping sound emitted by the destroyed eyeball was buried beneath the agonizing scream the man let out.

Anya nudged Johnny Mac away and placed her knee between the man's shoulder blades. "Shh . . . Shh . . . The pain will go away soon. You will not die, but you will remember that I am invisible to him who will not see. You have done terrible things, and for these things, you must pay. I will come to collect your payments in pounds of flesh. Today it is your eye. Next time, it will be the other extreme."

She grabbed a handful of his hair, raised his head as far as his neck would stretch, and drove his face into the brick-paved alley. Vladimir's body relaxed as unconsciousness overtook him.

When Anya stood, she saw the stripper standing in the doorway with her mouth agape. "Look, lady. I don't know who you are, but I know you're not a cop. You can keep the extra thousand. I don't want it."

Anya stepped toward the terrified woman. "It is okay. I promised to you money, and you will have it." She slipped ten bills into the dancer's hand.

Frozen in fear and disbelief, the dancer eyed Anya. "I didn't see anything, and you'll never see me again." She squeezed the money in her palm and vanished back inside the club.

Anya roughly removed the cuffs from Vladimir's wrists and tossed them back to Johnny Mac. "You did well. I am impressed."

Beneath his baggy, filthy clothes, he shrugged. "I don't think we'll have any more trouble out of him."

Anya glared down at the unconscious form. "This is only first night of many terrible nights to come for him. He kicked Gwynn in head seven times, so I will make him pay six more nights, and he will beg for death to take him before I am finished."

21

STAN' NOCH'YU
(BECOME THE NIGHT)

Special Agent Johnathon "Johnny Mac" McIntyre knelt beside Vladimir's tortured body and felt for a pulse.

Anya said, "He is still alive, yes?"

"Yeah, he's still alive, but I don't envy the headache he'll have when he wakes up. That's not all. Take a look at the bruises on his wrists. That was quick."

"Bruises on wrist are from earlier today when Gwynn cuffed him to steering wheel of car. He broke steering wheel to escape, but I do not know how he got out of handcuffs."

"There's a thousand ways. Most likely, he unlocked them with his key. I've never met a mob muscle guy who didn't have one."

Anya shrugged. "Probably, but he will not be thinking of hands when he wakes up."

"No, not after that thing you did with his eye. That was disgusting."

"He should not have hurt my friend."

Johnny Mac checked over his shoulder. "I hope you consider me a friend, too."

"I do not think we are friends yet, but I trust you, and this is very rare thing from me."

"I'm okay with that. I'll definitely take trust for now, but does that mean you wouldn't do the same thing to somebody who kicked me in the head?"

"I think you would not put yourself in position for someone to kick you in head, so I will never have to make this choice."

"I think I'll take that as a compliment. Now, what do we do next?"

Anya pushed up her sleeve to check the time. "I think I do not need your help with rest of night. I have things to do, but I must do them alone."

"It's my job to watch your back during this op. I can't just let you wander off into the night. I've got to stay with you."

Anya smiled. "If you can keep up, you are welcome to come along, but I do not believe this is possible. When I work in darkness, I become the night."

"Whatever. I don't think I'll have any trouble keeping up."

Two blocks farther north, Johnny Mac realized he'd greatly overestimated his ability to track a former Russian SVR assassin. She had, indeed, become the night.

Nine blocks south of the intersection where Anya lost her DOJ tail, she scaled the concrete block wall of a storage building behind Eden's View restaurant and settled in for the long night. Well concealed, she allowed her body and mind to rest in short repetitions as the hours passed.

As the clock struck midnight, a pair of employees from the restaurant emerged carrying overstuffed black garbage bags. They tossed their bags into a dumpster and slid behind the enclosure. Seconds later, a plume of white smoke arose, and the aroma of marijuana filled the air. The two passed the joint back and forth as they came down from another long night shift in the kitchen. With the smell still wafting through the air, the pair returned to the kitchen, a little more carefree than when they'd exited.

From her vantage point on the roof, Anya watched as, one by one, the employees dragged themselves to their cars and drove away into the night. When only three cars remained in the lot; a 1965 convertible Mustang, an Audi, and a black BMW 700 series, Anya slipped from the rooftop, stretched her legs and torso, and found a second position of concealment only a few strides away from the parked cars.

The maître d was first to stroll across the parking lot. He leaned against the Audi and enjoyed a legal cigarette before slipping inside and making his way to wherever he goes after twelve hours in the restaurant.

Next came a man Anya didn't recognize. He moved with the stride and attention of a well-trained operative. In his left hand, he carried a thick briefcase that would make a formidable weapon if wielded correctly. She had no doubt the man knew exactly how to put the briefcase in play as a lethal weapon, and the bulge beneath his left arm told her she had no interest in confronting him, regardless of what the briefcase contained. She wasn't surprised to see the man climb into the BMW, but what did surprise her was what he didn't do.

Instead of driving away like the maître d had done, the mystery man closed his door and laid his seat back until he was lying on his back, alone in the car. Anya's watch revealed it was just past one o'clock, and her mind revealed that the task that lay ahead just became exponentially more complex . . . and more deadly.

Another half hour passed before the back door of the restaurant opened to reveal the silhouette of Chef Christian Gerard. He tossed his jacket over his shoulder, closed and locked the door, and crossed the parking lot toward the waiting Mustang.

The armed man in the BMW showed no signs of moving, but his presence alone dictated the tactics. Instead of confronting the chef with force as he stepped into his car, Anya's approach would be aggressive in an entirely different manner.

The fence around the restaurant's dumpster provided only momentary cover between the back door and the parking lot, reducing Anya's window to intercept the chef before he came into sight from the BMW. She moved through the darkness, trading silence for speed, and stepped beneath an overhead light half a dozen steps in front of her target.

Chef Christian Gerard froze in his tracks, and Anya held up empty hands. "I am not going to hurt you. Do you remember me?"

Gerard squinted at the figure. "You're the runner with the sprained ankle."

"Yes, this is true, but I am better now. I want to talk with you. Can we go back inside restaurant?"

He shot a look back toward the door and then at the parking lot. "It's late. Can't we do this some other time?"

Rolling the dice, Anya said, "There is man in parking lot waiting for you. I think we should talk now."

"What man? Who's waiting for me in the parking lot?"

"It is man with briefcase inside BMW. He came from inside restaurant"—she checked her watch—"thirty-three minutes ago."

Gerard furrowed his brow. "You've been watching my restaurant for half an hour?"

"No, much longer than this."

"Look, I don't really know who you are. I don't want any trouble. God knows I've got enough already."

Anya interrupted. "This is why I want to talk with you. Perhaps we can help."

"We? Who's we?"

"Maybe this is not correct. Maybe *I* can help."

"I really need some sleep. It's been a long day. I'd be happy to talk with you tomorrow, but—"

She took a step toward him. "I think the man in parking lot is waiting to hurt you. I think you know this. I will make with you deal, yes?"

"What kind of deal?"

"First, I must ask question. Does man in parking lot have reason to shoot you without first talking to you?"

"What? No! Nobody has any reason to shoot me. What are you talking about?"

She took another step. "In this case, here is deal. You will go to car. If man in BMW does not confront you, you can get inside car and drive away.

But if he threatens you, I will stop him, and you will talk with me. We have deal, yes?"

Gerard leaned to see into the parking lot. "Are you saying he wants to kill me for some reason?"

"This is possible, but I can stop him if he tries."

Gerard shook his head. "How? I mean, what makes you think you can stop him?"

"You will trust me for this. He will not hurt you if I am here."

It was Gerard's turn to throw up both hands. "This is all too much for me. I didn't sign up for any of this. I had no idea—"

Anya closed the distance and took his hands in hers. "I know this. This why I am here. I can help you. Is what I do. We should go back inside now and talk."

The chef bowed his head and squeezed his eyelids against his world. "Look, lady. I don't know who you are. All I know is that you sound just like them when you talk. I don't know whose side you're on."

Anya squeezed his hands. "I may sound like them, but I am not like them." She pulled the miniature American flag from her pocket and slid it between his fingers. "Open your eyes, Christian. I am not what you fear."

He looked down at the tiny plastic flag and sighed. "Not tonight. I can't do it. I just can't. But if you keep your word and don't let him hurt me, I'll talk to you, and I'll tell you everything."

Anya pulled the flag from his fingertips and slid it back into her pocket. "I promise to you I will not let him hurt you, and even more than this, I will not let him follow you."

"How are you . . . ? You're going to kill him, aren't you?"

"I will only kill him if is necessary and there is no other way."

The chef swallowed the lump in his throat. "Okay, what do you want me to do?"

"I want you to walk to car, just as normal. This is all. But wait half of minute before you do. I must have time to get into position."

Without waiting for a response, she slunk back into the shadows, leaving the chef alone in the dim light. Certain he'd waited the thirty seconds she'd asked, he took a long, deep breath and stepped around the fence. The BMW and its occupant waited in the poorly lit parking lot, but the Russian woman was nowhere in sight.

Gerard felt the tremble in his knees as he grew ever closer to his car. The BMW sat only inches away from his driver-side door, making it impossible to get into his Mustang and escape without the man knowing. He scanned the edges of the lot in hopes of finding the woman, but she simply wasn't there.

Did she just deliver me into the hands of my assassin? Was she there only to kill me if the man in the BMW failed?

Gerard pulled his keys from his pocket and squeezed a pair of the metal implements between his fingers. If the confrontation turned into a fight, the keys were better weapons than his hands alone.

Why did I not bring a knife from the kitchen?

He reached for his door handle, extending the key to unlock the classic car's door, but before the key slid into the slot, the driver's door of the BMW swung open, and the man stepped from the car. He shoved a hand into Gerard's chest, pinning him to the convertible top of the Mustang. "You shouldn't have to be reminded to keep your mouth shut. I came here tonight in good faith. You know that, right?"

He slapped the chef's face almost playfully. "Say it, kitchen boy. Say you know I came here in good faith."

Gerard tried to resist, but he was pinned in such a position that fighting back was impossible. He squirmed and twisted, but the man shoved a knee into his crotch, forcing the air from his lungs. "Say it!"

Gerard moaned, "Okay, you came in good faith."

"That's right. No one forced you to do anything. You've been a willing participant and our partner from day one. Don't you forget that, cook!"

"What do you want from me?"

The sound of a pistol sliding from a holster and the hammer being cocked echoed through the darkness. The man pressed the pistol beneath Gerard's chin. "It's just another example of senseless violence on the streets of New Orleans. That's what the paper will say when they find your body. You're in this way too deep to—"

In an instant, the assailant was gone. Just as promised, from beneath the BMW, Anya slit the man's Achilles tendon of his left leg and pulled him from his feet. He struck the rough asphalt like a felled tree. Before he came to rest, Anya vaulted from beneath the car and planted her knee on the side of the man's face. She wiped the blood from the blade of her knife across his forehead.

"Get off of me," the man roared, but his demands fell on merciless and compassionless ears.

Anya locked eyes with the chef and motioned for him to escape. Without hesitation, he unlocked the door, jumped inside, and left the battle behind him.

The man pawed for the pistol he dropped when he was dragged to the ground. Anya patiently watched his struggle, and she let his finger find their prize. The instant his hand enveloped the weapon, she drove the point of her knife through the back of his hand. He bellowed in pain and jerked his hand away from the pistol. The motion served only to drag the razor-sharp blade through his flesh, opening the wound to the cold night air.

She withdrew the blade from his hand and sliced the length of his torso, freeing a long strip of cloth. With blinding speed, she grabbed the pistol, forced the barrel into the man's mouth, and wrapped the cloth around the butt of the gun and the man's head, driving the barrel deeper into his throat. With a second slice, she produced another strip from his jacket and hurriedly wrapped the bleeding hand.

With the bleeding slowed, she leapt to her feet, rolled the man faceup, and planted herself on his chest with each knee pinning an arm to the pavement. Anya grabbed the butt of the pistol and stared into the man's terrified eyes. Gagging, twisting, and clawing for purchase with his feet, he fought with all his strength, but he was no match for the Russian. Her training, skill, and precision left him defenseless.

With her finger on the trigger, she pressed her thumb into the magazine release, dropping the supply of ammunition from the gun. She raised the loaded magazine above her head and brought it crashing down like a hammer against the man's face. Blood exploded from his nose as bullets sprang from the magazine and fell to the ground around his head.

With her left hand, she racked the slide, ejecting the bullet that had been chambered into the assailant's mouth. With blood pouring from his nose and the temporary bandage on his hand soaking through, Anya rose from his chest and planted a mighty heel kick directly to the man's elbow on the only usable arm he had left. The blow shattered the joint, leaving him whimpering in agony.

Sheathing her knife, Anya reached inside the car and lifted the briefcase from the seat. The assault had taken only seconds, and the Russian, once again, stepped from the world of dim light and into the darkness, where she was not only most dangerous, but also most at home.

22

GDE ONA?
(WHERE IS SHE?)

U.S. Marine Corporal Blake Adams rose from his seat beside Special Agent Gwynn Davis's hospital room door. "This area is controlled access only, sir. State your name and the nature of your business."

The approaching man produced a cred-pack and flashed his badge to the guard. "Supervisory Special Agent Ray White. I'm on your list, and the nature of my business is classified."

He planted a foot with the intention to push past the Marine, but the combat-hardened corporal stood his ground. "Stand down, sir. If you're on the list, I'll grant access. Otherwise, I will prevent you from entering."

Uninterested in going fisticuffs with a Marine half his age, White took a step back and waited for Adams to check the access roster.

After finding Ray White's name on the roster, Corporal Adams stepped aside and held open the door. "I'm sure you understand I'm only doing my job, sir."

"I do, and I appreciate it. Those are my agents in there, and I'm anxious to make sure they're all right."

Adams said, "There's only one, sir."

"Only one what?"

"Only one agent in the room. The one with the Russian accent isn't in there."

White peered through the door. "Where is she?"

"I don't know, sir. She left just after I came on duty. My orders are to guard the door and allow only authorized visitors."

White stepped into the room to find Gwynn squinting toward him. "Is that you, Agent White?"

"Yes, where's Anya?"

"I don't know," she answered softly. "She left several hours ago, and I was in no shape to stop her."

White ground his palms against his temples. "Was she going after the guy who did this to you?"

Gwynn raised the bed. "Probably, but I don't know for sure."

"What was the guy's name?"

"I only know his first name. It's Vladimir. That's all I've got."

White plucked his phone from his pocket and crossed the room to examine the bruises on Gwynn's head and face. "Are you all right?"

She tried to force a smile, but it wouldn't come. "I'm pretty sure I'm better than Vladimir if Anya found him tonight."

"It looks like you're lucky to be alive."

"I wouldn't be alive it wasn't for Anya. She saved my life . . . again."

"That's becoming a regular thing. "I'm starting to think that sticking you with her was the worst thing I could've done to you."

"No! I wouldn't have it any other way. Johnny Mac is a great partner, but he and I went through the same training. Like you always say, we're just lawyers with guns and badges, but working with Anya gives me the chance to build skills I'd otherwise never learn. Don't split us up just because I got hurt."

White held up a finger. "Don't start handing out assignment orders, Davis. This is still my operation."

"Yes, sir. I'm sorry. I didn't mean to . . ."

"It's all right. We'll chalk it up to the head injuries this time. Does Anya have her phone?"

"Probably not. I doubt iPhones survive trips to the bottom of the Mississippi River."

White mumbled something inaudible, but he tried the number anyway. It appeared to be ringing, but no one answered. He thumbed another number and waited. Finally, he said, "This is Supervisory Special Agent Ray White with Justice. I need to speak with the desk sergeant."

Silence consumed the next thirty seconds, then he said, "Sergeant Whittaker, Special Agent Ray White with Justice. I need to know if you've responded to any attacks on Russian immigrants tonight."

Whittaker said, "Not that I know of, but they wouldn't come across my desk as immigrants. All I would see is Caucasian on the report."

"How about any attacks with knives?"

"Oh, sure. There's never a shortage of stabbings around here. We had a lawyer who got mugged in a parking lot in the Quarter. He was stabbed through the left hand, and one of his ankles was sliced open. That's not the weird part of that one, though."

"It gets weirder than sliced ankles and stabbed hands?"

"Oh, yeah. This one had a pistol stuck in his mouth and a rag tied around his head, holding the gun in there. It looked like he may have tried to wrap his wounded hand because there was another rag wrapped around his hand. His right elbow was broken, too."

"What did the perp steal?"

"That's even weirder. He didn't steal anything, apparently. The guy's wallet, watch, and car were all still there."

"What kind of attorney is he?"

"*Was* might be the more appropriate answer."

"Is he dead?"

Whittaker shuffled through some papers. "No, not yet. At least, not as far as I know. He was unconscious from blood loss when the bus delivered him to the ER."

"Back to my question . . . What kind of lawyer is, or was, he?"

"He is, or was, a defense attorney with a long list of clients with one thing in common."

"Let me guess. They were all mobbed up."

"You got it, Special Agent. We've got plenty of that kind of thing going on down here, so it's not a big surprise that one of their attorneys would wind up dead in a parking lot at Eden's View."

"What did you say?" White demanded.

"I said it's not surprising they'd have one of their own attorneys killed right down there where they hang out. I'm not talking about the Italians. That part of the Quarter belongs to the Russians, and wasn't that your original question?"

"Yes, it was. What time did this happen?"

"Just before one o'clock, so that would make it an hour ago. And before you ask, we interviewed the owner, Christian Gerard, but he wasn't giving up anything useful, so we'll keep looking into it, of course. But chances are it was a mob hit, and those things tend to take care of themselves. I'm sure you know what I mean."

"I know all too well. Thanks for the info. Are you sure there's nothing else that could be connected to the Russians?"

Whittaker groaned. "There *was* one other thing, but it turned out to be nothing."

"Sometimes nothing is exactly the something I'm looking for. Let's have it."

Whittaker slipped a sheet from his stack of reports. "Here it is. The only thing that brought this one to mind was the Russian thing. An anonymous caller reported a guy getting roughed up behind a strip club. Most of the girls who dance in that club are Eastern European. When the patrolmen responded, though, nobody had anything to say about it. Like I said, it was anonymous, so that one just goes in the file with no further action required."

"What time was that one?"

"It was ten minutes after nine."

Without realizing he was talking out loud, White said, "So, that could've been the same perp."

"No, probably not. The caller said it was a bum and a tall, thin guy. I can't imagine a homeless guy attacking a lawyer and leaving two grand in cash and a ten-thousand-dollar Rolex behind."

"Sorry," White said. "I was just thinking out loud. Thanks for your help, Sergeant."

Just as they hung up, a knock came, and White turned to see a second Marine standing in the open doorway.

"I'm sorry to bother you, but I'm the guard relief, Lance Corporal Dennison. Is everything okay in here?"

White waved him off. "We're fine, Corporal. Thanks."

"It's Lance Corporal, sir. I'll be right out here if you need me."

Gwynn opened her eyes. "Those Marines sure have a way of making a girl feel protected."

White pulled a chair beside her bed. "Something tells me it isn't *you* who needs protection tonight. I'm afraid I made a huge mistake."

Gwynn rubbed her eyes. "What are you talking about?"

"I told Anya to make Vladimir pay. I'm afraid she's casting a wider net than I expected. It's not just Vladimir she went after. It looks like she killed a lawyer in the parking lot at Eden's View."

Gwynn covered her mouth. "Oh, no. Did she really kill him?"

White shrugged. "The desk sergeant said he was alive when they got him to the emergency room, but he'd lost a lot of blood, and it wasn't looking good."

"That doesn't sound like Anya to me, Agent White. I know I've only been working with her for two missions, but she's weird about leaving wounded people behind, even when she's making a point. I've seen her tie tourniquets on guys she just finished slashing up. I don't think she would've left somebody lying there like that."

White shook his head. "I know, Davis. Somebody tied a rag around the stab wound on the guy's hand."

Gwynn said, "He could've tied it himself before he passed out."

"There's just one problem with that theory. The guy's other arm was broken at the elbow."

Gwynn turned pale. "She's out there running wild. We've got to stop her, Agent White."

"To stop her, we've got to find her before she gets to Orlov, and I don't have access to enough agents to lock down the French Quarter."

Gwynn closed her eyes, imagining what her partner might do next. "I don't think she's going after Orlov."

"What?"

"Hear me out. Orlov is a soft target for Anya. She could get to him in ten minutes and kill him before he knows he's dead, but I don't think that's what she's doing."

White motioned for Gwynn to continue. "Come on. Spit it out."

"I don't mean for this to sound arrogant, but I don't think she's working the mission. I think she's avenging me."

"What are you talking about?"

Gwynn swung her legs over the edge of the bed and sat up. "Think about it. Who did she go after? First, it was Vladimir, the guy who tried to kill me. Well, actually, he tried to kill both of us, but I got the brunt of it. It's obvious that Anya recruited Johnny Mac into helping her with Vladimir. He had to be the homeless guy in the police report."

White focused on Gwynn's eyes. "Okay, I'm with you so far, but why would she kill a lawyer in the parking lot at Eden's View?"

"That's just it. She didn't kill him. She cut him up, broke his arm, and then tried to stop the bleeding. She wasn't trying to kill him. She was leaving a message."

"A message for whom, and what message?"

"For me," Gwynn said. "She's smart, and she knows I know her MO. The lawyer has something to do with this whole thing, and Anya wants me . . . us . . . to know. What else could it be?"

"It could be a crazy Russian assassin on a killing spree in the French Quarter."

"No, that's not it at all. She's not killing people. She probably didn't even hurt Vladimir that badly. I'll bet she just roughed him up a bit and put a little fear in his heart. It's what she does. It's a cat-and-mouse game with her. Sure, she could rip out his heart, but what's the fun in that? She's going to terrorize him until she's extracted her pound of flesh for what he did to me."

"I think you're giving her way too much credit. She's a scorpion, and scorpions sting. It's what they do."

Gwynn pulled the oxygen cannula from her nose. "No, that's not right. You've got to understand. I'm the only real friend she's ever had. I've spent more time with her than anyone else. We've got a thing . . .a bond. What she's doing makes perfect sense if you look at it through that lens."

White leaned back and ran his hands through his hair. "I don't know. I think maybe you're sculpting the events to fit your narrative instead of the other way around. Look at it objectively."

"I can't look at it objectively. That's precisely the point. Anya knows exactly what I'll think and what I'll do."

"If that's true, Davis, then you should know the same about her."

Gwynn smiled. "I do. I know exactly where she'll go next."

23

Ty Nastoyashchiy?
(Are You Real?)

Anya Burinkova lay in the shadows watching the parking lot at Eden's View. Two paramedics worked feverishly over the flaccid form lying beside the open door of the black BMW. Three police officers shone lights in every direction as if expecting to see the assailant waiting to be apprehended. Radio chatter rang through the night air, and another sound she couldn't recognize approached from the northeast.

Lying motionless, she listened as the sound grew ever closer. Finally, the New Orleans Police Department mounted patrol clopped onto the parking lot. The pair of massive horses sniffed the air and swished their tails in wasted attempts to keep the swarming insects at bay.

The pair of officers stepped down from their mounts in practiced unison, but before they could join the melee, an older officer who'd clearly spent too many hours at Café Du Monde yelled, "Get those horses out of here. I've got the canine unit in route, and nothing screws up a dog's nose worse than the filthy smell of a horse."

One of the mounted officers yelled back, "Our horses are cleaner than your car, but if you don't want our help, we're out of here."

The two climbed into their saddles and ambled back toward the wasted crowd on Bourbon Street.

The threat of the canine unit was more than enough to send Anya scampering from her concealment. The time she'd spent lying beneath the BMW before attacking the attorney was sufficient to load the dogs' noses with her scent. Evading the officers wasn't a challenge, but escaping the bloodhounds was outside even Anya's skillset. Her need to get inside the restaurant had just become priority number two, right behind her need to avoid involvement with a police dog's sense of smell.

The throngs of revelers on one of the world's most famous party streets absorbed her as she scooped up a paper hat with a rubber band from the sidewalk. With the hat on her head, she would be challenging to identify, even from above. The only remaining disguise she needed was a half-empty cup of anything. She found the necessary accessory in the hand of a frat boy who was too drunk to realize he had hands, let alone noticing a KGB-trained operative lifting the cup from his grasp. Disguise complete, she moved without apparent purpose to the untrained eye, but everything about her course was planned to the finest point and executed with precision.

A change of clothes from a souvenir shop changed her appearance and her scent, but the cigar from a corner shop was the ultimate anti-bloodhound weapon. She let the cigar burn in her hands, periodically switching from right to left, ensuring her skin, hair, and clothes absorbed the aromatic white plumes. She placed the cigar between her lips only long enough to breathe new life into the ember every ninety seconds.

Confident she hadn't been followed, she crossed the street and headed southwest and back toward Eden's View restaurant.

Unlike its neighbors, the building housing the restaurant was a single-story, squatty building with a flat roof. The structure to the left was a three-story hotel, while the building on the right was a two-story, mostly abandoned warehouse. Anya chose the warehouse and crept inside with the agility and silence of a church mouse. The space was riddled with debris, from long-forgotten mattresses to rusted barrels used as firepits. The stairway to the second story was a dilapidated wooden relic that appeared likely to surrender to gravity under its own weight, and certain to do so if Anya added an additional hundred thirty pounds to its skeletal form.

Instead of risking the stairs, she found a wooden pallet with most of its boards still in place and propped it against the wall beside the stairway. The climb was easy enough, but the obstacle she discovered as she scampered to her feet on the second floor was daunting. Iron bars encaged each window, making it impossible for her to slip through. She pulled on several of the welded iron barricades, but none offered to move. A ladder attached to the rear wall of the building led to an overhead hatch that likely opened onto the roof. She stood at the base of the ladder, scanning the area in hopes of finding any other option, but the ladder and hatch seemed to be her only access to the outside world, and ultimately, onto the roof of the restaurant.

The hatch wore an ancient padlock that was far too rusty to pick. She doubted even its original key could open the clump of brown filth. Since finesse wasn't going to work, she turned to force and pressed her shoulders against the hatch while driving hard with her legs against the ladder. The hatch creaked and moved a few inches on the first attempt. Rotten, mildewed wood and flakes of copper-colored rust cascaded from the hatch that clearly hadn't been disturbed in years. Another thrust rendered even more debris but very little extra sacrifice. Finally, on the fifth attempt, the hinges collapsed under the unexpected force, and the hatch flew open with a crash and a rising cloud of dust.

Anya climbed through the opening, dusted herself off, and evaluated her position. The bulging-bellied cop's threat of canines came true, and Anya watched a pair of dogs scour the parking lot, crisscrossing and backtracking in seemingly random, scent-filled chaos. The ambulance was gone, presumably to carry her victim to the hospital, and the two dogs were the only interested parties left at the scene. The uniformed officers each wore the look of a man who'd seen far too many stabbings and caught far too few perpetrators.

Anya moved to the adjacent knee wall overlooking the restaurant and mentally measured both the distance and her likelihood of making the jump without injury. The memory of pretending to have a broken ankle just inside the front door of the restaurant played through her mind as she faced the probability of *actually* having at least one broken ankle in the coming minutes before making her way inside Eden's View.

In the soft tone she reserved only for herself, Anya whispered, "Is only six meters . . . maybe less. I have done this and higher many times. Is only matter of forward motion and not falling."

Adequately convinced, she gave one final glance toward the parking lot, then bounded forward for three accelerating strides before launching herself over the knee wall. The tar and gravel flat roof of the restaurant rushed upward toward her, and after landing on the balls of her feet, she allowed her forward momentum to carry her into a violent shoulder roll that ended in a collision with an air conditioning unit. The noise of the crash was enough to wake the dead, so she remained low and crawled to the rear of the building. She listened closely for barking dogs or excitement from the previously bored officers. Neither came, so she raised herself barely far enough to see the tops of the officers' heads. Their demeanor hadn't changed, and the pair of dogs still looked as if they were chasing a mouse through a maze.

Staying low enough to avoid catching any attention from the ground, Anya moved meticulously toward a collection of ventilation stacks, hoping to find the perfect fit. As she stuck her head and shoulders into the third stack, she pointed her toes, forcing her torso into the shaft. When her shoulders made their way through the restriction in the vent, the rest of her body followed like a snake slithering into the henhouse. The darkness inside the shaft finally surrendered to the soft light from inside the restaurant's kitchen, and the cleanliness of the commercial kitchen stood in stark contrast to the filth of grease and grime inside the vent.

Contorting her body, she left the vent feet first and landed silently on the tiled floor. The serenity of the abandoned space made the thought of the kitchen buzzing with cooks, dishwashers, and waiters almost impossible to imagine. The only sounds came from the fans and compressors of the freezers and coolers preserving what would become tomorrow's delicacies. The kitchen, however, was not Anya's goal. She had a much smaller room in mind.

It took only seconds to find the door to Chef Christian Gerard's office. The lock inside the doorknob delayed her for only seconds and quickly gave way, allowing her access to the financial soul of one of New Orleans' premier fine-dining restaurants.

A desk lamp illuminated the space with soft, yellow light, and Anya allowed herself a moment of curiosity. The photographs on the wall behind the desk showed Gerard shaking hands with some of the world's greatest chefs, as well as the centerpiece of the collection featuring a shot of the chef standing between Bill and Hillary Clinton. The crown of the collection wasn't a photograph, though. It was an ornately framed certificate granting Chef Christian J. Gerard and Eden's View two Michelin Stars, a coveted rating held by fewer than four hundred restaurants worldwide.

Refocused, Anya sorted through each drawer in Gerard's meager desk and finally found what she'd been searching for. She held up the folded copy of the current registration for the chef's 1965 convertible Mustang. Staring at the top of the document, she memorized Gerard's home address. Her next stop before the sun sliced through the predawn abyss would be Chef Gerard's bedroom, where she would give him no option to postpone their conversation.

Remembering the rear door of the restaurant being hidden from the parking lot by the fence, she left the office, relocked the door, and crossed the kitchen. The police officers wouldn't present a problem, but the dogs' noses weren't their only keen sense. Any sounds she made leaving the building would echo in the bloodhounds' ears, and their nose-down search for their prize would end with their ears perked upward and resounding barks. Silence was the crucial element of her escape.

Six strides before she would've reached the door, the compressors and fans came to a momentary halt, and the sound of soft incantation played on the otherwise silent space. Anya froze and listened with focused intensity.

Are these sounds real or imagined? Could they be coming from the street?

The longer she listened, the clearer the sound became, and it was wafting through the solid door of the walk-in cooler. Mesmerized, Anya abandoned her attempt at a silent escape and moved instead toward the chanting voice. The closer she moved to the cooler, the more defined the mysterious tone became.

Drawn to the melody of the incantation, despite the chant being in a language she couldn't identify, Anya slid a hand around the stainless-steel handle and pulled in silent slow motion. The latch withdrew, freeing the door, and the Russian continued the methodical pull on the door until she created an opening barely wide enough for her body.

The chanting continued as if incapable of stopping. The light from the kitchen cut a swath through the darkened interior of the cooler until the shadows gave way to the revelation of a dark, hooded form kneeling on the floor of the frigid cavern.

The unearthly sounds that had beckoned to Anya like the siren's song rose from the mystical form until resting at her feet.

Is this real? Am I trapped inside a dream?

As if sensing Anya's presence, the chant ceased, and the dark figure turned to face the intruder. The penetrating light illuminated a pair of haunting blue eyes protruding from within obsidian folds of flesh and garment. The eyes narrowed and fixed themselves like daggers on the soul of the tall, lean assassin. The voice that had, only seconds earlier, been filling the space with chanting reverence, turned cold and accusatory. "You've come for me, haven't you?"

Anya stood motionless with disbelief and utter confusion as the kneeling form extended a pair of hands wrapped in rags as if surrendering. "I see inside you only pieces of your light. You come to draw out the life and extinguish the light, but with every soul you deprive of its carnal breath, you surrender part of what remains within you."

Anya stared down at the woman who'd looked into her soul and known her emptiness. "*Ty nastoyashchiy?*"

The woman withdrew her hands and pulled the hood from her head, revealing mounds of dreadlocks adorned with slivers of bone. "Yes, I am quite real, but I fear you are not."

Anya ignored the accusation. "What are you doing?"

A quizzical expression overtook the woman's face as if her purpose should've been obvious, and she moved, seemingly without effort, to reveal a neat stack of burlap wrapping on the floor of the cooler. Before it lay the dismembered body of a massive orange and black tiger lying in seven severed pieces of flesh, pelt, and bone.

"I am communing with the tiger."

For the assassin who'd never known the taste of fear or allowed the supernatural to encroach upon her rational mind, the scene and revelation before her left her incapable of comprehending what she was witnessing. She was left wordless with only one exception. "Why?"

The crouching woman smiled, revealing teeth almost as black as her skin. "You were not sent for me. You don't understand why you're here, do you?"

Anya couldn't look away from the macabre tableau. "Why? Why are you doing this?"

The woman reached for Anya, and unable to resist, she gave the old woman her hands. She then squeezed the Russian's hands and spoke in flowing, beautiful Russian. "I soothe the animal's spirit before his bones are introduced into the wine. If this isn't done, the result is only poison."

Anya whispered, "Why do you speak Russian?"

The old woman widened her smile. "I am not speaking Russian, my girl. You are only hearing with your heart, and this is how we truly listen. This is how I can commune with the tiger."

Anya felt a shiver run the length of her spine, and she backed away from the woman, leaving her alone with the spirit of the tiger and the frigid air of the cooler.

24

CHTO NE TAK SO MNOY?
(WHAT'S WRONG WITH ME?)

Supervisory Special Agent Ray White and Special Agent Gwynn Davis pulled into the parking lot of Eden's View restaurant and stepped from their Suburban with their DOJ credentials in hand. "Who's in charge?"

The senior officer on the scene lit a cigarette. "I am."

Ray stepped in front of him. "SSA White with Justice. I have the scene, and the suspect is in custody. You can call off the dogs."

The sergeant examined White's credentials and pulled a small, spiral-bound notepad from his pocket, then noted the time. "Fine with me. It's all yours, Agent White." He turned to the canine officer. "Load 'em up, Carl. The mighty feds are takin' over."

The canine officer gave a whistle and a command in German, and the two bloodhounds galloped to his side as if someone had rung the dinner bell. Seconds later, White and Gwynn were left standing alone in the parking lot with the NOPD nowhere in sight.

"All right, Davis. Where is she?"

"She's here, Agent White. Trust me."

Gwynn led her boss toward the back door of the restaurant, and as they rounded the fence, their target stepped through the door as if in a trance.

Gwynn ran to her partner. "Anya! Are you all right?"

Anya looked between the kitchen and her partner as Gwynn approached.

"Anya! What's wrong?"

The Russian stared at Gwynn without a word, and the special agent inside Gwynn Davis came to life. She turned and ordered, "Bring the Suburban over here, and get out the med bag, quick!"

Instead of correcting the junior agent on her insubordination, he turned on a heel and sprinted for the vehicle. Seconds later, Anya was sitting on the tailgate of the SUV as Gwynn pumped up the blood pressure cuff. White stepped between her knees and shone a penlight in each of Anya's eyes, testing for pupil reaction. He stepped back and handed her an uncapped bottle of water, and she stared at it for a long moment before raising it to her lips.

Gwynn deflated the cuff and looked up at White. "We've got to get her to the ER. Her BP is two twenty over one twenty-five, and her heart rate is well over a hundred."

"Get the door!" White ordered as he scooped Anya from the tailgate. He placed her on the back seat, and Gwynn climbed in beside her.

White pulled the vehicle into gear and pulled from the parking lot, already accelerating through sixty miles per hour. "Keep her drinking, and keep your fingers on her pulse."

Navigating the narrow city streets in the eight-thousand-pound Suburban at high speed, White narrowly missed a dozen parked cars and ran countless pedestrians from the streets.

"We're two minutes out. How's she doing?"

"Her heart rate is down, and she seems to be relaxing."

Anya slowly turned to face Gwynn and spoke in a child's tone. "There was a woman . . . inside restaurant. We must go back."

White hit the brakes and slid to a stop with the red sign of the emergency room only hundreds of feet away. "What did you say?"

Gwynn answered. "She said there was a woman in the restaurant, and we have to go back."

White threw the vehicle into park. "What woman? What are you talking about?"

Anya looked down at her hands as if discovering them for the first time. "What is wrong with me?"

"You appear to be in shock," Gwynn said. "Tell me about the woman in the restaurant."

Anya blinked rapidly for several seconds before saying, "She was talking to tiger."

"Tiger?" Gwynn said, remembering their first Marine guard at the Navy hospital. "Do you mean Corporal Adams?"

"No. She was dressed all in black, and she spoke Russian and another language I do not know."

"Forget about the woman," White ordered. "What's this about a tiger?"

Anya shook her head and touched Gwynn's face. "You should be in hospital. Why are you here?"

"I'm fine. We're worried about you right now. Try to tell us what you saw inside the restaurant."

Anya pulled her hand from Gwynn's face and placed it against her own. "I think maybe I have also concussion from jumping onto roof."

"Did you hit your head?"

Anya squeezed her eyes closed and held up a hand. "Listen to me. We must go back to restaurant. Is important for you to see what is inside."

Gwynn said, "We can't just go inside without a warrant. If we do, nothing we see is admissible in court."

"What is inside is not for court. It is for you to understand because I do not."

White held up a finger. "Just stop talking. Gwynn, check her vitals while I think."

Gwynn slid the cuff onto Anya's arm and pumped the bulb. She read the dial and listened for the heartbeat. "One forty-two over eighty, heart rate forty. Respirations, twelve."

White spun in his seat. "Look at me, Anya."

She stared into his eyes with regained confidence.

"Tell me exactly what you saw in there."

Anya sighed. "Is better if you see. I cannot trust my eyes."

He placed two fingers beneath her chin. "Keep looking at me, and tell me what you saw."

She tried to look away, but he redirected her gaze. "Say it, Anya. No matter what it is, just say it."

She lifted the bottle of water back to her lips and savored the drink. "I went inside restaurant to find address for chef. I had only short talk with him, but I think he is afraid."

"Afraid of what?" White asked.

Anya continued. "I do not know yet, but terrible things are happening inside his restaurant, and I do not think he is in control of this."

White motioned for her to continue. "Get back on track, and tell me what you saw in there."

"I am sorry to say this, but I heard sound inside cooler when I was leaving. I stopped to listen, and I went inside. There was small woman dressed in black rags. She was chanting in language I do not understand. It did not sound like any language, just maybe sounds. In front of her were stacks of burlap wrapping Gwynn saw, and also was body of tiger cut into pieces. The woman said she was talking with tiger, and she spoke to me in Russian, but she said to me something very strange. She said I was only listening in Russian, and she could not speak this language. This is not how listening works."

White chuckled. "I think you may have hit your head on the roof, but that story is just weird enough for me to want to see it for myself. We're going back, but you're staying in the vehicle. And when we finish, both of you are going back to the hospital."

White pulled the Suburban into gear and turned back for the restaurant. Arriving at Eden's View, he parked near the back door and pointed a finger at Anya. "Stay here, and don't move. We'll be back in three minutes."

White and Gwynn stepped from the vehicle and moved toward the door with their pistols at the ready. White twisted the doorknob to find it unlocked, and they cautiously stepped inside. Anya slid from the back seat and crept toward the door, unable to resist her curiosity. She peered through the sliver left between the door and the jamb.

Suddenly, the door flew open, and White stood glaring down at her. "I knew you'd never listen. Get in here."

She stepped through the door and pulled it closed behind her. Pointing toward the first cooler, Anya said, "This one."

White motioned for Gwynn to open the door to the cooler. He held his pistol high with his flashlight, just below his line of sight. Gwynn looked up for the signal, and White nodded. She pulled the handle and threw the door open to its limit. White shuffled forward, and Gwynn stepped to his side, sweeping the interior of the cooler with her weapon's light. Anya drew her knife and stepped between the two agents.

White exhaled and lowered his pistol, and Gwynn did the same. "Are you sure it was this cooler, Anya?"

The Russian stepped forward and knelt on the floor. She slid her hand across the smooth, cold surface. "She was here. I know I saw her."

"Are you sure this is the right cooler?" Gwynn asked.

Before Anya could answer, White said, "We're checking the other coolers."

They entered the two remaining coolers with the same result. With his pistol holstered, he met Anya's eyes again. "Tell me you didn't imagine it."

Anya shook her head. "I did not. I am now certain of this."

"What makes you certain now?"

She held up a single orange hair between her thumb and index finger. White focused on the hair and lifted it from her fingertips. He motioned toward the door with his chin, and Gwynn closed the door of the cooler. White locked the back door of the restaurant as they stepped back outside.

At the Suburban, White took Anya's arm and turned her to face him. "There's something you need to know."

She looked up with a hint of concern on her face, and White said, "I believed you even before you showed me the hair."

She tried to smile. "Thank you, but I did not."

He opened the door for her. "Get in, Catwoman. I'm taking you and your trusty sidekick back to the hospital. You can tell me about Vladimir and the lawyer after we get you checked out."

Anya shook her head. "I do not need doctor. I only scratched my shoulder and hand jumping onto roof from other roof. It was only six or maybe seven meters."

Gwynn huffed. "You jumped twenty feet onto a roof, and all you got were a couple of scratches? That's insane! Who does that?"

Anya cocked her head. "They did not teach you this inside Academy?"

"No! Nobody ever taught me to survive a twenty-foot jump onto a roof."

"I will teach you this."

White broke in. "Hey! When did this turn into a negotiation? Both of you are going back to the hospital." He shot a finger toward Anya. "*You* are getting a full exam." He spun to face Gwynn. "And *you* are getting back in the bed until the doctors say you can officially leave the hospital."

Anya smiled at her partner. "You broke out of hospital just to find me?"

Gwynn laughed. "Actually, *he* broke me out so I could help him stop you from burning the whole city to the ground."

Anya smirked. "I think maybe now I have two lawyers with guns to help me burn down city."

25

Kak Ty Uznal?
(How Did You Know?)

Anya Burinkova strolled into Gwynn's hospital room, where she should've found the special agent recuperating in bed, but the scene barely resembled a hospital room at all.

SSA Ray White leaned across a folding table and pointed to a document under the attentive eyes of Gwynn, First Officer Dave Young from MV *Morning Star*, and Peter, the former driver and State Department representative.

White looked up. "Oh, good. You're back. You've got to see this."

Anya held up a single sheet of paper. "The doctor—or someone who looked like doctor—said to me my brain is healthy. I do not think they know very much about my brain, but machine was terrible. It was like tunnel with horrible sounds."

White chuckled. "Yeah, that's an MRI machine, and everybody hates them. I'm glad to hear you're okay. Now, get over here and get back to work. Maybe you can explain this to me."

Gwynn slid a stack of aerial photos toward Anya, but she ignored them, focusing on Peter, and switching to Russian. "You are alive. This is very good. I was concerned for you."

He looked up from his wheelchair. "Yes, I am alive, but only because of you."

"It was not only me. Gwynn and also pilots were there."

Peter lowered his chin. "They told me what you did, and I would have died out there in the swamp if you hadn't saved me. I am in your debt."

"There is no debt," Anya said. "You would do same for me."

Dave Young said, "Hey! Excuse me, but could you two comrades speak a language all of us know?"

Peter switched back to English and laid a hand on Dave's shoulder. "This conversation was not for you. It was for the soldier who saved my life."

Appropriately scorned, Dave turned back to the photos.

Anya leaned over the table. "What am I supposed to explain to you?"

Gwynn sorted through the stack of shots and placed them in order. "We were able to nab satellite photos of the boat we believe carried the contraband in a load of cargo to Grand Isle. Actually, it went to Port Fourchon. We even got lucky on the timing and picked up a shot of the crew unloading the boat. As you can see in these shots"—Gwynn slid two more photos to Anya—"the cargo is being offloaded by hand instead of a crane or forklift. It's not great resolution, but if you'll look closely, you can see these shots look a lot like burlap bundles."

Anya lifted a magnifying glass from the table and studied the pictures. After several minutes, she laid down the glass and turned back to Peter. "How did you know about the tiger?"

White slapped the table. "What? You knew about the tiger? When and why didn't you brief me the second you knew?"

Peter swallowed hard. "I will answer Anya's question first. I didn't actually *know*. I only suspected. I am sorry I wrote in Cyrillic. I was losing blood, and I couldn't think in English."

"Do not apologize," Anya said. "I had trouble only because it looked like English letters, but I realized later it was Cyrillic."

White knocked twice on the table. "*When* did you know?"

Peter looked up at White's reddening face. "When I was assigned to this task force from State, I plowed through mountains of files on traffic into New Orleans. Most of it was benign, but a few files stood out. The ones that sent up red flags for me were poached exotic animals from China and southeastern Russia. I didn't mention it to anyone because it sounded so outlandish, but when I believed I was dying in the bayou, the thought wouldn't leave my mind, and I had to tell someone."

White pulled his tie loose. "Why would the State Department have files on poached exotic animals?'

"We have files on everything, sir. Everybody thinks the CIA is the storehouse for all international intelligence, but State has mounds of research and intel the Agency will never see."

White said, "I want to be furious because you didn't tell me, but if you had, I wouldn't have believed you. But don't let that stop you in the future. If you have so much as a hunch that something isn't right, I want it in my ear before you finish the thought. Got it?"

Peter furrowed his brow. "No disrespect, sir, but I don't work for you. I report to the under secretary of state for Arms Control and International Security Affairs."

White stepped away from the table and pulled out his phone. Suddenly, the focus left the satellite imagery and turned to SSA White. He pressed the phone to his ear. "This is Supervisory Special Agent Ray White. Put the under secretary on the phone." He paused only briefly before belting out, "Is she in with the president? No? Then put her on the phone, now." A few more tense seconds passed. "My next call is to the White House, and you're going to need to get your résumé in order."

Everyone held their breath.

"Patricia, hello. Ray White from Justice. I have one of your officers on a detail with me in New Orleans. His name is Peter . . ." White paused and eyed the man.

Peter said, "Evans, sir."

White spoke into the phone, "Peter Evans. Probably Pyotr Evanoff, originally." A few more seconds passed. "He's under the misguided belief that he reports to anyone other than me on this operation. I'm sure you know I'm assigned by the attorney general at the behest of the president.

I'd like for you to have a conversation with Mr. Evans concerning his chain of command."

Without listening for a reply, White handed the phone to Peter, and he raised it to his ear. "Peter Evans . . . Yes, ma'am . . . I understand, ma'am . . . Of course I understand. Thank you . . . Yes, ma'am. Here he is."

He handed the phone back to White. "She would like to speak with you again."

White covered the microphone. "Did she tell you that you now report to me?"

"Yes, sir. She did."

White thumbed the red end button and pocketed the phone.

Gwynn covered her mouth to avoid laughing out loud. "Did you really just hang up on the under secretary of state?"

White shrugged. "I got what I needed from her. There was nothing left to discuss. Now, we're all on the same team."

Gwynn said, "I can't wait until I get to that point in my career."

"That's enough interruptions. Let's get back to work."

"Agent White," Peter said, "please understand that I meant no disrespect. It was just that—"

"Relax, Peter. It's taken care of. You were following the chain of command, and now I'm the link above you in the chain. Now, shut up while those of us who haven't been shot on this mission talk about grown-up stuff."

Peter turned to Anya. "It's a Russian thing, isn't it? He hates Russians."

Anya laid a hand on his thigh. "No, he hates everyone equally, except maybe sometimes he hates me a little more than everyone else."

Gwynn called the meeting back to order. "Here's what we know. The boat left Puerto Cortés, Honduras, with a couple thousand pounds of fish and whatever is in those bundles. My bet is it's one deconstructed tiger, but why? Why kill a tiger in China or Russia, ship it to Honduras somehow, and pack it on a small boat like that just to bring it to New Orleans?"

Anya said, "I have these answers."

White motioned for her to keep talking.

"I think chef is making tiger bone wine for Vasily Orlov."

White frowned. "What's tiger bone wine?"

Peter spoke up. "It's an ancient elixir that started in China a few thousand years ago. It's made by grinding up tiger bones and soaking them in wine for eight years."

"Eight years?" Gwynn said.

"Yes, always at least eight years. It's said that aficionados can tell by taste and smell if the wine is aged even one day less than eight years."

Gwynn asked, "Why? I mean, what's the purpose of it?"

Anya said, "In the East, it is believed that tiger wine makes men virile and strong and also cures disease."

"What kinds of diseases?" Dave asked.

Anya said, "Every disease. Tigers have no natural enemy. Nothing kills tigers except other tigers, and they are afraid of nothing. In Chinese medicine, it is believed spirit and strength of tiger is drawn from inside bones by wine and given to person who drinks it."

Gwynn shuddered. "Okay, that's just nasty and weird."

White said, "It may be, but the important thing for us is that it's a violation of federal law. To import, possess, or transport an exotic animal—living or dead, especially if poached—into or within the U.S. without appropriate licensing is a felony."

"So, we have them," Anya said. "You can now arrest them, and we are finished, yes?"

"Slow down, Red Sonja. We're a long way from an arrest."

Anya held up a stack of satellite photos. "But you have pictures and also hair from inside cooler."

White said, "Explain it to her, Davis."

Gwynn took the photos from Anya. "It's like this. The pictures don't show anything illegal. We don't know what kind of fish are in those crates, and we don't know what the bundles are. It could be tuna and coffee, for all we know."

"But what about woman and tiger parts I saw inside restaurant?"

"Take us to them," Gwynn said. "You can't. And if we can't present them in court, as far as the legal system is concerned, they never existed."

"But I saw them inside cooler. I can testify."

Gwynn shook her head. "Without physical evidence, your testimony is meaningless."

"Then what do we have to do?" Anya asked.

"We've got a couple of options. First, we can try to flip one of the participants and get them to testify against the rest of the ring. For example, if we could get Chef Gerard to testify against Vasily Orlov, if he has knowledge of a crime, that would be a good start, but even that might not be enough. We still need physical evidence to support the testimony."

"What is second option?" Anya asked.

"You and I get inside the organization, just like we did in Miami and New York, and tear it apart from the inside."

Anya sighed. "This is not possible. These people think you and I are dead."

Gwynn turned to White. "Do you have any ideas?"

White smiled. "Hey, Anya. Where were you headed when we picked you up at the back door of the restaurant?"

"I was going to talk with chef at his home. I have now his address."

White nodded. "Yep, exactly. He doesn't know the two of you are dead. Only Orlov and Vladimir believe that, unless they're all three in bed together and the chef is wrapped up in this thing deeper than we know. By the way, next time you need someone's address, don't break into a restaurant to find it. Just ask me. We're pretty good at finding people."

Anya smirked. "You did not find me when I was gone before mission."

"Yes," White admitted, "but there's a big difference in a chef and a former Russian assassin."

The look on Peter's face showed a light had just come on inside his head. "You're Anastasia Burinkova . . . You're a legend in—"

Anya held up a hand. "No! I am only Anya or Ana, and last name is Fulton."

Peter smiled as if his favorite character had just walked off a movie screen in front of him. "We should have tea and talk about . . . things."

"Yes, I think we should do this, but first, I must have talk with Chef Christian Gerard."

26

Net Vreda v Razgovore
(No Harm in Talking)

Ray White gave a single clap of his hands. "Okay, any questions? Good. Get to work. Except Peter and Davis. The two of you are still on bed rest until the doctor says otherwise."

Gwynn glanced between Anya and White. "But, Agent White, I'm good. The headache is gone, and I need to be with Anya when she interviews the chef."

Ray placed a finger to his chin and stared toward the ceiling. "In case you're wondering, Davis, I'm not thinking about my answer. I'm trying to remember what I said that would lead you to believe any of this is negotiable. Give me just a minute to replay the mental voice recording."

Gwynn stood and moved toward the hospital bed.

White said, "Ah, good. You remember it the same as I do."

Anya stacked the aerial photos neatly into one file and turned to Peter. "You were in civilian hospital. Why are you here now?"

He looked up from his wheelchair and motioned toward White. "He did it. As soon as it was safe for me to be moved, they brought me here so I could work with the team while I'm recuperating."

"I will push you back to your room, and we will talk, yes?"

Peter smiled. "Yeah, I'd like that. But don't you think we should clear it with Agent White?"

Anya grabbed the handles of Peter's chair and rolled toward the door. "There is no harm in talking, and I need to know where your room is in case we need you."

White checked his watch. "Ten minutes, comrades, and then you're hitting the street to find Gerard."

"He will not be difficult to find. I will talk with Peter for thirty minutes and then go to Gerard's house, where I will find him barely awake having morning coffee."

Without another word, she rolled Peter through the door and into the hallway. Before she'd made it ten strides, White stuck his head through the door. "Twenty minutes, and not a minute longer. Got it?"

She ignored the order and continued down the hallway. "Which is your room?"

"It's the other way," Peter said, "but I'm learning you don't take direction very well, so I was going to let you push me anywhere you wanted."

Anya brought the wheelchair through a one-hundred-eighty-degree turn, and Peter motioned toward the left. "I'm in four seventy-seven."

She rolled through the door and helped Peter back onto his bed, then she leaned across him to reach the controller, leaving their faces only inches apart and frozen for a moment.

Peter swallowed hard.

Anya recoiled. "I am sorry. That was . . ."

Peter shook his head. "No, don't be sorry. There's not a man on Earth who wouldn't . . . well, you know."

In a rare, involuntary reaction, Anya blushed and smiled down at her countryman. "Yes, I know, but you are married man, yes?"

He shook his head. "No. My job doesn't lend itself to a family life."

"This is true also of my job."

"Speaking of your job," he said, "I've read a little of your file—the parts that weren't redacted. Is it true what you did?"

"I have not read my file. Is what true?"

He motioned toward a chair by the window. "Pull up a chair. We still have sixteen minutes, by my estimation."

"This is not correct. We have twenty-six minutes."

"But White said twenty minutes and no more."

"Yes, this is true, but I said thirty. So, what do you want to know if is true inside file?"

Peter sucked air through his teeth. "Is it true that you defected because of the agent you were, uh . . ."

"Is okay," she said. "I am trained sparrow. It is true I was to seduce American agent and recruit him into service to Kremlin, but this is not what happened."

"You're the first one."

She frowned. "First one, what?"

He stared down at his feet beneath the cover. "You're the first sparrow I've ever met. I have heard about them, but I wasn't sure they were real."

"Is very real, and school for seduction is terrible. I was trained in this school, but this was only small part of training for me. I am assassin, not whore."

Peter's eyes turned to saucers. "I didn't mean to imply that . . ."

Anya didn't have to fake the smile she offered. "Is okay. I know this is not what you asked, but I have nothing to hide. We are on same team now."

"I just didn't want you to think I was accusing you of anything. I left the Soviet Union when I was only eleven years old, so I never knew the socialists as an adult."

Anya cocked her head. "How did you leave when you were eleven?"

Peter straightened himself in his bed. "You've not read my file?"

"I did not know you existed, so why would I read your file?"

"Fair enough. I was eleven when my father defected. He was a mid-level Communist Party official and probably former KGB. I don't know, but it doesn't matter. He defected into the arms of the CIA in nineteen seventy-nine, and it was well planned. My mother and I were on holiday in Greece. Two men from the American embassy came to our hotel room and told us my father had stepped from behind the Iron Curtain in Switzerland, and we were to meet him in Paris."

He paused to replay the memory.

"I'll never forget the relief on my mother's face when those two men came. She knew it was to happen, but I was only a child, so she didn't tell me. On the ride back to the embassy in the back seat of the car, she held me in her arms and cried the whole time. I thought, back then, those were tears of sadness because we were leaving our home, but I understand now they were tears of relief."

Anya listened intently, hanging on every word as he continued the narrative.

"My mother never got to see America. An assassin killed her in Paris. We were inside a safe house, awaiting our flight to America, when I heard a dog yelping as if he were hurt, so my father took me into the edge of the woods to find the dog. We never found him. The house exploded while we were searching for him, killing my mother and an embassy Marine guard instantly. My father and I were on a plane within two hours."

"I am so sorry, Peter. I had no idea. That is terrible story."

Peter nodded slowly. "Thank you, but that wasn't the first time, nor the last."

"What do you mean?"

He pressed his lips into a thin line, preparing himself for the rest of the story. "Two years earlier, my older sister was killed because my father had disobeyed an order from the Kremlin. I think that was the day he decided to defect. They took everything from him."

"Oh, Peter. I do not know what to say." She rose from her chair and nestled beside him, taking his hands in hers.

"There is nothing to say. When I was fourteen, my father allegedly shot himself inside our home in Virginia, and I was instantly orphaned."

Anya sighed. "Then it is you who they have taken everything from, and not your father. Even if they did not kill him directly, what they did made him take his own life and left you, a teenaged boy, alone in a country far from home."

Peter's eyes glazed over. "He did not kill himself."

"What?"

"My father was left-handed, and the pistol that killed him was in his right hand when I found him."

Anya leaned in and pulled him close. "If you want, I will find man who did this, and I will bring to you his heart in paper bag."

Peter moaned as his wounds reminded him why he was still in a hospital bed. "There was a time I would have loved nothing more, but if I asked you to do that, it would make me no better than them, and I can't let myself become the thing I hate the most."

"Look to me in eyes," she whispered. "You did not ask me to do this. I made offer."

"No, Anya . . . Or Ana. Which is it?"

"For you, it is Anya."

"Thank you for the offer, Anya. It means a great deal to me, but it's not what I want."

"Then I am correct about you. You *are* spy, no?"

He looked away. "My country—the country who saved me from Moscow—asked for my help, and I gave myself to them because they tried to rescue my family in the name of freedom. They failed. They saved only me, but they tried, and for that, I owe them everything. I do the work the State Department asks of me. If this is spying, I spy. If this is driving beautiful special agents around New Orleans, I drive. America is my country because they gave me something no one else on Earth could do. They gave me freedom, and without freedom, nothing else matters."

Anya reached inside her pocket and produced the small plastic American flag. She twirled it between her fingers. "Me, too."

He lifted the flag from her hand and held it against his chest. "They don't know the value of their own country, do they?"

Anya laid a hand across his. "Some of them do. There are courageous people who are willing to sacrifice everything for this country. I know some of these people, and they are the best people in all of world."

Peter sighed. "Him?"

She nodded. "He gave to me this flag, and also this country, when he did not have to. Even after he knew I was horrible person, he did these things for me when he should have taken my life. I would not have stopped him if he had tried."

Peter let her words soak into his mind. "It sounds like you and I have far more in common than just the country of our birth."

She stood, and he raised the miniature flag toward her. She pushed his hand away. "You keep it. I have more."

He tucked the flag behind his ear. "When all this is over—if we survive it—maybe we can have a drink or beignets and coffee."

She paused in the doorway. "I would like that, but I will buy because you have only civil servant pay."

"Maybe we can go Dutch."

She frowned. "Beignets are French, but we can have Dutch if you want. I think I have never eaten Dutch food."

"Get out of here," he said. "Go talk a chef into ruining what's left of his life."

27

Sadovyy Rayon
(The Garden District)

Anya stepped from the car and onto a tree-lined street in New Orleans' wealthiest neighborhood, the Garden District, and gazed up at the century-old home on a corner lot. The cameras affixed to each corner of the second floor gave her pause as she turned the corner and continued surveilling her target. The midday sun made it impossible to identify the rooms that had lights turned on, but lights weren't the indicators of occupancy she was looking for.

The row of trees delineating the property line to the north offered excellent concealment as she made her way to the first of her two objectives for the morning. She stayed low, winding her way through the hedges and trees that still held their leaves, despite the calendar. When she reached a point where no security cameras were visible, she slipped silently from the tree line and approached the detached garage. A glance through the side window of the structure revealed Gerard's beloved Mustang resting peacefully in her stable.

Staying tightly against the garage, she rounded the building and eased her way toward the house. The crawl space was more of a standing space. Obviously, the original builder had the wisdom to anticipate the hurricanes that would batter the city until the storms drove the occupants to higher ground permanently or the Earth stopped producing tropical storms. Neither scenario was likely.

Anya slipped through a hinged door constructed of lattice and exterior framing until she was beneath the beautiful old house. She moved with cat-like patience around the perimeter, listening closely for sounds of inhabitance above. Finally, as she approached the rear of the house, a chorus of clicks sounded overhead, followed by shoes striking the floor. She followed the sounds to the rear of the house until she could hear the squeak of an ancient door opening. The clicks from inside the house turned to galloping strides on the wooden slats of the back porch. Solid footfalls followed the previous sounds, and the door closed against its jamb.

The clicks of the animal's footsteps on the interior hardwood floor that morphed into gallops on the decks and rear stairs gave way to full-on barking from the golden retriever.

Anya had no fear of the animal's aggression. Befriending that breed of dog took no more effort than a friendly nuzzle behind the ear, but the barking, especially the specific intruder-induced tone of the bark, would give away her position in seconds.

"Hey! Cut it out! What are you barking at, Dore'e?"

Hearing the dog's name, Anya knelt beside the steps, rubbed her fingertips together, and whispered the French word for *golden*. "Dore'e, good girl. Come . . .come."

The dog's tail waved like a flag in the wind, and Dore'e danced toward the Russian until they were only inches apart and the dog was sniffing her hands.

"Dore'e! What are you doing down there, girl?"

Footsteps on the wooden stairs changed Anya's plan. Instead of confronting the chef on her terms, she was left to improvise because of a curious golden retriever. She looped two fingers through the dog's collar after rubbing her head with several loving strokes, then the animal let Anya lead her into the darkened depths beneath the stairs. Chef Christian Gerard bounded from the bottom step and knelt to peer beneath his house. "Dore'e! Come out of there. Come on, girl."

The dog lunged toward her owner, but Anya held the collar, preventing her from striding toward Gerard.

His beseeching continued. "Come on, Dore'e. What are you doing under there? What have you found?"

Gerard took a knee and leaned into the space. Dore'e whined with desire to run to him, but Anya held fast. Finally, Gerard scooted through the triangular opening into the space, and Anya released the dog. Dore'e lunged for Gerard and planted a wet tongue solidly on his face. It was just the distraction Anya needed. She pounced, landing with one knee on the back of the chef's left hand and driving a forearm against his neck, robbing him of the ability to move or strike her with his right hand.

He yelled out in surprise and pain, but Anya whispered, "Relax. I am not going to hurt you. I only want to talk."

His surprise became disbelief, and he tried to escape back toward the light. The dog frolicked, enjoying the game, but Gerard belted out, "Who are you? And what are you doing under my house?"

Anya eased her aggression and took some of the pressure from his hand. "I am woman from restaurant with hurt ankle. I am not going to hurt you, but we need to talk."

He recoiled. "Are you stalking me or something? What's wrong with you?"

She leaned close enough for him to feel her breath on his skin. "Tell me about tiger wine."

"I don't know who you are, lady, but I'm going to yell for help if you don't let me go right now."

"This would be terrible mistake," she said just as he inhaled in preparation for the audible alarm. She drove a thumb into the notch at the top of his sternum, preventing the air he'd inhaled from escaping past the vocal cords.

Gerard instinctually tried to pull away, but with his hand pinned beneath her knee, the man was her prisoner until she decided to release him. He made gagging sounds until she withdrew her thumb.

"Do not yell. I only wish to talk with you. Nothing more. We can do it here in darkness beneath house, or inside. This is your choice."

"Let's go inside," he managed to cough up.

She released the pressure of her knee from his hand and held up an arm to protect her face should he lash out. Thankfully, he didn't. Doing so would've turned the encounter into an incident Gerard most certainly didn't want.

He withdrew from the space, and Anya followed, never letting his hands out of sight. The dog ran for the tree line to accomplish the original meaning of her excursion, and Gerard led Anya up the stairs and through the back door of the house.

He motioned toward an antique oak table. "Let me guess. You drink tea and not coffee."

"Yes, with honey, please."

He poured steaming water into a pair of mugs, dropped a teabag into each, and produced a small plastic container in the shape of a bear. "Here's your honey. How do you know about the tiger wine?"

"Thank you. I know many things, and most important, I know you are in position you never wanted. I can help you from this position if you will let me."

"You're a cop, aren't you?"

"Not today. Today I am woman who appreciates what you did for my ankle and also for tea. Bear with honey is cute. I like."

Gerard took the first tentative sip of his tea and slid down in his seat until his head rested on the top of the ladder-back chair. "I knew this day would come, but I didn't think it would be anybody like you."

"What do you mean?"

Gerard sighed. "I understand what's going on here. You're a Russian, just like the rest of them, and there's no chance I'm going to live through this, is there?"

"Do you believe I am here to kill you?"

"Why else would you be here?"

"If I wanted to kill you, I would have done it, and you would never have seen my face. I am not with Vasily Orlov. He is dangerous man who believes American laws do not apply for him, but you know this already."

"If you're not here to kill me, then what do you want?"

Anya sipped her tea. "This is very good. Thank you. First, I want for you to tell me how you became involved with Vasily Orlov."

He continued staring at the ceiling. "Aren't you going to show me your badge and read me my rights?"

"No, I am not going to do those things. If I did, this would be interrogation, and I could not help you. Instead, this is grateful woman who is trying to help man who is in trouble."

"So, you are a cop."

Anya leaned forward and tapped on the table. "Look at me. If I were police officer, I would say to you, 'We saw your witch and dead tiger inside restaurant,' but this is not what I am saying. Do you understand?"

"No, I don't understand any of this, but I am thankful it's over now."

"What is over?"

He waved his hands through the air above his head. "All of it. The whole messed-up thing is over, and we're all going to prison. Will you take my dog when I go away? She seems to like you."

"Stop this. You are not going to prison. You are simply going to tell me about what happened when you first met Vasily Orlov. This is all."

"Is it going to be like witness protection or something?"

Remembering the effect Ray White's fist on the table had, Anya rapped on the ancient oak with her knuckles. "Listen to me. My name is Ana, and I can make all of this go away. You will not go into prison or witness security. This is what it is called and not witness protection. Many people get this wrong."

Gerard took another drink. "What if I don't want to talk?"

"Then I am wrong, and you will go into prison."

He glared down at Anya's feet. "Your ankle was never hurt, was it?"

"No, it was ruse to get inside restaurant."

"The other woman with you, is it true that she drowned in the car that ran off the seawall?"

"This is not important just now. Tell me of Vasily."

Gerard drove the heels of his hands into his eyes and let out an animalistic roar.

Anya took advantage of the moment. "I understand. I have been also in situation like yours. Is terrible decision, and fear is everywhere. You saw what I did to man in parking lot at restaurant. I am dangerous woman, and I have no fear left inside me. I am probably only person in whole of world who can protect you. You were kind to me, and I saw in your eyes, it was sincere kindness. You are good person in bad situation, and this I can end for you. When all of it is over and gone, you will still be good person inside. No one can take away goodness from you. It can only be given away by you. Remember this."

He closed his eyes and began to talk. "I met Vasily Orlov when I was working in Vancouver under Chef Pierre Toussaint. He was the best chef in Canada, and nobody disagreed, and I was the only person on Earth who could tolerate his rage. I just let it roll off my back because I was learning so much. I'm a graduate of the Culinary Institute of American and Cordon Bleu. I've got one hell of a culinary pedigree, but working under Chef Toussaint was the cherry on top. Vasily was a regular. I didn't know anything about him back then. He was just a flashy Russian guy who got fatter every time I saw him. That's all I knew. You've got to believe me."

Anya sat stone-faced. "Do not lie to me, and I will believe you, but I am very good at knowing when someone is lying."

He wiped a bead of sweat from his brow. "I'm not going to lie to you. What good would it do?"

"It would only do harm," she said.

He continued. "So, this one night, Chef Toussaint sent me to Vasily's table. No one ever went to Vasily's table other than the chef or his personal waiter. I knew something wasn't right, but I refused to disobey Chef Toussaint. When I got to Vasily's table, he never looked up at me. He simply reached for the hem of my apron, lifted it up, and read the embroidery."

Anya found herself intrigued but tried to appear disinterested. "What did it say?"

"NOLA."

"NOLA? What does this mean?"

"Look around," he said. "It's all around you. It means New Orleans, Louisiana, but specifically, it meant Emeril Lagasse's restaurant here. I was a guest chef on Chef Lagasse's television show a long time ago, and he gave me the apron. It's always been a prized possession of mine. I still wear it every day."

Anya gave him the icy Russian gaze. "I do not care about apron. I care about Vasily Orlov."

"You may not care about the apron now, but you will when you understand what it means."

"Continue. Why did Vasily care about apron?"

"I had no idea at the time, but it became a huge turning point in my career and my life. He looked at the name and waved me away without a word. When I got back to the kitchen, the chef asked me what I said to Mr. Orlov. I said, 'Nothing. He just looked at my apron and sent me away.'"

"What did Toussaint say?"

"He ordered me to wash my hands and get back to work, so that's what I did. I forgot all about the strange encounter for a couple of months. Then late one night after I'd closed the kitchen, a big Russian guy met me at the back door, a lot like you did, but he didn't have the personality. He told me his boss wanted to talk to me, and he pointed toward the back seat of a big, black sedan. I told him I didn't know who he was and that I wasn't getting in the car with him in the middle of the night. He shrugged and said, 'You are getting in car—either on your own, or I will put you in car. Is up to you.' I'll never forget it."

"Did you get in?"

"No, he put me in and drove me to a warehouse down by the docks in Vancouver. I was terrified. I cook. That's it. That's all I do. It's all I know how to do. Now, I'm in the back of a car with some crazy Russian driving me into a warehouse. I didn't know what was happening. I didn't have any money, so unless these guys wanted a soufflé, I had nothing to offer them."

Anya continued her stoic demeanor, so Gerard kept talking.

"So, the crazy Russian driver yanks me out of the car and shoves me toward a pair of swinging metal doors. I asked him what his boss wanted with me, but he didn't offer an answer. He just stood in front of the doors with his arms crossed until Vasily Orlov walks in and sits down. The muscle said, 'That's all, Vladimir,' and he disappeared. Vasily looked at me and said, 'Are you okay, Chef? You look like you're about to soil yourself.' He didn't put it quite that nice, but you get the picture."

Anya said, "This is same Vladimir who is now here in New Orleans with Orlov, no?"

"Yeah, same guy. Anyway, he said, 'I've got a proposition for you, NOLA. Take a look at this.' He opened an envelope of pictures and dumped them on the table. They were pictures of a building. It turned out to be Eden's View, but I didn't know it at the time. He told me that he and a partner wanted to provide the financing and the real estate for me to start my own restaurant in New Orleans. That's when he introduced me to a guy named Zakhar Belyaev."

The name immediately caught Anya's attention as the same man whose life she'd saved in Vancouver when a Russian assassin had tried to kill him.

"What?" Gerard asked. "What's that look about?. Do you know Belyaev?"

"Continue with story," Anya ordered.

"To make a long story short, the two of them gave me a million dollars to remodel a building they owned here in New Orleans and turn it into a world-class fine-dining restaurant. I took their money, turned in my notice to Chef Toussaint, and moved to New Orleans."

"One million dollars is a lot of money. How long will it take you to pay them back?"

"That's the thing," he said. "They didn't want their money back. They owned the building, so they were essentially financing the remodel of their own building. All they wanted was to make sure I served some traditional Russian dishes and that they and their friends always ate for free. At least that's all they wanted at first, but it didn't take long for the other demands to begin."

"What were other demands?"

"Initially, it was some caviar. They wanted to import some caviar for the restaurant, but they wouldn't tell me where they were getting it. It was the good stuff . . . some of the highest quality I've ever seen. When I asked about it, they told me I didn't need to worry about it. Since I wasn't paying for it or placing the orders, nobody would ever care where it was coming from. It was Russian beluga caviar, and it was arriving by the truckload. It came and went, but I sold thousands of dollars worth of the stuff. After that, the fish came."

"What fish?"

"Chilean sea bass. It's one of the most highly regulated commercial fish in the world. It can only be imported under strict—"

"Yes, I know this. What is next after fish?"

He shook his head. "This is where it really gets weird. They sent me to China to learn about an exotic wine from Asia."

"This is tiger wine, yes?"

Gerard emptied his tea mug into his mouth. "Yes. I learned to grind the bones and blend the wine, and I also learned the precise ratios of the formulas for a dozen different kinds of tiger bone wine. I'd never heard of the stuff until then, but when I got home, they had a voodoo high priestess and a dead tiger in my kitchen. That was the limit for me. I told them I wouldn't do it. I wasn't going to prison for them. That's when Orlov stood up and walked out. I thought that might be the end of it, but Vladimir came in with a stack of invoices for tons of caviar and illegal Chilean sea bass with my name all over them. At the bottom of the stack were a dozen pictures of my mother in her nursing home. Vladimir said, 'It would be a shame to see something terrible happen to your mother, especially while her only son was sitting in prison for poaching and illegal importation and distribution of contraband fish and caviar.'"

28

Nozh i T'ma
(Knife and Darkness)

Anya listened intently as Chef Christian Gerard laid out his history with Vasily Orlov. The longer the chef spoke, the more fluid the story became.

Anya said, "I think phrase for this in English is *victim of circumstance*. There are many things I can do to help you. I will begin first with Vladimir. I have other business with him that is also unfinished. For now, I need from you only one thing."

Gerard laid his head in his hands. "What is it?"

"I need for you to act normally, as if no one knows this secret. If you change how you behave with Orlov or Vladimir, they will be suspicious. This is understood, yes?"

"Yeah, I got it. But I have a question for you."

"I will give answer, if possible."

"How long?"

"This I cannot tell you because I do not know. There are many variables, and this is serious situation. I promise to you, though, I will protect you, and I will not tell Orlov or Vladimir about our discussion. This is good for you, yes?"

He slowly rocked his head in his hands. "None of this is good for me. They'll kill me if they suspect I've ratted them out. You don't know these kinds of people. They're more dangerous than you can understand."

Anya took his hands. "These are exactly the kinds of people I understand. I know everything about them, and I am far more dangerous than all of them combined. They have only one fear. This fear is losing their power and money. I do not have such fear, so this makes me very dangerous for these people. Is important that you trust me. You have seen what I can do with darkness and knife. These are my weapons."

* * *

Back at the hospital on Naval Air Station New Orleans, Anya stepped from the elevator and onto the fourth floor, then turned instinctually toward room 477. She tapped on the heavy oak door, but no one answered from inside. Moving silently, she turned the handle and stepped into the room. Pyotr Evanoff lay on his side, her tiny American flag still tucked behind his ear, and breathing in sleep's long, deep rhythm. Anya crossed the room and watched the defector's chiseled features in perfect peace. The narcotics in his body provided the sleep, but his Eastern European lineage shaped the features of his face. Anya's mind flashed back to a time when she'd watched the American covert operative, Chase Fulton, sleeping like a child aboard the boat he called his home. The affection she'd felt for Chase in those moments had been the first taste of humanity she'd ever known. Kindness and sincerity were concepts beyond her realm of understanding. She'd known only emotionless service to the Kremlin, but Chase had shown her a tenderness she hadn't dreamed existed. Their worlds had been diametrically opposed all those years before, but now, with every new mission with the Justice Department, she became a little more American, a little more sincere, and perhaps even more human.

The man lying in sleep's merciful embrace before her had known the bitter truths of life behind the Iron Curtain, and he'd sacrificed everything he'd known to become an American. Like her, his family had been stolen from him, and the concept of home had become a choice rather than a foundation. His body would heal in time, but the ravages of his memories would forever cut new scars until he drew his final breath. Perhaps that perpetual sword laying waste to Peter's childhood was the same blade Anya felt every time she longed to know a childhood innocence and humanity she could never experience.

Without a sound, she left the room and closed the door without disturbing the man inside—the man who may represent the part of her that had always been empty and longing to know anything other than loneliness.

Gwynn hadn't surrendered to drug-induced sleep, and Anya found her pacing the floor of her room in street clothes with a notepad and pen poised in her hands.

"Why are you not in bed as Agent White directed?"

She looked up and lightly touched her hairline with the tips of her fingers. "Hey, you. I'm feeling much better. The nurse told me I could get dressed. I think the doctors are going to release me anytime now. Where have you been?"

"I have been with the chef, and he told me fascinating story, but I will tell to whole team only once instead of many times. Where are Ray and Dave?"

Gwynn checked her watch. "They should be back any minute. They went to find something to eat. And I guess Peter's in his room. I haven't seen him since you left this morning."

"Yes, he is sleeping. I checked on him."

"What's that look about?" Gwynn asked.

"I do not know what you are asking. I have no look."

Gwynn giggled. "Oh, yes, you do. You've got what my father used to call the 'googly eyes.' You've got a crush on Peter. Admit it."

"Googly eyes? This is not real word. I am only concerned for Peter. He is badly hurt and needs time to heal. This is all."

Gwynn continued grinning. "Googly eyes are very real, and you've got them. The only other time I've ever seen you like this is when you talk about Chase."

"No, this is not true. I cannot think of relationship with man. I have too many responsibilities. Responsibilities you cannot understand."

Gwynn surrendered. "Okay, okay, I won't push it. But Peter's crushing on you, too. And that's all I'm going to say about it."

Anya pointed toward Gwynn's pad. "What are you writing?"

"Oh, this? Just some notes and questions I have about the case."

Anya held out a hand, and Gwynn placed the pad in her palm.

Anya skimmed through the list and looked up. "I think I will have answers for all of these questions when I tell you about Gerard."

"Good," Gwynn said. "It's about time we get some answers. This case is falling apart around us."

Anya surrendered the pad back to Gwynn. "I think case is coming together nicely. You will feel same after briefing."

White and Dave Young came through the door, balancing three bags and four drinks.

White handed a bag to Anya. "There you are. What took you so long?"

She took the bag and peered inside. "Unlike you, I have been working. What is this in bag?"

"I'm always working, Red Sonja. It's a full-time job keeping track of you and your band of shot-up, beat-up misfits. Speaking of shot-up, your boyfriend down the hall is apparently tough as ball bearings."

Anya pulled a sandwich from the bag. "First, he is not my boyfriend, and then I do not know this phrase, *tough as ball bearings.*"

White unrolled a shrimp po' boy from its paper and took his first bite. "Mmm. First, if he's not your boyfriend yet, he sure wants to be, and second, he's apparently hard to kill."

Anya unrolled her sandwich and joined White in diving into the sandwich. "You are right. This is delicious."

White wiped his mouth. "It's called a po' boy down here, and there's no other sandwich like it anywhere in the world."

"Is very good. I would like to now give briefing while we eat."

Without slowing his po' boy consumption, White motioned for her to continue.

She began. "I spoke with Chef Gerard, and I think he is pleased we are here. He is, as you say, in over his head."

White said, "Do you really mean *we*, or is he glad *you* are here?"

"He does not know about you yet. He only knows of me, but I told him I could help, and he gave to me long story."

"Okay. Let's have it."

She spent the next twenty minutes laying out the story Gerard had told her. Everyone listened carefully but only interrupted a few times for clarification.

White said, "So, how did you tell him you were going to help?"

"I gave him nothing specific, but he is afraid. He fears Orlov will have him killed if he involves police."

Gwynn asked, "Does he know you're a fed?"

Anya let out a hesitant sound. "He asked if I was police officer, and I gave only vague answer."

Gwynn turned to White. "So, how do we handle this? Do we start flashing badges and cuffs, or do we leave it to Anya and save the lights and sirens for the grand finale?"

"For now, it's all Anya. Gerard thinks he has an ally, so I'd like to keep that illusion floating as long as possible. Once it sinks, our cover is busted. As long as it's Anya's gig, we can stay in the shadows and provide support and cover. She's got a lot of latitude the rest of us don't have."

Gwynn said, "We'll really be walking a tight rope with any evidence Anya gathers through untraditional means."

White took a long breath and let it out. "Something tells me this one won't ever see the inside of a courtroom. There are too many heavy hitters with overblown egos in the game. I suspect they'll run home to the motherland or kill each other before this is all over."

"We will not arrest Vladimir," Anya said. "My knife and darkness of night will make him pay for what he has done, especially what he did to Gwynn."

White narrowed his eyes. "We're not vigilantes, Anya. We're federal law enforcement officers."

Anya returned his gaze and pulled her credential pack from her pocket, then slid it across the table. "No one tries to kill my friend without paying highest price. You will keep badge for me until I am no longer Avenging Angel."

White lifted his cup and used the bottom edge to slide the credentials back to Anya. "Those are safer with you, and if anyone ever kicks me in the head . . ." Instead of finishing the statement, he shrugged and made his exit.

Anya gave Gwynn a knowing glance. "That was permission, yes?"

Gwynn laughed. "That's how I'd take it."

The Russian re-pocketed the credentials and gave Gwynn a wink. "I have things to do, so I will leave you and Dave alone while you are waiting for doctor to say you can come with me tonight."

"*The* doctor," Gwynn said. "You're waiting for *the* doctor."

"Yes, I know," Anya said. "But is better if I sound like real Russian while we are here."

"All right, I'll give you that one. But we're going to fix your English when this is over."

"I have better idea. When this is over, I will take you to place to work on your Russian."

Gwynn looked at Dave and then back at Anya, then she gave her partner a friendly wave of the fingertips.

Anya took the hint. "Call me when *the* doctor says you are finished being patient."

29

ZASHCHITNOYE ZAKLYUCHENIYE
(PROTECTIVE CUSTODY)

Anya slipped silently back into room 477 to find Peter in the same position she left him. She eased onto the chair near the window and reclined as quietly as possible. The sleep of which she'd been deprived the prior night reclaimed its territory, and she drifted into slumber.

Two hours later, she woke to the sound of restless motion from Peter's bed and pain replacing narcotic bliss. She stretched and stood from the chair. "Are you okay?"

Peter opened his eyes and grimaced. "You're not my nurse."

She stepped closer. "No, but I can get her for you."

"I think I prefer you."

Anya smiled and found herself surprised by her reaction to Peter's discomfort. "Are you hurting?"

He smacked his lips. "I'm thirsty."

She poured a cup of water and helped him sit up as a gentle knock came at the door, followed by the entrance of a nurse in blue scrubs. Anya eyed the young woman. "You are not same as before. Other nurse wore green."

The nurse kept coming. "Nope, we had a shift change. I'm the evening nurse. My name is Tera, and I'll be here until eleven o'clock tonight. I just need to chart your vitals. How are you feeling?"

Before Peter could respond, Anya said, "He is in pain and needs more morphine."

Tera raised an eyebrow. "And are you Mr. Evans's wife?"

"Yes. Give to him more morphine."

"Well, ma'am, your, uh, *husband* isn't on morphine. He's on Tramadol, and I'll take care of that after I take his vitals."

Peter smiled up at Anya, amused by her concern.

The nurse checked his blood pressure and pulled the sheet down to check the bandages on his abdomen. "It looks like you're having a little bleeding, but that's normal. The doctor will take a look when he does afternoon rounds. Other than pain meds, is there anything you need?"

"Maybe a blanket for my, uh . . . wife, if you have one. She didn't get much sleep last night."

The nurse installed a new bag of IV fluid and added a syringe of Tramadol into the line before pulling a blanket from the overhead cabinet. "Here you go, Mrs. Evans. The doctor will be in between three and four. Just ring if you need anything."

Through the narcotic haze, Peter said, "Why did you tell her you were my wife?"

"You do not have wife, do you?"

"Apparently, I do, but I don't remember the honeymoon."

Anya smirked. "Trust me, you would never forget honeymoon with me."

"I have no doubt," he said as the drug took its toll and he drifted off again.

Anya curled up beneath the blanket and slept for another ninety minutes before her phone chirped. She whispered, "Yes?"

"Hey, it's Gwynn. The doctor just discharged me. Where are you?" Anya blinked and surveyed the room. "I am still inside hospital. I will come to your room."

"I'm not in my room. I'm downstairs in the lobby."

"Okay, I will be there in minutes."

She left her "husband" sleeping peacefully in his room and headed for the stairs. The three flights of stairs stole the look of sleep from her eyes and prevented her from appearing out of the elevator and having to answer questions.

"There you are," Gwynn said. "Where have you been?"

"I was back there," Anya said. "How would you like beignet and coffee before we go to work?"

"I'm always up for beignets and coffee, but what are you planning for tonight?"

"Is simple plan. We will find Vladimir, and he will tell us everything."

"Oh, it's that easy, is it?"

"It is for me when I am holding man's life in my hands. He will tell to us truth, or he will die inside of lie."

* * *

The stop at Café Du Monde killed ninety minutes and gave the Earth time to rotate beneath the sun. When darkness overtakes the city of New Orleans, ageless spirits come out to play—some joyful and harmless, but some, like the pair of avenging angels, frolicked beneath a sinister cold the light of day cannot contain.

They found their prey waiting outside Eden's View and smoking a Turkish cigarette beside the dumpster. Anya approached from behind the man, and Gwynn followed half a dozen steps behind.

Vladimir took a long draw on his cigarette and let his hand fall to his side. Seconds later, a plume of foul-smelling gray smoke rose from his lips. The black elastic band of his eyepatch encircled his head, reminding the approaching Russian of the deadly garrote she'd mastered under the terrifying direction of her former Soviet masters. Would she exact her final revenge on the man who attacked her friend and partner, or would she only continue his torture for the deed he would regret for the short time he had left on Earth?

With the decision made, Anya slowed her pace, and Gwynn matched the new stride. Anya stepped behind the man and laced her right arm around his neck, locking the hold with her left. "Remember me?"

The man jerked and twisted against the coming sleep into which he would dissolve. Anya let him pull her from her feet and sling her like a rag-doll, but she never released the hold she had on his neck.

Gwynn drew her pistol in preparation for the second Anya would be thrown free of the man's back, but that moment never came. With every twist of his body and stride of his feet, he grew weaker until tunnel vision overtook the one good eye he had left and darkness fell on him. His knees softened, and Anya followed him to the ground, her arms still locked around his head. The hold, designed to render a man unconscious in seconds, worked flawlessly, leaving Vladimir little more than two hundred pounds of Russian putty in Anya's hands.

She let his head fall to the ground and turned to see Gwynn standing only a few feet away with her pistol drawn and focused intently on the man.

"How long will he be out?"

Anya stood. "Not long, but long enough for us to get him inside car for interrogation."

"Whatever you say. I'll get the Suburban."

Gwynn holstered her Glock and jogged toward the parking lot. She was back in minutes, and the two hefted their prisoner into the back seat.

"Give to me two pairs of handcuffs."

Gwynn produced the stainless-steel restraints and passed them to her partner. Anya laced one cuff around Vladimir's right hand and pulled his arm across his chest. She connected the other cuff to the headrest and repeated the process with the other set of cuffs, leaving his arms drawn across his chest and affixed to opposing headrests.

As he started to squirm, Anya slapped his face far more violently than Gwynn expected. The sting and sound of the attack brought Vladimir from his slumber.

Anya slipped across the seat, taking up a position behind the man while Gwynn knelt on the front seat, facing their prisoner.

"Welcome back, sleepyhead. I hope you enjoyed your nap."

The man glared at Gwynn through his one good eye as recognition overtook him. He stammered, "I thought you were . . ."

Gwynn smiled. "What? Dead? Whatever gave you that idea?"

He strained against his restraints. "Are you the one who . . . ?"

Gwynn widened her smile. "Nope. That would be my guardian angel. She hates it when people try to hurt me, so I'll pray for your soul. In the meantime, I have a few questions."

He spat, sending spittle into Gwynn's face, and Anya leapt into action. From behind him, she slid his eyepatch across his nose and mouth, forcing it beneath his chin. She slipped a hand beneath the strap, twisted, and pulled.

He bucked and pulled against the makeshift garrote until Anya pressed the tip of her middle finger of her right hand against his eye. Accepting his coming fate, he gagged and settled against the seatback.

"Very good," Anya said. "I am going to allow you to breathe, and you will apologize. Nod if you understand."

He didn't move, so she pulled the eyepatch a little tighter until submission took hold and he nodded in compliance. She eased the stress on the garrote until Vladimir took in a horrified breath.

With his lungs filled with enough air to speak, he whispered, "*Mne zhal'.*"

Anya extended her arm and withdrew a powerful hammer fist into her captive's nose, crushing cartilage and sending blood in every direction. "English!"

Amid his agonized admission, guttural sounds like those of a wounded animal poured from his mouth. "I am sorry."

Anya gave the garrote a pull to remind him of the control she held over him. "You will now answer every question with only truth. You understand this, yes?"

"Yes."

"If you had answered questions for us inside car instead of trying to kill us, this would not be happening to you. All of this is your fault."

He gasped and tried to shake off the pain of the broken nose. What do you want to know?"

Gwynn turned into the master interrogator she was born to be but could never become inside a locked room with cameras and microphones. "Let's start with how long you've worked for Vasily Orlov."

He groaned. "I don't remember."

She lifted the baton from beside the seat and inspected it closely, making sure Vladimir could see and almost feel the club. "One more try, Vlad. How long?"

He squeezed his eyelids closed, the left one partially covering the hole where his eye had once been. "I was going to say, I do not remember a time when I did not work for him. I was orphaned, and he took me in."

Gwynn rolled her eyes. "Aww, isn't that sweet? Did he also teach you to kick women in the head?" Before he could spit out a response, Gwynn landed the butt of the baton in his gut hard enough to garner a sickening groan. "You're not going to get any pity from us, Vlad. There are only two possible outcomes from this interview. One, my partner will kill you slowly and play in your blood, or two, you'll tell us everything we want to know, and you'll spend the rest of your life right here in America where you belong, albeit behind the bars of a federal prison."

"You two are not police. Police cannot do things like this."

Gwynn tapped the baton against his knee. "Believe what you'd like, Vlad, but if that's the path you want to walk, I guess there's only *one* way this is going to end." He swallowed hard, and Gwynn continued. "Let's get down to business, Vlad. You don't mind if I call you Vlad, do you? Good. I thought not. Tell us about the caviar."

Behind the battered surface of his rutty face, confusion appeared. "What?"

Gwynn gripped the club and scowled. "Don't make me hit you again, Vlad. I'm aiming lower next time."

"What do you want to know about caviar?"

"When did Orlov start smuggling it into the country?"

Vladimir looked even more confused than before. "What do you mean? Mr. Orlov isn't smuggling anything. He's a businessman."

Just as promised, Gwynn delivered the blow a foot lower than the previous strike, and the man gagged, heaving in pain.

When he caught his breath, Gwynn leaned close. "No more lies, Vlad! We'll come back to the caviar. Let's talk about the Chilean seabass."

Vladimir whimpered. "All of this for caviar and seabass? What is happening to me?"

Gwynn slid the tip of the baton beneath his chin. "Oh, I think you know quite well what this is about, but we'll get to that. For now, how about telling us exactly what you do for Vasily Orlov."

"Please let me breathe," he begged.

Gwynn met Anya's eyes and gave her a nod. She loosened the eyepatch band around his neck, and he inhaled a long, deep breath. "Thank you. I drive. Sometimes I do surveillance when Mr. Orlov needs to know what someone is doing. That's what I was doing the morning you two—"

Gwynn tapped his forehead with the baton. "Yeah, Vlad. We know that part. What else?"

"I run the clubs."

"Clubs?" Gwynn asked. "Which clubs?"

"The one where your friend put out my eye, and two more like that one."

Gwynn nodded. "So, we'll add prostitution to your long list of sins."

"No! We let some low-level drug stuff happen in the clubs, but the girls are clean. If we catch any of them hooking, they're out. Mr. Orlov detests prostitution."

"Okay, you can pretend we believe you on that one, but you can bet your other eye we're going to check it out."

"I've got no reason to lie about that."

"Let's get back to the fish."

He groaned and shook his head. "What do you want to know about fish? They're just fish the chef brings in. That's all I know about them. Sometimes I drive down to Grand Isle to meet the ship, but they're just fish."

Gwynn glanced at Anya and mouthed, "The chef?"

Anya leaned close to Vladimir's ear. "What do you mean chef brings in the fish? This is Vasily Orlov who brings fish and caviar into country, yes?"

Vladimir jerked his head away and drove it violently back toward Anya's forehead. Anya and Gwynn reacted in the same instant. Anya met the coming blow with her elbow crashing into his temple, while Gwynn drove the baton into the man's face where his nose had once been. His neck went limp, and his chin fell to his chest. The rise and fall of his chest said he was alive but unconscious.

Gwynn took advantage of the moment. "Did he say the chef was bringing in the caviar and fish?"

"Yes, this is what he said, but this cannot be true."

"What if we've got this whole thing backward? What if Orlov isn't the smuggler and Gerard *is* at the heart of the whole scheme?"

Anya cocked her head in thought. "I do not know. If this is so, chef is very good liar. I believed him."

Gwynn motioned toward their prisoner. "So, what do we do with this guy while we figure out what's really going on?"

"You are supposed to know these things. You are lawyer with gun and badge, and you have been to Academy."

"Yeah, well, they never covered this at the Academy, but I guess we could stick him in protective custody while we sort it out."

"I have more questions first. Where is medical kit?"

Gwynn said, "It's beside you in the orange and white bag, but this guy needs more help than a little first aid."

Anya pulled open the bag, slipped a pack of smelling salts from its wrapper, and cracked the capsule. She stuck it beneath Vladimir's nose and waited for him to inhale. As the ammonia poured into his sinuses, the man jerked away and growled.

"Hit him with water again," Anya ordered.

Gwynn obeyed, sending half a bottle of cold water splashing into his battered face.

Anya spoke barely above a whisper. "We hurt you because you tried to hurt me. This will not happen again, yes?" He nodded, and she said, "No! You will answer with words!"

"No, it won't happen again."

"Good, now tell me how Vasily Orlov makes money."

"He owns buildings and ships. He's a commercial real estate guy. Everybody knows that."

"What kinds of ships?" Anya said.

"I don't know, like tugboats and small freighters, I think. I don't know anything about boats."

She said, "Now tell us about Zakhar Belyaev."

"No! You can kill me. Do whatever you want, but I'm not ratting on Belyaev. If you're looking for a bad guy, he's the one. But you're not getting the goods from me."

"Why are you afraid of him but you are not afraid of Orlov?"

"Because Mr. Orlov is a businessman, not a *psikhopat*."

"Why do you think Belyaev is a psychopath?"

"I told you, you can kill me, whatever, but I ain't talking about Belyaev."

"That's enough," Gwynn said. "Get him down from the headrests and cuff him. Our little New Orleans gig just turned international."

Gwynn slid behind the wheel of the Suburban, and Anya climbed across the seat to join her in the front after rearranging Vladimir's handcuffs into a more traditional configuration. Ten minutes later, they pulled into the parking garage of the United States District Court for the Eastern District of Louisiana on Poydras Street.

Two uniformed officers pulled Vladimir from the back seat and inspected the damage to his face. "We'll get you cleaned up and tucked away someplace safe. You're not under arrest. You're being provided protection in the custody of the United States Department of Justice. Do you understand?"

Vladimir said, "I'm not under arrest?"

"No," said one of the officers. "You're being provided protection by the United States. You'll be safe here."

Vladimir motioned toward Gwynn and Anya. "Safe from them?"

Before the officer could investigate the situation any further, Gwynn pulled away, leaving Vladimir even more confused than before.

"We have to brief Agent White," Gwynn said as she pulled back onto the street.

Anya picked up her phone and dialed White's number. "Hello, it is Anya. We have briefing for you, but we should not do it on phone. It is very confusion."

White said, "Pick me up at Jackson Square."

They arrived only minutes later, and White kicked Anya out of the front seat. "Okay, let's hear it."

They detailed their encounter with Vladimir practically word for word, and White listened intently.

"You've got to be kidding me," he said. "What are the chances that you'd save Zakhar Belyaev's life in Vancouver only days before starting this mission?"

Anya ignored the question. "I have to speak with chef again. I will not let him lie to me this time."

White said, "No! Not yet. We'll get to that, but for now, we're just going to watch him. If he's the victim in all of this, he won't change his routine, but if he's the real mastermind, he'll run. And if he runs, we'll catch him."

Gwynn said, "I think it's time to bring Johnny Mac in out of the cold. With the mission changing, we need him in a suit more than we need him sleeping in a cardboard box. Don't you agree?"

"I'm already on it, but that's good thinking, Davis. You're learning. While you're on a roll, what would be your next call if you were in charge?"

Gwynn let the rare compliment from White roll around inside her head for a moment. "I'd pick up Vasily Orlov for questioning."

"So, you think the rest of the op should be by the book?"

"I don't know about the rest of the operation, but I think we need Orlov on the record. If Gerard is the bad guy, our cover is blown already. If he's not, he'll likely warn Orlov that we're asking a lot of questions. Either way, the only sensible next move is to put Orlov under the spotlight."

White almost smiled. "Go get him. Do you need any additional muscle?"

Gwynn grimaced. "Maybe it would be better if someone else picked him up. Even if we're blown, that doesn't necessarily mean Orlov knows exactly what Anya and I are . . . yet."

White couldn't suppress the smile any longer. "I was afraid Anya was going to ruin you, but I was wrong. You're on your way up, Special Agent Davis. I'll have Johnny Mac and uniforms pick up Orlov, then I'll interrogate him, and you two can play voyeur from behind the looking glass."

Anya held up a finger. "I have one question before all of this happens."

"Let's hear it."

"How is Peter?"

Gwynn hissed. "Anya, no. This isn't the time."

White said, "Relax. He's going to be fine. I checked on him last night, and he had a few questions about you, Ms. Burinkova. Be careful what you step into, though. You never know what you're getting with those State Department guys."

She almost blushed.

White made a telephone call and turned to face Gwynn and Anya. "We've got a few of hours before they'll have Orlov rolled up, so if you two want to get some rest, I'll meet you at the federal courthouse at eight thirty."

Gwynn asked, "Where are we supposed to rest? Our yacht sailed away."

White pulled a hotel key from his pocket and tossed it to Gwynn. "We picked up an adjoining room at my hotel. You two can crash there."

White stepped from the Suburban and disappeared into the crowd.

Gwynn grabbed Anya's arm. "That sounded like jealousy, if you ask me."

Anya screwed up her face. "What are you talking about?"

"You know, Agent White. He sounded a little jealous about Peter. I think he probably thinks about you more than you know."

"This is ridiculous. He hates me, and he will be glad when I am no longer problem for him."

"Believe what you want, but I see how he looks at you."

"Stop this silliness. I am tired."

Sleep came quickly for the pair while Johnny Mac and White spent the remaining hours of darkness encouraging Vasily Orlov to have a little chat with them.

Just before 9:00 a.m., White ushered the bulbous Russian into a white-collar interrogation room. The seats were padded, and the light was anything but harsh. Special Agents Gwynn Davis and Ana Fulton remained hidden behind the two-way mirror consuming one wall of the room.

White asked Orlov, "Is there anything I can get you?"

"You can get me out of here. I have rights in this country, and you haven't Mirandized me."

White said, "You're not under arrest, Mr. Orlov. We just have a few questions, and then you can be on your way. That's all."

White left the room and joined Anya and Gwynn.

"Aren't you going to question him?" Gwynn asked.

"Eventually, I will, but Johnny Mac is going to take the first crack at him. You know the routine—a little good cop, bad cop."

Gwynn said, "For Orlov's sake, I hope you're the good cop."

White grinned. "Never."

After letting the miserably obese Russian sit alone in the interrogation room for half an hour, Johnny Mac strolled in and took off his jacket. An empty shoulder holster hung beneath his left arm, and a pair of gleaming handcuffs dangled from the back of his belt.

He held up his DOJ credentials for Orlov to examine. "I'm Special Agent Johnathon McIntyre, and I'm going to ask you some questions. Is that all right with you, Mr. Orlov?"

"No! It is not all right. If I am not under arrest, I demand to be released."

Johnny Mac pulled a handcuff key from his pocket and leaned down. "Sure. Give me your hands, and I'll uncuff you. You're free to walk right out of the United States federal courthouse in broad daylight with two of Zakhar Belyaev's men sitting across the street."

Orlov searched the agent's face for any sign of deceit, and Johnny Mac urged, "Come on. Give me your hands. I'll show you the way out."

Orlov glared toward the mirrored glass. "Who is behind there?"

Johnny shrugged. "I don't know. I didn't look, but it's probably a federal prosecutor, my boss, and maybe a criminal psychologist watching every move you make. If it'll make you feel better, I'll turn the table so they can only see your back."

Orlov licked his lips as perspiration began to form on his forehead. "Why would a federal prosecutor have any interest in me?"

"I don't know, but I'm sure we can figure it out together. Let's start with your tax returns."

He pulled a stack of file folders from inside a box beside the table and thumbed through the first collection of returns. "You seem to be doing pretty well here in New Orleans. I'd say you're living the American dream, wouldn't you?"

Orlov rattled his handcuffs. "Are these really necessary?"

Johnny Mac didn't look up. "No, I'll be glad to take them off if you'd like, but then we have to bring a couple of armed guards in to protect me in case you decide you want things to turn violent. Are you a violent man, Mr. Orlov?"

"No! I'm just a businessman. My competition may perceive me as dangerous, but I'm no threat to you."

Johnny checked his watch and gave a yawn. "I didn't ask if you were dangerous. I asked if you were violent."

"They are the same," Orlov grunted.

Finally, Johnny looked up. "Oh, I see you don't have the command of the English language you think you have. *Violent* means you tend to lash out and hurt people around you. *Dangerous* means something entirely different. *Dangerous* means you have power over someone else and you can do great harm to that person. Harm doesn't always come through violence. Sometimes it comes in the form of forensic accountants and field agents from the Internal Revenue Service. Sometimes it comes wearing a robe and sitting on the federal bench. Sometimes it even comes in the form of people you thought were your friends. Do you have many close friends, Vasily?"

The Russian scowled. "You're threatening me with an audit and a federal judge. Is that what you're doing?"

"No, I was merely explaining the difference between violence and danger. That's all. So, tell me why you think you're here."

"I think I'm here because of a terrible decision made by one or more of your superiors, Special Agent."

Johnny ignored the jab and continued thumbing through Orlov's tax returns. "Tell me about the chef at Eden's View."

"What about him?"

"What do you know about him? That's all."

Orlov shot a glance back toward the mirror. "I know he is a brilliant and creative chef."

Johnny let his eyes roam over Orlov's massive body. "You look like a man who knows a thing or two about good food."

"Are you calling me fat, Special Agent?"

"No, you don't need me to point that out. Why did you finance Gerard's restaurant?"

"What? Why would you think I financed anything for him?"

"Are you saying you don't own the building?"

"Yes. I'm saying exactly that. I have never financed anything for Gerard or any other chef. The restaurant business is the most volatile business in the world. I'm a practical man, and I deal in practical scenarios. I would never invest in a restaurant. It would appear I am not the only one who has eaten too much. Clearly, you've been fed some very bad information, and you seem to have swallowed every bite."

Johnny tried to remain steadfast, but Orlov had planted a seed of doubt, leaving the young agent dealing with the fact that the whole investigation could hinge on what he did next.

"So, tell me, Mr. Orlov, when did you first meet Chef Gerard?"

"When he approached me about leasing one of my buildings."

"And where was this meeting?"

"In my office."

Johnny paused. "In New Orleans?"

"Yes, of course in New Orleans. What are you fishing for, Special Agent?"

Behind the glass, Ray White leapt to his feet, but he wasn't fast enough to stop Johnny's next question. "Are you sure you didn't meet Chef Gerard in Vancouver?"

Before Orlov could answer, White burst through the door and into the interrogation room. "Get out, Agent McIntyre."

Without hesitation, Johnny left the room, closing the door as he went. Behind the glass, he said, "Why did he jerk me out of there? I thought I was gaining ground."

Gwynn put her hand on Johnny's shoulder. "You have no idea how this thing just turned inside out. If Orlov is telling the truth, we've made a huge mistake."

"What are you talking about?"

Gwynn shot her finger to her lips. "Shh. Listen."

Orlov looked up at White. "Let me guess . . ." He eyed White for a long moment. "You're definitely not the prosecutor. Your suit isn't good enough. I don't think you're a shrink, so that must mean you're in charge and your whole case is falling apart."

"Very astute, Vasily, but we've got statements contradicting yours, and I tend to believe the word of productive members of society over Russian mobsters."

Orlov lowered his eyebrows. "Because I have a slight accent I'm still working on and I was born in the Soviet Union, you think I'm Russian mafia?"

"The whole world knows you're Russian mafia, Vasily. I know my colleague said you weren't under arrest, but that's about to change."

"And what charges will you bring against me?"

"We'll start with making a false statement to police, interfering with a federal investigation, and obstruction of justice. That'll be enough for me to hold you for a few days while we stack up the RICO charges."

Orlov smiled. "I love this part."

"What part?" White demanded.

Orlov pointed toward the files still resting on the table. "Take a look at those. If they really are my tax returns, you'll see that I'm far more than just a productive member of society."

"Is this the part where you brag about paying my salary because you pay your taxes?"

"No, even I wouldn't stoop that low, whatever your name is. This is the part where I have absolutely nothing to hide. I am, as you say here in America, an open book."

Changing tactics, White leaned back in his chair and tossed his credential pack onto the table. "I'm Supervisory Special Agent Ray White with Justice, and I have your man, Vladimir, down the hall. He's singing like a bird."

Orlov read White's credential carefully. "I guess that means the Russian girl and her beautiful friend were undercover officers. I am sorry to hear of their demise. I'm sure Vladimir will say anything he has to say to avoid charges of murder for what happened on the street."

For the first time, White smiled. He curled a finger toward the mirrored glass, and seconds later, the door to the interrogation room opened. Gwynn and Anya stepped into the room, and White said, "Do you mean these two women?"

Orlov examined their faces and chewed on his bottom lip. "Yes, but they are clearly not dead."

"Oh, no, they're quite alive. Do you know what that means?"

Orlov pondered the question but didn't respond.

"It means there are no charges pending against Vladimir. He's spilling his guts because it's the right thing to do."

Orlov ignored White and continued examining the two women. "Which one of you gouged out Vladimir's eye?"

White said, "Vladimir is a violent and dangerous man, Vasily. You of all people know this. That's why you hired him. If anyone hurt him, it was done only in self-defense."

Vasily locked eyes with White. "You are making a terrible mistake, Agent White. You seem to believe you know things that simply aren't true. I have never financed Chef Gerard's endeavors. I have never broken any federal laws of the United States, unless, of course, speeding on the interstate is a federal crime. And most of all"—Orlov smiled as if he'd just won the Powerball—"Vladimir is not my employee. I've never hired him for anything. He is my adopted son. I will confess that he has ideas about running a business that I do not share, but he is still my son. His clubs are, shall we say, a bit unappealing to most, but they, and he, are quite legal. It is a valorous attempt to make me believe my own son is providing damning information about me just down the hall, but I am not a small-minded street thug. I am a businessman, a father, and nothing more."

In a wasted attempt to come up with another avenue to approach Orlov, White ran his hands through his hair. "Look. Here's what's going to happen—"

Before he could finish his statement, Johnny Mac came bursting through the door to the interrogation room. "Gerard is running!"

31

POGONYA
(THE CHASE)

Supervisory Special Agent Ray White drove a finger through the air toward Vasily Orlov. "I'm not finished with you. If you leave the state of Louisiana before I get back, I will burn you to the ground. Do you hear me?"

Orlov sighed. "The truth is happening right under your nose, and you're too arrogant to see it. Go catch Gerard, Agent White. He's your enemy, not me."

White led the way from the interrogation room, and Gwynn grabbed the arm of the first uniform she spotted. "Cut the guy in interrogation room six loose."

"What about the guy in protective custody?" the officer asked.

Gwynn yelled, "Agent White! What about Vladimir?"

"Deal with it."

Gwynn considered her options. "Surrender him to the guy we were interrogating, and tell them both that they're free to go."

"Are you sure?"

"Just do it!" Gwynn ordered as she sprinted to catch up with her team.

When she caught them, Johnny Mac leapt behind the wheel of the Suburban with White in the front and Anya on the back seat.

Gwynn jumped in and slammed the door behind her. "Where's he going?"

Johnny Mac motioned toward White. "We don't know yet, but we'll know soon."

They pulled from the parking garage and accelerated through the congested streets with the blue light flashing on the dash and the siren blasting its piercing wail from behind the front grill of the SUV.

White pulled the phone away from his ear and tossed it to Gwynn. "Take care of that."

Gwynn caught the phone and stuck it to her ear. "Agent Davis."

"What happened to Agent White?" came a voice through the tiny speaker.

"Who is this?" Gwynn asked.

"It's the ops center. We're tracking your target. A team is in pursuit, but they lost him near the Louis Armstrong International Airport."

Gwynn covered the mouthpiece. "They lost him near Louis Armstrong."

Johnny stood on the brake and turned the eight-thousand-pound vehicle around in its own distance. Smoke poured from the tires as they fought for purchase on the asphalt. Horns blared and obscenities filled the air, but worrying about pissed-off motorists wasn't on Johnny Mac's mind.

"He's got to be flying private," White said. "Find the FBO, and get Homeland Security rolling!"

Gwynn said, "I can't do both!"

Johnny Mac clawed at his pocket and produced his phone. He tossed it to White as he weaved through traffic with the speedometer bouncing above one hundred.

Gwynn handed White's phone to Anya and yanked hers from her pocket. "Stay on with the ops center, and report anything they tell you."

Anya nodded and pressed the phone to her face. "This is Special Agent Fulton."

Gwynn said, "He has to be headed for Atlantic Aviation." She dialed furiously, then yelled into the phone, "This is Special Agent Gwynn Davis with the Justice Department. We're in pursuit of a suspect named Christian Gerard, and we have reason to believe he'll attempt to escape on a jet from your facility. Do not let him take off!"

The terrified voice on the phone said, "I can't stop anyone from taking off. I'm just the—"

Gwynn didn't listen for her to finish. She hung up and turned to Anya. "Get the control tower's number from the ops center."

Anya called out the number, and Gwynn dialed. Repeating the same instructions she'd given the woman at the fixed base operator, she ordered, "Do not clear any jets for takeoff!"

"Ma'am, I don't think you understand. This is an international airport. I don't have the authority to delay any flights."

"Okay, then. Don't delay any commercial flights, but don't you dare clear any private jets for takeoff. If you do, your career with the FAA is over."

White yelled over the siren into the phone. "Open the gate at Atlantic Aviation, and stop any jet trying to taxi out." He turned in his seat and asked, "Who's on with the ops center?"

"I am," Anya said.

White reached for the phone, and she stuck it in his hand. "This is White. Get somebody at the FAA to close that airport, now!"

He threw the phone back toward Anya, and she caught it on the first bounce. The voice on the other end was reciting reasons why that couldn't be done, but Anya cut in. "Trust me, you do not want to be reason we lose our suspect. Make it happen!"

White pointed through the windshield. "There! Get us through that gate!"

Johnny Mac maneuvered the truck like a sports car and hit the gate at seventy miles per hour. The tires squealed as they made the ninety-degree turn toward the Atlantic Aviation hangars. Dodging airplanes and fuel trucks, Johnny continued to accelerate across the parking apron.

Gwynn yelled, "There he is!"

Johnny and White looked up to see the nose of a mid-sized business jet taxiing from the main hangar at Atlantic. The twin turbines pushed the jet onto the taxiway westbound toward runway one one.

"Get the tower back on the phone," White ordered, and Gwynn had the controller on the line in seconds and stuck the phone into White's hand. He commanded, "Stop the jet in front of Atlantic Aviation and shut down this taxiway. I'm in a black SUV with blue lights and a siren." Without waiting for a response, he threw the phone back to Gwynn. "Get in front of him! Don't let him get to the runway."

Johnny pressed the accelerator to the floor, and the big engine of the Suburban howled as Johnny turned toward the jet. "I don't think I can make it beneath his wings. What do you think?"

White peered down the taxiway, mentally measuring the height. "It'll be close, but we have to try."

Johnny allowed the SUV to drift to the side of the taxiway to get the most vertical clearance possible beneath the jet's wing. The closer they came, the lower the wing appeared. "We'll never make it."

"Hit the grass and go around," White ordered, and Johnny let the tires leave the pavement.

The rear of the Suburban fishtailed, and grass and mud flew from the tires. He fought the wheel and accelerator to keep the vehicle moving toward the jet. "Hang on! This is going to hurt."

Everyone braced as the front tires hit the edge of the concrete, sending the Suburban bouncing and sliding back onto the pavement. Losing control, Johnny stepped on the brakes in a wasted effort to keep the SUV upright. The rear tires lost all traction and slid to the right. Johnny furiously fought the wheel, desperately trying to recover, but it wasn't enough. A tire finally found purchase, and the vehicle's momentum sent it tumbling and rolling across the ramp.

When they finally stopped tumbling, the Suburban came to rest upside down with bodies, equipment, and weapons spread all over the interior. Anya hung upside down in her seatbelt with the taste of blood in her mouth and chaos all around her. A quick inventory of her situation revealed Gwynn conscious but bleeding and the two front-seat passengers covered in white powder from the airbags. Neither White nor Johnny appeared to be conscious, but the powder floating near their mouths and noses said they were still alive.

Anya drove a thumb into the seatbelt release and fell onto her shoulders in the inverted vehicle. She braced Gwynn's body with her left arm and shoulder as she released her belt. Gwynn slid from the belt into Anya's waiting arms, and she laid her on her back. "Just relax. I do not think you are badly hurt, but do not move. I will get you out if there is fire."

Anya sniffed for the smell of fuel or flames, but the blast from the jet was all she could smell. Continuing her assessment of her situation, she discovered a rifle that had been concealed in the back of the SUV. She pulled it from its case and cycled the bolt. A .308 Winchester round fed from the magazine into the chamber, and she pulled the door handle. Her effort was rewarded with the sound of the handle breaking off in her hand. She threw a powerful kick to the window, but it withstood the blow without breaking. She tried several more times with the same result. Should a fire begin, the Suburban would become a flaming coffin for four, and the likelihood of escaping grew more distant with every attempt.

Gwynn reached up with a wilting hand and touched Anya's arm. In a weak, whispering voice, she said, "Glass is hardened."

Anya rolled onto her back, pulled the rifle to her shoulder, and closed her eyes. "Cover your ears if you can." She squeezed the trigger, and the massive concussion of the rifle filled the vehicle. She opened her eyes to see a small hole pierced through the center of the glass. Following up the shot with repeated kicks folded the glass outward in sheets of tiny shards until the hole was large enough for her body.

She grabbed a pistol from the debris and crawled through the opening, pulling the rifle behind her. She moved away from the inverted truck and positioned herself in the sniper's preferred position, lying prone with the rifle poised on its bipod. She cycled the bolt as the wail of sirens flooded her dampened hearing from the close shot from within the vehicle. Bringing the right engine into perfect sight alignment, she squeezed the trigger, sending the one hundred eighty grain projectile racing through the air at over twenty-six hundred feet per second. Gerard's jet may have outrun the Suburban, but it wouldn't outrun Anya's lead.

Fire exploded from the jet's right engine, followed closely by the engine's automatic fire-suppression system, shutting the engine down and cooling it before the fire could spread. The shot stopped the taxiing jet the same instant the first firetruck arrived.

Firefighters in silver-reflective suits tore at the SUV until every door was open and the three federal agents inside were pulled to safety. As one of the first responders approached Anya, she shoved him away and crawled to her feet. Although her body rocked with pain, she didn't believe any major bones had been broken, and she staggered toward the crippled jet, each step becoming easier and less painful until she was almost jogging. By the time she reached the left side of the jet, the door was already open. She drew the pistol she'd taken from the Suburban and raised it to eye level just as a uniformed flight attendant stepped into the door. The woman froze and threw her hands into the air.

Anya yelled, "Come out, and lie down on ground!"

The woman followed Anya's command, and the two pilots did the same. With the flight crew well clear of the airplane, she climbed the stairs with her pistol at the ready. If Gerard was willing to run, he was likely willing to fight, but Anya knew it would be a fight he couldn't win.

Warm blood trickled from her face, leaving streaks of deep red tracing their way across her skin. She could taste the iron and salt, but nothing could keep her from boarding the plane and confronting Gerard.

She took the stairs carefully, clearing the front of the airplane as she made her way through the door. As she stepped into the aisle of the luxury jet, she was shocked to see the turbaned heads of two Middle Easterners with their hands in the air.

Trying to recall the limited amount of Arabic her mind contained, she ordered, "*La tataharak.*" She hoped she'd said, "Do not move," but she'd never be certain. The two men seemed to understand, and they obeyed like frightened children.

With her pistol leading the way, she cleared each seat and the lavatory. No one was aboard the plane except the crew and the two Arabs. If Gerard was on an airplane, it wasn't this one.

32

VINOGRADNIK
(THE VINEYARD)

Back beside the overturned Suburban, Anya submitted to an examination by a paramedic who wiped blood away from a small laceration at her hairline.

"It's going to need a few stitches, but I think you're going to be okay. You certainly fared better than your friends." The paramedic motioned toward the pair of ambulances where Johnny Mac and Ray White sat on gurneys.

"Where is Gwynn?" Anya asked.

"You mean the other woman?"

"Yes. She is my partner. Is she okay?"

The medic laughed. "Yeah, she's okay, but it looks like this isn't the first fight she's lost lately. Her head and neck show bruising at least several days old. She's on the phone over there."

Anya followed the woman's line of sight to find Gwynn sitting in the cab of a firetruck with two telephones pressed to her ears. "She did not lose fight," Anya said. "She only lost first round. In end, she was winner."

The paramedic chuckled. "She's one tough cookie, all right. She needs to get to a hospital so a doctor can check her out, but none of us could get her to sit still long enough to examine her. What's going on out here?"

"We are—or now, we *were*—chasing suspect. This was wrong airplane. He was not inside."

The medic whistled. "Ouch. That's gotta sting. This is going to cost somebody a lot of money. I don't envy whoever was in charge."

Anya looked out over the carnage, meeting the eyes of her team as she took in every detail. "I was in charge. They will blame only me, and I will pay for engine for jet."

"All that's fine and good, but do you think you could get your partner to let us at least give her a cursory exam?"

"I will try," Anya said as she stood and headed for the firetruck. She pulled open the door and looked up at Gwynn. "Are you okay?"

Gwynn nodded. "I'm on the phone with the FAA and the ops center. Gerard may not have been on that plane, but he's on one of them. I've got Homeland Security checking hangars, and we're tracking down every jet that took off within thirty minutes prior to this whole mess."

Anya said, "I know where he is going."

Gwynn raised an eyebrow. "Spill it!"

"He is running home to Zakhar Belyaev. If we find him, we will find Gerard."

Gwynn ended both calls and slid down from the truck. "Anya, that's brilliant, and there's no one on Earth Belyaev would rather see again than the woman who saved his life in Vancouver."

"Yes, I know this, and I know exactly how to find him."

Gwynn sighed. "Something tells me Agent White isn't going to love this plan as much as I do."

"Is not his plan. Is my plan."

Gwynn motioned toward the crippled airplane on the taxiway. "After your most recent plan, I'm not so sure the federal government is going to be quick to jump on board one of your ideas."

Anya glanced over her shoulder to see a small plume of smoke still wafting above the plane's right engine. "Then we will not tell them."

Gwynn took Anya's arm. "Come on. Let's go check on the boys."

Neither of "the boys" looked happy to be in their current predicament, but Ray White was angrier than usual.

"How are you feeling, Agent White?"

He ignored Gwynn and her question, focusing entirely on Anya. "Nice shootin', Annie Oakley. What were you thinking?"

"I was finishing mission to stop airplane."

He growled. "From now on, check with me before you finish any more missions."

Anya eyed the overturned Suburban. "I did check with you, and you did not tell me to stop."

He glared at the Russian and then at Gwynn. "So help me, God, if you start acting like her, I'll drown both of you in gasoline while smoking a Marlboro."

Anya frowned. "But you do not smoke."

Gwynn yanked her partner away from their boss. "Let's go see how Johnny Mac's doing."

The young agent sat with a look of bewilderment on his face as they approached.

Gwynn leaned against his gurney. "Are you okay, Johnny Mac?"

He stared into the distance. "How? What happened?"

Anya started to speak, but Gwynn stopped her. "We had an accident while chasing that plane. Are you hurting? I'm sure they could give you something for the pain."

"No, I'm not in any pain. I'm just working through my career options."

Gwynn said, "Relax, Johnny Mac. Your career is going to be just fine. Unlike our favorite Russian over here, you were following direct orders. At least you didn't shoot at some Saudi's private jet."

He looked up at Anya. "Did it work?"

She smiled. "It did, but I did not know if it would. Now I know how to kill jet airplane with rifle."

He grabbed his abdomen as he tried to stifle the laughter that wouldn't be quieted. "I guess in the big picture, wrecking a fifty-thousand-dollar Suburban isn't nearly as bad as killing a hundred-million-dollar jet."

Anya protested. "At least I did not flip it over . . . and over . . . and over."

Two medics interrupted. "If you'll excuse us, we need to get him to the hospital."

Gwynn and Anya stepped aside, and Johnny Mac was loaded aboard the ambulance.

One of the paramedics turned to Gwynn and threw a thumb toward the back of the ambulance. "You, too, ma'am. We have to take you to the hospital. It's procedure."

Gwynn shot a glance toward White's ambulance and then toward Anya. "You ride with Agent White. He's less likely to kill you, and I'll go with Johnny Mac."

After two hours in the emergency room, Anya was treated and released. The paramedic had been correct. The cut at her hairline took five stitches, but otherwise, she was perfectly healthy. The rest of the team was far less fortunate. White's and Johnny Mac's injuries would require at least an overnight stay, and Gwynn found herself back in the old familiar playgrounds of concussion protocols.

Anya squeezed Gwynn's hand. "You will be okay, yes?"

"Yeah, I'll be fine as long as my brain doesn't come dripping from my ear."

Anya put on a disgusting face. "That sounds terrible, but it will not happen. I will see you again soon."

Gwynn grabbed her wrist. "Wait. Where are you going?"

Anya pulled her wrist from Gwynn's grasp. "I am finishing mission."

* * *

Anya knocked on Peter's door, and he said, "Come in."

She walked through the door to find her State Department friend sitting by the window in his wheelchair.

He looked up and smiled broadly. "Hey. I didn't expect to see you. What happened to your head?"

Anya gently touched her stitched wound. "We had small accident, but is fine. How are you?"

He let his eyes fall from her wound to her blue eyes. "I'm a lot better now."

"You are very kind man. Thank you, but I am not here for social visit. I need your help."

Disappointment made its appearance in his eyes. "Okay, I'll do what I can."

She gave him a warm smile. "There will be time for social visiting for us, and I will like this."

His smile returned. "So will I."

"For today, I need to find Russian man named Zakhar Belyaev. You are American spy, so you can find him for me, yes?"

"I'm not a spy, Anya, but I have friends with access to a lot of information."

"This is exactly what spy would say, no?"

"Maybe, but there's only one spy in this room."

She let the comment drift by. "You will find this man for me, yes?"

"Yes, I'll find him for you, but first, do you know who he is?"

"Yes. He is wealthy Russian oligarch."

Peter shrugged. "Yes, he is that but also a lot more. He's a dangerous man—the kind of man who always gets what he wants."

"I will change that for him," Anya said, "but I have to first know where he is."

Peter held out a hand. "Give me your phone."

"Why?"

"Because I'm not using mine to call in this favor."

She pulled her phone from a pocket and slid it into his hand. Their fingers lingered on each other's a second longer than they should have before Peter dialed a number from memory.

"This is Peter Evans, two one six seven four."

The bored voice from the other end said, "Stand by, sir."

Thirty seconds later, another voice filled his ear. "Research."

"Zakhar Belyaev." He spelled the name. "I need his location and likely upcoming locations."

"Stand by."

The line went silent, and Anya wondered who was on the other end of the phone. Was it someone like Skipper, Chase Fulton's analyst, or was it an entire government department dedicated to keeping track of targets all over the world?

Peter listened closely when the disembodied voice came back on the line. Half a minute later, he hung up and tossed the phone back to Anya. "We believe he's at his winery on Lake Beleu in Slobozia Mare."

Anya let the information float around in her mind. "I do not know this place."

"Nobody knows this place," Peter said. "It's a tiny village in the Cahul District of Southwestern Moldova."

"Moldova? Why?"

"Apparently he fancies himself a winemaker. He bought the vineyard and winery a decade ago."

"This is strange," she said.

"I agree, but trying to think like a billionaire will never be something I can do. I held up my end of the bargain, so now it's your turn."

"My turn for what?"

"Your turn to tell me why you need to know where Belyaev is."

"Is very long story, but short version is I believe Vasily Orlov is not our bad guy. I think bad guy is chef."

Peter raised an eyebrow. "Christian Gerard?"

"Yes. I believe he lied to me and is working for Belyaev and not Orlov."

"How did you come to a conclusion like that?"

"As I said, it is very long story, but will tell you on plane to Moldova."

He looked down at his pajama pants, T-shirt, and wheelchair. "Why would you want me on the plane to Moldova with you? I'm a prisoner here until the doctors release me."

"You are only prisoner if you choose to be, and I do not speak Romanian. This is language of Moldova, no?"

Peter stood from his wheelchair. "You know? You're right."

"I am often right," Anya said. "But I am right about which thing?"

"Both. I'm tired of being a prisoner, and my Romanian isn't bad. But how did you get Agent White to authorize overseas travel?"

Ignoring the question, she asked, "Does Moldova have extradition treaty with United States?"

Peter slowly shook his head. "You don't have authorization, do you?"

"I have mission."

Peter pointed to his feet. "You used the wrong pronoun. I think you meant *we* have a mission. And I need some shoes."

33

Eto Plan
(This is the Plan)

Clothes, including shoes, were the easy part. Finding an airline flight from New Orleans to Moldova turned out to be the greatest immediate hurdle.

Anya stood in front of the ticket agent at Louis Armstrong International Airport.

The young man said, "Ma'am, you can't just fly to Moldova. My computer says Americans must register with the Moldovan government prior to arrival in the country, but that's not all. There's civil unrest, and the State Department recommends—"

Peter stepped to the counter and held up his State Department credentials. "We're not concerned about the recommendations of the State Department, and we'll register when we arrive."

The man examined Peter's credentials, and his fingers danced across the keyboard. After several seconds of typing, he studied the screen and shook his head. "I'm sorry, but without official government travel orders, I'm not allowed to sell you a ticket to Moldova."

Peter turned to Anya. "Is there any chance of getting a set of official orders cut?"

"I do not think so, but I have other idea." She laid a hand on the counter. "How about Bucharest in Romania? Can we have ticket there?"

Fingers flew across the keyboard again, and the man paused to read the screen. "Economy, business, or first class?"

Anya pulled a black credit card from her pocket and slid it across the counter. "First class."

The keys rattled. "And when will you be returning?"

Anya said, "This is not important. We only care about getting into country. We will buy new ticket to come back to United States."

"Okay, one-way it is, but it's cheaper to buy a round-trip ticket now."

Anya rapped a knuckle on the counter. "I said this is not important. Give to me tickets. We are wasting time."

The young man hit a few more keys, and a collection of tickets and boarding passes protruded from a printer. He slid the documents into paper envelopes and then across the counter. "You'll board at gate eleven in forty minutes. Will there be anything else, ma'am?"

Without answering, Anya turned, handed one set of tickets to Peter, and scanned the lobby for directions to gate eleven.

The next thirty hours were spent in layovers in Charlotte, New York, and Rome.

When the plane finally touched down at Henri Coandă International Airport in Bucharest, Anya came awake in the luxurious, first-class seat. "What time is it?"

Peter glanced at his watch in a wasted effort. "I have no idea, but it's noon in New Orleans."

The cabin lights came on, and the pilot said, "Welcome to Bucharest, where the local time is eight oh five under overcast skies, and the temperature is minus eleven degrees Celsius. Thank you for flying with us, and on behalf of the flight deck and cabin crew, we hope you enjoy your stay in Romania."

Anya shivered in her seat. "Minus eleven? This was terrible idea."

Peter stood and pulled their packs from the overhead compartment. "Come on, you soft American. A little cold air isn't going to kill you."

"Maybe not, but I do not want to take chances." She pulled a jacket from her pack and laced her arms into the sleeves.

They disembarked and headed for the rental car counter. A pleasant voice made announcements over the speakers in multiple languages, and Anya was surprised how few of the languages she recognized.

At the rental counter, Peter slid his international license, passport, and credit card across the counter to a stunning young woman who looked up as if mesmerized by Peter's sharp features and three-day growth of beard.

Anya stepped beside him and slid her arm through Peter's.

He glanced down and whispered in Russian, "Jealous much?"

"Is not jealousy. Is only tree pee."

Peter shuddered. "Tree pee? What does that mean?"

Anya pulled him close. "Animals leave scent on trees so other animals will know tree belongs to someone else."

Peter couldn't control his laughter, and the wounds in his stomach ached only slightly less than the day before.

The woman behind the counter looked up and pulled Peter's documents into her hands. Five minutes later, he held the keys for a 2003 Dacia Solenza.

Anya shivered on the walk through the parking garage until they arrived at their rental. "Is horrible looking car, but I do not care as long as heating works."

Peter held the door for her, and she climbed inside, thankful to be inside anything—even a horrible Romanian car. The engine came to life and produced warm air inside the car far more quickly than either of them expected. Soon, they were on the Autostrada Soarelui E81 and headed east.

Anya held her hands in front of the warm air from the heater. "How far is drive, and what is temperature in Moldova?"

"About four hours, I think, and the weather will be a lot like it is here."

"We should have waited until summer for this."

Peter held up both hands. "Hey, you bought the tickets. I'm just the translator."

"I think we should drive all the way to Slobozia Mare tonight."

He grimaced. "I don't think it's a good idea to cross the border in the middle of the night with American passports and civil unrest in the country. The city of Brăila is on the Danube River just southwest of the Moldovan border. We can get a room there for the night and cross in the morning when it wouldn't look quite so suspicious."

The nighttime traffic was light, and the car ran well enough to make the trip to Brăila in just under three hours.

Peter pulled up in front of La Casa Cu Stuf. "Do you want to wait in the car or brave the cold?"

"I think you know answer to this question."

"Right," he said. "I'll be right back. One room or two?"

She considered the question. "Maybe one room with two beds would be good, but leave car running, please."

Peter reemerged from the inn with one key. "They only had one room available. It has one double bed, but I can sleep on the floor. It'll be fine."

They shouldered their packs and found their room.

Anya gave the space a long, surveying look. "Bed is large enough for two people, yes?"

"That's up to you."

She shrugged. "Is only reasonable. Sleeping on floor would be uncomfortable for you, and you are still healing from shooting."

Anya woke as the sun shone through the short curtains to find Peter's arm draped across her body from behind. She closed her eyes and slid backward until their bodies were pressed lightly together, savoring the feeling of being held for the first time since she shared Chase Fulton's bed.

She drifted off into sleep until the smell of coffee woke her an hour later. Anya yawned and stretched, and for the first time, noticed she was alone in the bed.

Peter stood in front of the full-length mirror on the bathroom door wearing only a pair of shorts and cautiously probing at the wounds on his abdomen.

She watched him with silent admiration until he caught her looking.

"I'm sorry if I woke you," he said. "I was just making coffee and changing my bandages. How do you take your coffee?"

"Good morning. You did not wake me, and I do not drink coffee. Only tea."

"They have tea. I'll make you a cup."

She pulled her long sleeping shirt down and crawled from beneath the cover. On her way to the restroom, she let her hand brush across Peter's arm. "Thank you for being gentleman last night."

He caught her hand and lightly pressed her fingertips to his wounds. "I'd like to take credit for my gentlemanly behavior, but I couldn't act otherwise, even if I wanted."

She gave him a sly smile. "You are young and strong. You will soon heal, and I will still be here."

"I hope so."

Showers, caffeine, and back into the same clothes they wore the day before, Anya and Peter hit the road, heading for the Moldovan border.

As they approached the border crossing, Peter sighed. "Here comes our first obstacle. Break out your papers."

Anya handed him her Russian passport. "This is second obstacle. First was airplane flight."

Peter slipped his diplomatic passport on top of Anya's. "Something tells me the border guards don't care how we arrived in Romania."

Opening the window required rolling down the glass with a crank, but he soon had it down far enough to pass out the documents and allow the guards to see inside the car.

Without a word, the guard pulled the passports from Peter's hand and examined them closely. He let out a shrill whistle and waved for the second guard to approach. A man perhaps ten years older than the first guard mumbled something in Romanian and motioned toward the car. Anya didn't understand the language, but Peter seemed to relax as he accepted the passports back through the window. With extensive effort, he returned the glass back to the closed position and placed Anya's passport back in her hand.

She took the red-covered booklet. "What were you afraid of?"

He shoved his booklet back into his pocket. "There's some turmoil going on in the capital, and I was afraid we might be turned away, but thankfully it didn't happen."

"What did second guard say to first?"

Peter replayed the conversation in his head. "Oh, he just told the first guard to stop wasting his time."

"This is good. How far are we from vineyard?"

"It should be less than thirty minutes, but I'm not familiar with this area. The only map I have will get us close, but we'll have to do some self-navigation at some point."

"We will find it. I am certain of this. But we will need weapons."

"Weapons?" Peter asked. "Just what is your plan when we find Belyaev's vineyard?"

Anya turned in her seat. "I have only fluid plan. I think Belyaev will have guards, and we will have problem getting past them. I do not want to kill anyone, but if this becomes necessary, is easier with weapon than with only hands."

"What sort of weapons are we talking about?"

"I prefer knife. Gun is loud, and only military has them here."

"If Belyaev does have guards, they'll likely be armed."

"Is this possible in Moldova?" she asked.

"When you've got as much money as Belyaev, anything is possible. Don't forget that."

The community of Slobozia Mare came into view, and Peter suggested breakfast.

Anya quickly agreed, and they pulled into a parking place beneath the only sign in town Anya could read. She leaned forward and pointed upward. "English word and Romanian word are same for *restaurant*, no?"

Peter stepped out of the car. "Look at you, learning already. You'll be fluent by the time we leave."

"*If* we leave."

They pushed through the two-hundred-year-old door and shook off the cold. A roaring fire burned in a massive stone fireplace, and Anya wasted no time nestling on the hearth.

A woman almost as old as the building approached and spoke to Anya, but she turned to Peter in confusion. He continued the conversation, and the woman finally pointed at a small wooden table.

Peter pulled the table toward the fireplace until Anya nodded her approval, and they took their seats.

She leaned across the table. "Order for us tough meat with also honey and bread."

Peter relayed the order to the old woman.

When she left the table, Anya said, "Perhaps she knows where vineyard is."

Peter grunted. "Perhaps if we asked she would tell us, but she would also tell the authorities about the two Russians who ate at her restaurant the same day bodies started piling up at the vineyard."

"Yes, of course, you are right. This is bad idea."

Their meal arrived with mugs of hot tea, and the woman laid a pair of ancient steak knives beside their plates.

Peter smiled. "Excellent play ordering meat to score a pair of knives, but why honey?"

Anya sliced her meat with a hand far more delicate than she would bear should it become necessary to use the knife in defense. "Only because I like honey and bread. It was treat for me when I was child."

"I'd like to hear about your childhood sometime."

She met his gaze. "No, you would not. My childhood ended when my mother was killed when I was four or maybe five. From that day, I became adult."

"I'm sorry, Anya. I guess I should've known."

"Is okay. Do not be sorry. It was not done by you. You are very kind man, and I enjoy being with you. Why is your English so much better than mine?"

He chuckled. "Because you learned English from Soviets. I learned it from watching American television. You should try it."

"I detest television. Is waste of time."

"Not if it teaches you to sound like you're from Athens, Georgia."

She paused. "How do you know about Athens?"

"Even though I didn't dig deep enough to learn about your mother, I did my research."

"I think I like this because it means you are curious and also good at job."

He swallowed a bite and washed it down with the steaming tea. "This is really good, whatever it is."

When they finished their breakfast, Anya pocketed both knives and stacked their plates so the absence of the knives wouldn't be noticed immediately. Peter paid the old woman, and she handed him a bag.

"What's this?" he asked in Romanian.

She answered, and he added another folded bill to the stack.

As she stepped into the car, Anya lifted a smooth, gray rock from the ground. By the time Peter rounded the car and slid behind the wheel, Anya had one of the knives held tightly in her hand, rubbing it against the stone.

He watched for a moment. "I guess knives really are your thing, huh?"

Without looking up, she said, "Knife is most versatile and deadly weapon when close to opponent. From distance, is no good, but from distance, I can escape without fighting."

He pulled the car into gear and accelerated onto the two-lane road. With one more glance at the map, he said, "This is where we strike out on our own."

Anya tested the sharpness of the first blade and gestured toward the bag. "What is inside package?"

"I thought you'd never ask. Go ahead. Take a look. It's for you."

She unrolled the top of the bag and peered inside, where she found two small loaves of bread and a pot of honey.

She pulled herself across the seat and kissed Peter on his cheek. The instant he felt her lips touch his skin, he pulled the car from the road and set the brake. Turning to face her, he took her face in his hands, and they kissed . . . hesitantly at first, but more passionately with every passing moment.

A strange horn sounded from behind them, and Peter jumped, turning toward the sound. Seeing the car trying to pull onto the road, but blocked by their rear bumper, he reached for the gear shift. They laughed like teenagers as he pulled back onto the asphalt and continued through the countryside to the northwest.

Still reveling in the aftermath of the kiss, Anya pulled the bread and honey from the paper bag. She drizzled honey onto the bread and held it in front of Peter's mouth. He playfully attacked the bread, nibbling on her fingers as he did, and they shared the bread until the first loaf was gone.

Anya capped the honey pot and returned it to the bag.

Peter protested. "Hey, I thought there were two loaves in there."

"Yes, there were two. We ate yours, and now only mine is left."

He started to continue the inquest, but as they crossed a small hill, hundreds of rows of dormant grapevines lay out in front of them.

"I think we found our vineyard," he said.

Anya looked up and gasped. "Yes, this has to be it. We should keep driving until we find gate."

"I agree," Peter said, "but what do we do when we find it?"

Anya studied the landscape, and her girlish persona was instantly replaced by the focus of one of the world's deadliest assassins. "After finding gate, we will move to hill and observe for a time. I will make plan after this."

"You're the boss," he said as he continued down the winding road, the taste of Anya's lips still on his.

She memorized every detail of the area from the slope of the road to the angle of the shadows. Nothing escaped her eye.

Rounding a sharp curve to the left, she pointed through the windshield. "There is gate, but I do not see guards."

Peter pulled slowly toward the gate and saw a massive lock laced through heavy chains wrapped around the hinged gates. "If anyone is here, they're locked in."

Anya narrowed her eyes and surveyed the drive beyond the locked gate. "No. This is not gate for leaving. Is only for coming."

"How could you possibly know that?"

She pointed toward the stones scattered on the road. "Look at rocks. They are only tossed onto road when a vehicle stops, someone unlocks gate, and car continues onto path. There are no stones thrown back toward gate from road. This means gate is only used for coming and not for going."

Peter shook his head. "You're terrifying."

"Yes, I am. Do not forget this."

He changed the subject by pointing out the border wall. "The fence is just stones and timbers. It's not going to stop anyone from getting into the vineyard."

"This is true only if person is walking, but it would be impossible to take car through fence. This means we must walk or find gate made for going."

"I think there might be one more option," he said, pointing up the slope to the right.

Anya followed his finger to a small barn with a pair of horses nibbling at a trough full of hay. She nodded. "Yes, this could be useful, but car is better and faster."

Peter drove farther north as Anya committed every inch of the vineyard to memory. As they drove, she drew the second knife across the stone until, like the first one, it was razor sharp. When she finished, she sliced two pieces of carpet from the floor of the car.

"What are you doing?" Peter demanded.

"I am making sheath for knives. I cannot carry them safely in pockets without sheath."

"This car is never going back to Romania, is it?"

Anya noticed a narrow path to the right. "Put car inside there. I have plan."

He followed her order and pulled onto the path partially covered with gravel.

Turning to judge the visibility behind the car, she said, "This is good. You will wait for me here. If I do not come back in two hours, I am dead, and you will take car back to Romania. If I come back, I will have with me Christian Gerard, and we will take him to country with extradition treaty. This is plan."

34

Vyderzhannyy do Sovershenstva
(Aged to Perfection)

Peter grabbed Anya's arm. "No! You're not going in there alone!"

She glared down at his hand encircling her wrist. "Take hand from my arm, now." He loosened his grip, and she yanked her wrist away. She said, "You are injured. You cannot run. You cannot fight, and I cannot carry you from vineyard while at same time forcing Gerard to come with me. You are here to drive and speak language. This is all. I am here to bring back fugitive to have trial and prison inside United States. This is not to be challenged."

"But, Anya—"

She pressed her finger to his lips. "I care for you, Pyotr Evanoff. You will be safe here, and I will return to you. Do this for me, and we will find warm place in sun where you can heal and we can play together."

She leaned in and kissed him once more before stepping from the car and closing the door behind her. He watched her move like a cat as she ran down the gravel path, crossed the road, and leapt over the stone fence. She was soon out of sight and deep inside the vineyard.

The minutes passed like hours for Peter as he sat in silence scanning the valley and praying for Anya's return. She'd been correct. He would be nothing but a liability on foot inside the vineyard.

For Anya, the minutes ticked from the clock at a blinding pace. She ran quickly enough to cover the ground in time to complete her work and return to Peter on schedule, but slowly enough to have the energy to fight should she encounter resistance. Judging her distance based on her pace, she believed she'd put three quarters of a mile behind her when she topped a small knoll in the undulating landscape. From the high ground, she could see the entrance drive winding to the south and four large buildings in the distance, perhaps half a mile away. She focused on the area surrounding the buildings and found no signs of life stirring.

Checking that her knives were still firmly seated in their makeshift sheaths, she continued running toward the buildings. If Gerard was on the property, he would be somewhere warm and dry. The four buildings of the winery were an excellent place to start.

She reached the compound in five minutes and slowed to catch her breath and calm her heart rate. A minute later, she crept around the first building and pressed her ear to the wall beside the door. As her heart slowed and her breathing softened, she listened carefully but heard nothing. She reached for the knob of the windowless door, and it turned freely in her hand. Lifting the weight of the door from the hinges to reduce the chance of squeaking, she pulled the door open only far enough for her to slip inside.

Her eyes adjusted to the darkness, revealing row after row of stacked barrels on heavy wooden racks where thousands of gallons of wine rested, aging to perfection. She moved silently through the space, using her ears more than her eyes to scan for any living soul, but she found nothing but barrel after barrel.

Back at the door, she moved outside and to the next structure, taking her time. She reached a sliding door on the side of the second building and gave it a gentle push. It moved a foot and froze. She forced her body through the opening and found herself inside a very different building than the first.

Enormous vats and tanks filled the space. There were no interior walls, only vast open space where the grapes began their long journey toward becoming fine wine. In the rear corner of the building, she discovered a pair of horizontal doors in the floor with a locked hasp securing them closed. From beneath her, the gentle hum of machinery rose through the locked doors.

Anya quickly scanned the space and discovered a long metal pole. She bounced it in her hand, judging its strength and diameter before sliding the narrow tip into the hasp behind the lock. She leaned against the pole with all her weight, prying against the closure. The pole held, but so did the hasp until she bounced herself against the lever, sending the hasp shattering beneath the force. The noise was enough to garner the attention of anyone in the building, but she still heard nothing.

Convinced she was still alone, Anya gently pulled open the left door, revealing a set of metal stairs descending into the darkness of the pit below. Carefully, she took each tread as if she expected each to explode beneath her weight. By the time she reached the bottom, her eyes had adjusted to the even darker surroundings, and the mechanical hum presented itself to be the compressor and fans of a walk-in cooler.

She pulled the lever, unlocking the door, and stepped inside. Stacked from floor to ceiling were dozens of burlap-wrapped packages just like the ones she'd seen in Gerard's cooler in New Orleans. She drew her knife from its carpeted sheath and sliced into the closest bundle. As she pulled the burlap away, she heard footsteps overhead and a second set descending the stairs. Cornered, she drew her second knife and pressed herself against the front wall of the cooler.

The footsteps drew ever nearer until a hand threw back the cooler door and demanded in Russian, "Who's in here?"

Anya held her position and barely breathed as a shadowy form stepped through the opening, the beam of his light slicing through the darkness of the space. There had been at least two sets of footsteps. If she killed only one of the men, the other would sound the alarm, and her mission would fail before it had truly begun.

Pushing her patience to its absolute limit, she waited for the man to redirect the beam of light on her, at which point, she would be forced to take his life.

Still in Russian, the second man said, "What are you doing?"

"Someone has been in here," the first man said.

"Are they still there?"

"I don't know."

The second man grabbed the other man's light and burst through the open cooler door, sweeping the light ahead of him as he moved.

Anya raised an arm and came down hard on the man's wrist, knocking the light from his hand and sending it skittering across the floor. The gig was up, and the men had sealed their fate the instant they came through the door.

Anya spun through the dark with lightning speed and delivered a plunging blow with the knife in her left hand to the base of the first man's skull, where his spine became his brainstem. He melted like molten lava to the cold, unforgiving floor of the freezer. The second man heard, more than saw what happened, inside the giant metal box.

Anya could see him in silhouette as he drew his pistol with his left hand. An instant later, the blade from her right punctured the flesh and muscle of his left shoulder, rendering the arm all but useless for firing the threatening weapon. He staggered backward, grasping for the knife protruding from his shoulder. Anya took full advantage of his confusion and closed the distance between them. Her final step landed simultaneously with the thrust of her second knife. The polished steel disappeared into the man's chest just below his solar plexus. A second thrust, lifting the blade upward, left the man's heart incapable of continued toil. As he fell, she caught the collar of his jacket and dragged his corpse into the cooler alongside his partner.

A quick search of the two bodies convinced Anya that neither man had notified anyone else of their discovery of her in the cooler. Neither carried a radio or phone.

With the man's light tucked beneath her arm, Anya turned back to the burlap bundle she'd cut before the interruption. She focused the beam on her original slit and pulled back the cloth to reveal the long, coarse hair of a once-majestic tiger.

She closed the cooler door behind her and climbed the stairs back onto the ground floor of the structure. Closing the horizontal doors, she positioned the latch to appear unaltered.

More convinced than ever that she was on the trail of the true culprit behind the importation of poached tigers from China and Siberia, Anya checked her watch, revealing only seventy minutes to finish her work and return to the car. If she didn't make the deadline, the State Department spy —and whatever else he was destined to become for her—would face the dilemma of waiting longer or leaving her behind, believing her to be dead inside Belyaev's compound.

She moved back through the door and heard the rumble of trucks approaching. A small structure that could've been a storage shed for tools, or possibly a shelter for pumps used to bring water to the surface, stood less than twenty-five meters away. Her decision would be final, no matter which building she chose. Back inside the huge open structure offered the best possibility of quickly hiding but was also the likely destination of the coming trucks.

Her decision was made, and she sprinted across the open space, keeping as low as possible during the dash. Reaching the small building, she dove and slid beside the structure. The door proved to be less than an obstacle as it was held closed by a stone the size of Anya's fist. She slipped inside and pulled the door behind her. A small window gave her the visibility she needed without exposing her to the drivers of the coming trucks. She watched carefully, noting the size of each man as they climbed from the vehicles. None were large enough to create an issue one on one, but the five of them combined represented a formidable threat. She could most likely defeat all of them if she could retain possession of her blades, but the possibility of at least one of the men escaping to warn others was too high to risk.

Anya watched as the five men leaned against the trucks, smoking cigarettes and exchanging stories in her native Russian. Fifteen minutes into the episode, one of the men retrieved a clear glass bottle from behind the seat of his truck and pulled the cork from its neck. They passed the bottle and continued their revelry as the minutes ticked by. Her window of time was closing quickly, and her only avenue of escape was obstructed by five smoking, drinking laborers who seemed to be in no hurry to be anywhere else.

The minutes continued to stack as desperation set in and she could wait no longer. Something had to be done before time ran out and she was left ten thousand miles from home in the arms of her enemy. The contents of the shed offered no solutions, but a glimpse through the door brought a glimmer of hope.

She moved between the door, away from the men and the window facing them. The third large building of the compound lay only fifty meters directly out the door, but judging the line of sight of the carousing men was all but impossible from within the small structure. The slope of the ground offered some protection as it fell away from the high ground where the men stood. The decision to go had been made, but to run or crawl was only a coin toss. Either or neither could be better than the other, so she chose speed over stealth and left the shed in a sprint, doing her best to keep the small building between her and the men surrounding the trucks.

She traversed the distance in seconds and turned the corner behind the building that had been her goal, but suddenly, her objective changed as the sight of an elaborate, two-story house appeared only three hundred meters down the slope toward the lake. Lights filled several windows, and smoke rose from two of the four chimneys. Somebody was nice and warm inside, and Anya was about to find out who.

She double-checked, and both of her knives were still where they belonged, but a glance at her watch revealed just how much time she'd wasted by hiding in the shed. There was no way to complete the mission in time to get back to Peter, and the men behind her made it impossible to backtrack and let him know she needed more time. She was committed, and there was no turning back. Peter would simply have to leave without her. If she survived, she would make her way into Ukraine, where she knew the language and customs. From there she could contact Agent White or maybe even find an American embassy.

She gave a quick check around the end of the building she would use as cover, and the men were still enjoying themselves and their bottle. They were no longer a factor, so she sprinted down the slope toward the welcoming house, praying there were no dogs to alert the occupants of her presence.

The barks didn't come, and no eyes appeared in the windows. She threw herself to the ground beside the stacked stone of one of the chimneys to catch her breath. Habit sent her eyes to her watch, and the countdown sent spikes through her belly. The clock could no longer be an element of the mission. She'd come too far—ten thousand miles too far—to turn back now.

The steps of the house were constructed of massive stones, so climbing them silently was child's play. The porch surrounding the house was at least four meters deep and built of heavy timbers. She moved on the balls of her feet, peering into corners of windows at every opportunity. When she made her way three quarters of the way around the house, one final look inside a massive window gave her the answers she needed.

Her gut had been right. Sitting on the stone hearth was Chef Christian Gerard, warming himself by the roaring fire. Across the room sat the man whose life she'd saved in Vancouver only days before. In his right hand rested a long, dark cigar, and in his left, he held a snifter of honey-colored liquor. She saw no one else through the window, but the chance of only two people being inside such a massive home was slim. She would have more to contend with than just Gerard and Belyaev, but the odds no longer mattered. The confrontation was inevitable.

She retraced her steps back around the house and crept inside through a kitchen door after slipping the lock with her knife. Easing the door closed behind her, her eyes flashed again to the watch on her wrist. Peter would be gone by now, and she hoped she'd be back in his arms somewhere warm in the days to come. But her mission demanded absolute focus, so she put those thoughts away and moved toward her objective.

The hardwood floor was smooth and silent beneath her feet as she moved painfully slowly across its surface. The smell of the cigar and the wood fire filled her senses and hardened her resolve. Reaching the wide opening to the great room where Gerard and Belyaev sat in comfort and believed security, she stepped through the opening with her blades drawn.

The old Russian jerked his head to face her, recognition gleaming in his eyes, and he raised both hands into the air. He bellowed in Russian, "My savior! How have you found me? Come, come . . . You must meet my son, Alexi."

Anya shifted her attention to Gerard, who was standing with terror instead of jubilance dancing in his eyes. Disbelief consumed him as he gazed between Anya and Belyaev.

In trembling Russian, the chef yelled, "Father, this woman is a killer!"

Before the words left his mouth, he sprang onto the hearth and reached above the mantle for the shotgun hanging from an ornate rack. He thumb-cocked the double hammers and raised the weapon to bear on Anya as Belyaev growled, "No!"

In the instant before Gerard pulled the first trigger, the front door exploded inward, and Anya dove behind a massive wood carving of a life-size grizzly bear. Four shots rang out in intermingled succession: two unmistakable shotgun blasts and two smaller-caliber rounds.

In the silence following the shots, Anya stood, breaking cover from behind the carving and struggling to piece together the gruesome scene in front of her. Belyaev lay across the arm of his chair, his cigar and glass rolling across the floor at his feet and blood pouring from his head. Across the room, Gerard stood on the hearth, shoving two more shells into the double-barreled shotgun. And lying on his back with his legs still inside the room and his torso sprawled across the porch was what remained of Pyotr Evanoff with an ancient revolver still clamped in his lifeless hand.

Anya hurled her blade across the room and sprinted for Gerard, who was raising the shotgun for his second murderous assault. The thrown blade sank into the soft flesh of his neck the same instant he pulled the first trigger. The shock of the piercing knife and recoil of the weapon sent the shot high and right, missing Anya as she closed the short remaining distance. As Gerard began to weaken and sink beneath the killing blow of the knife, Anya yanked the shotgun from his hand and turned the massive weapon on Gerard. She squeezed the remaining trigger, sending heavy, killing lead flying through the man's chest and driving him backward toward the roaring fire. Anya left the ground in a mighty arc, throwing a front kick with every ounce of rage inside her and landing a foot squarely in his face, finishing the job the shotgun blast had begun. His soulless body folded and collapsed into the raging fire.

Turning on a heel, Anya ran to Peter and fell at his side. He lay lifeless and cold at her fingertips as her tears fell on his face.

ALKHATIMA
(EPILOGUE)

Five days later and half a world away, Supervisory Special Agent Ray White sat at his desk with Special Agents Guinevere "Gwynn" Davis and Johnathon "Johnny Mac" McIntyre sitting across from him, each bearing the scars—both physical and psychological—of the previous days of their lives.

"Can either of you read Romanian?" White asked, holding a copy of the *Moldova Suverană*, the daily newspaper of Chișinău, the capital city of Moldova.

"Something tells me this article holds the answers to both of our questions. Where did they go, and why hasn't Anya checked in?"

Both junior agents shook their heads.

White pressed the intercom button on his phone. "Get a Romanian interpreter up here, now."

Minutes later, a young man in a dark suit and thick glasses stepped through the door.

White asked, "Are you the interpreter?"

"Yes, sir. I'm Clayton Fairburn. They told me you have a Romanian document for me to translate."

White held up the paper. "Read this front-page article to me in English."

The man straightened his glasses and lifted the paper from White's hand. "Okay, give me a minute to read through the article for context."

"To hell with context," White yelled. "Just read us the article."

"Yes, sir. It says, In a bizarre scene, the bodies of nine men were found at the winery and vineyard owned by multi-national business mogul Zakhar Belyaev early this morning. The two bodies discovered inside the main house on the property were that of Zakhar Belyaev and his son, Alexi Belyaev, known in the United States as Chef Christian Gerard, whose body was found partially burned in the home's fireplace. Seven additional bodies of unknown men (likely Russian) were found, and all had been killed by multiple knife wounds. Police have no leads in the horrific case, but early supposition is that the scene is somehow tied to the body left on the altar of Saint Michael's Cathedral late last night. The body is believed to be that of a former Russian citizen, Pyotr Evanoff, who is believed to have been an American State Department diplomat at the time of his death. The reason for Evanoff's presence in Moldova is yet unknown. If you have any information about either of these discoveries, officials ask that you contact the Moldovan State Police immediately."

ABOUT THE AUTHOR

CAP DANIELS

Cap Daniels is a former sailing charter captain, scuba and sailing instructor, pilot, Air Force combat veteran, and civil servant of the U.S. Department of Defense. Raised far from the ocean in rural East Tennessee, his early infatuation with salt water was sparked by the fascinating, and sometimes true, sea stories told by his father, a retired Navy Chief Petty Officer. Those stories of adventure on the high seas sent Cap in search of adventure of his own, which eventually landed him on Florida's Gulf Coast where he spends as much time as possible on, in, and under the waters of the Emerald Coast.

With a headful of larger-than-life characters and their thrilling exploits, Cap pours his love of adventure and passion for the ocean onto the pages of his work.

Visit www.CapDaniels.com to join the mailing list to receive newsletter and release updates.

Connect with Cap Daniels

Facebook: www.Facebook.com/WriterCapDaniels
Instagram: https://www.instagram.com/authorcapdaniels/
BookBub: https://www.bookbub.com/profile/cap-daniels